A LONG WAY FROM HELP . . .

"Jesse! Answer me," she demanded, turning in a lonely circle. Beneath the mesa the vista was empty, without a sign of Detective Nick Powell's sedan or a posse of rescuers. Had he found her note and understood where she meant?

Ruby returned to the Jeep and blasted the horn. What had Hank once told her? If she was ever lost in the woods, three of anything signaled an emergency: three whistles, three shouts, three gunshots. Three times she leaned on the horn, holding it while she counted to three, waiting between each honk while she counted to three again. Then she paused and did it all over again. And again.

"I hear you."

Ruby whirled around. A man stood twenty feet behind her, on an outcropping of rocks. Relaxed, casual, a slight smile on his face . . .

Dell Books by Jo Dereske

SAVAGE CUT
CUT AND DRY
SHORT CUT

SHORT CUT

Jo Dereske

A Dell Book

Published by
Dell Publishing
a division of
Bantam Doubleday Dell Publishing Group, Inc.
1540 Broadway
New York, New York 10036

ISBN: 0-440-22223-0

Printed in the United States of America

Published simultaneously in Canada

July 1998

10 9 8 7 6 5 4 3 2 1

WCD

For my dear sister, Mary Lee

I can't thank Bill Vreeke and Mary Lee Dereske enough for generously explaining the mysteries of civil engineering to me, for the many tours of works-in-progress, and for patiently answering my endless questions. Thank you to Mary for her keen eye, her generous heart, and her relentless search for the key to this novel.

I'm grateful for the encouragement of my agent, Ruth Cohen, and the wisdom of my editor, Jacquie Miller.

And I especially thank my husband and best friend, Kip Winsett, for his clarity of perception and uncommon good humor.

Chapter 1

Ruby Crane stood in front of the frost-edged window of her cabin, holding a mug of hot coffee in both hands and watching a solitary person walk casually onto the punky ice of Blue Lake.

"I hope you know what you're doing," she said aloud to the distant dark figure, and took another sip of black coffee. She'd skipped her usual generous splash of milk, recalling vague warnings about avoiding milk products when you had a cold. "Clog you up good." This was the disgusting phase, and she was ripe to try any advice or superstition, desperate even, sick of toting around boxes of tissues and breathing through her mouth, her head feeling like an overstretched balloon.

Behind her a fire crackled in the fieldstone fireplace. She'd kept it burning at full tilt during these two days she'd stayed inside, overheating the cabin, which was as good as any medicine from a bottle. A small door in the log wall beside the fireplace opened onto a woodbox that could be filled from outside. It usually held enough oak and beech logs for a week, but not at the rate she was burning the wood.

Dirty snow, gone flat and crusty, still surrounded the cabin, revealing whatever had lain beneath each snowfall all winter long like stratified life: a blue rag kicked from Ruby's car, twigs blown from the trees, dog manure, acorns and pinecones, a bright spot of pink that might be Jesse's lost glove.

Around the base of the trees, and in open patches, the snow had melted, exposing muddy tracts of earth that froze solid each night and softened to muck by noon the next day. No matter how hard she prodded her imagination, Ruby couldn't make out the slightest hint of green: the world seemed dead to living things.

March in Michigan dragged on, a month of false hope, when the sun teased with warmth that turned to subfreezing temperatures during the night, when balmy winds suddenly whipped into gales, and snow shovels were put away too soon.

Ruby had caught sight of the figure on the ice a few minutes earlier, walking below the public boat ramp across the lake, a dark shape moving against the white landscape. There was probably a car parked up near the picnic shelter. The ice was still solid, but it had taken on a treacherous dull gray and pocked appearance. Now, whoever it was, was heading farther out toward the center of Blue Lake, where the natural springs had weakened the ice even more. Ruby tapped her fingernails against her cup and frowned, willing the idiot to turn back.

A week ago, during a sudden warm spell, she'd been awakened in the night by the crack and boom of the shifting ice, at first thinking she'd heard gunshots. And as if all of Waters County had heard the ominous sounds, too, the next day fishermen began hauling their fish shanties off the lake on sled skids. No more snowmobiles buzzed out from the trees and whined across the tempting flats. People who ventured out stayed close to shore, where they at least had a chance in the shallower water.

But now, here was someone heading straight toward the softest ice and not walking casually either, but striding purposefully, without caution, as if they had no idea of the ice's danger, or didn't care. She couldn't make out whether it was a man or woman. What she'd thought was a black jacket now proved to be deep burgundy—a hooded parka—covering the figure from head to thigh. She glimpsed the blue of denim jeans.

Ruby's log cabin was the oldest structure on Blue Lake, occupying an acre of land that jutted into the lake. A peninsula, almost an island if she counted the little swamp her driveway crossed to reach Blue Road, a wooden bridge she sometimes fantasized raising like a castle drawbridge.

Ruby gasped as the figure on the ice suddenly halted, raising its arms like a tightrope walker about to lose balance in a precarious spot. She held her breath, watching the still figure stand like a dark cruciform. Finally the figure moved and Ruby breathed again, watching it skirt a section of ice and, instead of turning back, continue onward, straight toward Ruby's cabin.

"You fool," she said, and set her coffee on the windowsill so hard that liquid sloshed unheeded onto her hand. She glanced down at her slippered feet. She wore a sweater over the flannel pajamas she'd worn for two days, but there wasn't time to change now. Her jacket hung beside the kitchen door, and she kicked off her slippers as she raced across the cabin toward the jumble of winter clothes that belonged to her and Jesse.

She jammed her bare feet into a pair of fleece-lined boots and pulled on her jacket, then fumbled for gloves, finding one red mitten and one blue glove; good enough. A leash she'd bought for Spot but never used hung on the wall, and Ruby snatched up that, too.

The three-legged collie clambered up from beneath the kitchen table, barking once, her tail wagging, then her hackles rising as she tried to read Ruby's intent.

"No, Spot," Ruby said, reaching for the doorknob. "Stay."

After the warm cabin, the outdoor air knifed her to the bone. The frigid wind snatched her breath away, gusting straight into her face. Jesse's red plastic saucer sled leaned against the cabin wall, and Ruby grabbed its pull rope, dragging it behind her toward the shore. It was important to distribute weight on soft ice. If the fool on the lake broke through the ice, she might be able to lie flat on the saucer and push herself to him, then throw out Spot's leash. She'd watched a similar maneuver during the rescue of a drunk snowmobiler when she was a child.

She clumsily tried to zip her jacket as she ran across the rough lawn. It was still early in the day and the crusty snow held her weight, crunching beneath her feet. The saucer bumped behind her, slipping every which way on the crust and then dragging as she crossed hard, bare ground. Ruby's reddish gold hair whipped across her face, obscuring her view of the ice and for a horrible moment she thought she was too late, that the idiot had already fallen through.

But no, when she pushed back her hair, she saw the figure striding onward as determined as before. Ruby took two steps onto the pocked and milky ice, watching, gathering up her nerve to attempt a rescue.

It was a woman; she could see that now. The poised stride, one foot in front of the other. Slender and upright, calf-high leather boots too stylish for real winter.

A stinging blast of wind from across the lake forced Ruby to close her eyes. When she opened them, the burgundy hood had blown off the woman's head. Her features were still indistinct, but her hair blazed in the drab day.

Reddish gold, the same color as Ruby's, the same as Jesse's. The same color Ruby's mother had once claimed hers had been, before Ruby's father had driven every vestige of color out of her.

Ruby dropped the saucer's rope and stared, ignoring the bump of the saucer against her shin. Her sister Phyllis lived in Albuquerque, and Ruby hadn't seen her in thirteen years, but she was positive that was who now crossed the lake toward her. The hair was shorter, cropped close to her head. She recognized the slope of her shoulders, the upright position of her head as if her chin were raised, that familiar determined walk: Ice be damned.

Phyllis didn't pause in her stride, but continued

toward Ruby, and she felt the intensity of her sister's stare. No smile flashed there.

Ruby watched, biting her lip, until Phyllis reached the firmer ice a hundred feet from shore. Then Phyllis stopped, shoved her black-gloved hands into her jacket pockets, and gazed at Ruby. From this distance she appeared thinner than Ruby recalled, but as striking as ever, as if no time had passed since their last heated meeting.

"That was a very dramatic entrance," Ruby said. Her voice easily carried across the ice; there was no need to shout.

"What's wrong with your voice?" Phyllis asked. The wind feathered her hair.

Sounds and smells, Ruby had read once, were the most evocative of memories. Hearing the clear tones and rhythm of Phyllis's voice, Ruby felt the past wash over her. She helplessly shook her head to banish the images and said, "I have a cold."

"I can see why." Phyllis removed a leather-gloved hand from her pocket and waved it to encompass Ruby's half-zipped jacket, her flannel pajamas, the saucer, mismatched gloves, and bare head. "You're not exactly dressed for sledding."

"That ice is dangerous as hell," Ruby said, nodding toward the lake. She felt in her jacket pocket for a frazzled tissue and wiped her tender nose.

"Don't you think I know that?" Phyllis asked, her voice growing peevish. "I lived here longer than you did." She kicked at a hump of snow but made no move to come any closer to shore. "I bought these boots in Chicago," she said, turning her foot to admire the slouchy gray leather of her boot. Even from this distance they said expensive. "I knew I wouldn't find anything but mukluks and Russian grandmother boots around here."

"They'd be more appropriate," Ruby said.

"I made it across the lake in these, didn't I? That's appropriate enough for me."

"You could have driven in on the driveway," Ruby told her. The cold wind blew through the thin flannel covering her legs. She might as well be bare-legged. "You didn't have to risk your life."

"I wanted to see this place from the water side." Her voice faltered, and she glanced away. "Get the full effect."

Ruby squinted at her sister, now noticing the tense way she held her head. She repeatedly removed her hands from her pockets, made fists, and jammed them back into her pockets, stretching the fabric of her parka. Ruby had never seen Phyllis other than supremely confident, the cool head among the rabble, the woman who believed that any answer was better than indecisiveness.

"Do you remember calling me last summer?" Ruby asked. After having only spoken to each other twice in thirteen years, there had been two late-night phone calls that hadn't made any sense.

"Do you think I'm losing my memory?" Phyllis challenged, but there was a sting of defensiveness in her voice. "What about it?"

"You said you'd call me again, but you didn't."

"So? Here I am in the flesh." Phyllis removed her hands from her pocket again and gripped them together in front of her waist. Ruby would bet that beneath her gloves, Phyllis's knuckles were white.

Ruby couldn't stop shivering. "Are you coming ashore?" she asked.

"All ashore that's going ashore," Phyllis said in a soft singsong that barely reached Ruby's ears. Then louder, "Where's Jesse?"

"In school."

"Special school?"

"Regular school, special classes." Her cheeks were stiff. She coughed and reached down to pick up the rope of the saucer. "I'm freezing," she told Phyllis. "You'd better come in."

Phyllis firmly shook her head. "I'm not ready."

"Then let me give you a ride back to your car."

"I can do it."

"The road's a mess. It's a long walk around the lake to the public ramp," Ruby warned her.

Phyllis pulled up her jacket hood and turned her back to Ruby. "Not the way I came."

"Not on the ice, Phyllis," Ruby said. Without thinking, her voice dropped to the quiet, reasonable tone she used when Jesse became overexcited. "It's too dangerous. The ice is ready to give way."

Phyllis turned her head and said over her shoulder in a low flat voice, "I don't care." Then she began walking toward the center of Blue Lake.

"Phyllis, stop," Ruby called, but her sister didn't even pause. She continued onward, following her own tracks back toward the boat ramp. Ruby took three steps after her and then stopped. What was she going to do, wrestle Phyllis down on the dangerous ice? Tie her to the saucer with Spot's leash and drag her back to the cabin? She knew Phyllis; from this vantage point there wasn't one single thing Ruby could do to stop her.

So she stood in the bitter wind, hugging herself, feeling her teeth clicking together, and watched until Phyllis was safely across Blue Lake. Phyllis stepped on shore and disappeared into the trees without looking back.

Chapter 2

When Ruby stepped inside the cabin through the kitchen door, her phone was ringing, its old metallic bell jangling like an alarm. The Sable Telephone Company's promised upgrade to Touch-Tone service had been postponed for the third time, this time because customers were fighting the rate increase.

Spot sat beside the table regarding her with canine reproach as she slammed the door on a gust of wind.

"Feeling left out, are you?" Ruby asked through stiff lips, and rubbed Spot's ears with her gloved hands until the dog's tail wagged. "You're better off to stay out of this one, believe me," she said, and kicked off her boots but left her jacket on, still shivering, glancing out the window at barren Blue Lake to be sure Phyllis hadn't taken to the ice again. After two more rings, Ruby sighed and picked up the receiver.

"You sound like hell," her friend Mary Jean said.

"That's exactly what I feel like," Ruby said, reaching for a fresh tissue from one of the boxes she'd scattered around the cabin.

"Guess who blew into town this morning?" Mary Jean asked gleefully. She was a real estate agent and her office sat on Sable's two-block-long main street with a grandstand view of all its comings and goings. Sable was the closest town to Blue Lake, a mile south of Ruby's cabin.

"My sister Phyllis," Ruby said. She slipped off her mismatched gloves and tossed them across the room toward the box. Both landed wide.

"You already know?" Mary Jean asked, her voice dropping in disappointment.

"I saw her."

"Really? I wish I'd witnessed *that*. What's her story?"

"All I know is that she's here."

"I thought you were supposed to be some kind of sleuth," Mary Jean said. "Did she say what's going on? Why does she look so rough?"

"Rough?" Ruby repeated. "We didn't get close enough for a detailed inspection. She looked fine to me." Spot leaned against her leg, then sat on her foot.

"Not true," Mary Jean disagreed. "Rough as sandpaper. I ran into her coming out of Paulas's Drug Store. She didn't recognize me, or chose not to, anyway. Haggard and jumpy, that's my prognosis, ma'am. When I saw her three years ago, before you moved back, she was in top form. Classy, very Southwest, nose in the air." Mary Jean paused, and Ruby pictured her tipping her curly dark head, considering what she was about to say. "She smelled of alcohol."

"Are you sure?" Ruby asked. "This morning?"

"Unless she's discovered some weird new perfume. But I *know* that smell."

Ruby didn't answer, trying to imagine Phyllis looking haggard and smelling of alcohol; it didn't fit.

"It's pretty weird," Mary Jean went on. "Both of you in Sable at the same time. Ears must be burning around town. Are you going to see her again?"

"I don't know."

"Well, I'm here if you need to talk," Mary Jean said more gently. Other people in Sable might mull over Ruby's connections to her sister and her father, but only Mary Jean, Ruby's closest friend since she'd returned to Sable, knew the full story, and then only the bare bones.

"Thanks."

"What are you taking for that cold?"

"Aspirin and crates of tissues. But right now I think I'll take a nap."

"Good idea: Sleep it off. I'd like to take a nap until true spring shows up. This sucks. Is Hank there to rub Vicks on your chest?"

"He's coming by tonight. At the moment I'm unfit for human companionship."

"Jesse can spend the night here with Barbara if you want."

"That's okay. I'll be rejuvenated by the time the bus brings her home."

"Yeah, right. Good luck."

Ruby hung up and piled three more logs in the fireplace. The dry wood immediately snapped and caught fire, and she closed the mesh screen against the flying sparks, standing before the fire, her palms out, until she was finally warm enough to take off her jacket.

Twice more, before stretching out on the couch beneath one of Gram's quilts she'd finished herself, Ruby stood in front of the window that faced Blue Lake, gazing out at the empty white expanse. Nothing moved in the long, frigid sweeps of the March wind except tree branches. Outside, the air would be agitated by the click and whistle of the gusts through the naked trees.

Spot sat on the rug in front of the fireplace, watching Ruby pull the quilt to her chin. Phyllis returned to Sable every two or three years to see their father, Ruby knew that. If Ruby was lucky, Phyllis would stay at their old house in Sable for a few days and leave without their paths crossing again. If Phyllis had a problem that made her look "rough as sandpaper," Ruby didn't expect to hear about it.

One of Phyllis's lifelong talents had been to appear to slide smoothly and effortlessly through life, obstacles parting before her and her defenses closing in behind her. Whatever heartache, self-doubt, or rage Phyllis experienced—if she did—nobody else would detect a ripple in her confident surface. To the world Phyllis Crane lived the most charmed of lives. Ruby couldn't picture her sister haggard *or* drinking; either one would be too public a display.

Ruby had just dozed off, breathing through her mouth, tissues gripped in her hand, when the phone jangled again. Phyllis still disturbed her semiconsciousness, and Ruby found herself halfway to the stand between the kitchen and main room where the black phone sat before she was truly awake. By then she might as well answer it.

"Ruby?" the voice began. "This is Emma Lightner, the counselor at Sable High School."

Ruby leaned back against the comfort of the rounded and varnished logs of the cabin wall, her heart pounding. "Is Jesse all right?" she asked.

"Oh yes. I'm sure she is. I just thought I should let you know she left school early."

Ruby stepped away from the wall. "Why?" she demanded. "Where did she go?"

The woman's voice grew uncertain, apologetic, and Ruby imagined Emma Lightner's eyes widening behind her thick glasses. "Your sister Phyllis picked her up a few minutes ago. She said she forgot the note from you, but since Jesse was so happy to see her and she *is* your sister, well, we didn't see the harm in it, but I wanted to check with you."

"It's a little late for that, isn't it?" Ruby turned her hand into a fist and lightly pounded it against the countertop. "I didn't authorize this," she said, her voice helplessly rising. "Where did they go?"

"I don't know." The woman couldn't have sounded more contrite. "Well, I did hear Jesse mention her grandfather." Ruby briefly wondered if visions of lawsuits were passing through Emma Lightner's head.

"Please don't allow this to happen again," Ruby told her.

"We won't, I assure you. We just believed that—"

But Ruby hung up the phone before Emma Lightner had finished trying to appease her. Her hand shook. Phyllis had taken Jesse out of school. She must have gone directly from the ice on Blue Lake to the high school. That's why she'd asked if Jesse attended a special school. Ruby pictured her, charming Jesse right out the door of the brick building, a forgotten note just one more smooth lie to get what she wanted.

She climbed the narrow steps to the cabin loft, where she kept both her lab and her bedroom: L-shaped tables held her light table and lamps, and next to them the metal cabinet where she kept disputed handwriting cases and her stereoptic microscope. Her cramped bedroom was at the back of the loft, beneath the window that looked out toward Blue Lake. Instead of glancing out at the familiar view as she usually did, Ruby hurriedly pulled clean jeans from her bureau and a shirt from the rod that served as her closet.

What if Phyllis *hadn't* taken Jesse to their father's? Ruby paused as she pulled on wool socks; what if she'd *kidnapped* her? Phyllis had stayed in contact with Jesse from the moment she was born, despite their distance and the acrimony between the sisters. Phyllis didn't have children of her own, and Jesse was the closest related child in her life.

Ruby shrugged away the image of Phyllis as a kidnapper as she climbed back into the fleece-lined boots and jacket, shoving a fistful of tissues into her pocket and picking up the mismatched gloves. She could phone her father, but Ruby wasn't ready to hear her father's version of Phyllis's visit—nor to face the possibility that Jesse might not be there after all.

Her Pinto's engine caught, then died. She hadn't driven it in three days and she forced herself to slow down, pump the gas twice, and try again. It caught and died once more. "Don't do this to me," she told it aloud. "I'll buy you a nice oil change." She pumped twice, turned the key and it caught with a roar, then dropped to a peaceable rumble.

She pulled away from the cabin, bouncing over ruts and following the long single track through the trees to graveled Blue Road, which was in even worse shape because the county plows had haphazardly taken care of it all winter long. Only three families lived on Blue Lake year-round and the road was a low priority until the threat of summer tourists appeared on the horizon.

Ruby steered to the middle of the road, driving between the ruts, avoiding innocent-appearing, ice-skinned puddles that she already knew could be axle deep. Rills of plowed snow lined either side of the road, edges calving like glaciers.

It was a relief to turn onto the patchy paved road, free of ice and mud, and her grip on the steering wheel relaxed. She'd followed this route innumerable times during the first seventeen years of her life, between her house in Sable and the cabin on Blue Lake. By foot, bicycle, and car, a path so familiar that traveling it was a comfort, like a well-known melody.

At the edge of Sable she slowed, alert for any sign of Jesse or Phyllis. She had no idea what Phyllis was driving, probably a rental; her father had sold his car years ago.

A bright red and yellow billboard stood on the lot where the empty Chevrolet dealership had burned down last fall. COMING SOON: SILAS'S MINIATURE GOLF LAND!

Sable's two-block downtown stretched before her, brick and wooden storefronts, diagonal parking, dirty piles of snow melting on street corners. Pedestrians were bulky in their winter clothes, as drably colored as the weather; the sides of cars were crusted with winter grime and the road salt that turned snow and ice to liquid even when temperatures fell to subzero, fantailing behind cars after fresh snowfall.

No cars that looked like rentals were parked on the main street, at least not the kind of automobile Phyllis was likely to rent. She glanced toward Mary Jean's small real estate office and saw her friend talking on the phone. Mary Jean's chair faced the street and she waved. Ruby's twenty-year-old white Pinto had become signature in an area where most five-year-old cars were rusted out and ready for the junkyard.

She turned past the post office and drove two blocks to the gray house where she'd grown up. A teal Grand Am was parked in front, pulled in crookedly, one wheel canted onto the sidewalk.

In a bad mix of relief and anger, Ruby parked behind the Grand Am and turned off her engine. She sat there for a few moments while her car engine pinged, rapidly cooling, and ran her hands around the steering wheel as she looked at her old house, the wide front porch and gabled roof. In the year and a half since she'd returned to Sable, she'd only been inside that house three times. She and her father maintained, or maybe the better term was that they'd *attained,* a wary civility, with Jesse the glue. He hadn't met Jesse until eighteen months ago, when she was fourteen years old, but he was more tender toward Jesse than he'd ever been to Ruby, maybe even as much as toward Phyllis.

The front door was closed, the aluminum storm door flexing in the wind. Ruby glanced up at the double windows of her old bedroom above the porch; she'd last seen that room the night she'd run away twenty years ago, when she was seventeen. She'd never come back, she'd sworn back then. Not home, not Sable, not Michigan. Not ever.

She left her keys in the ignition and got out, pausing beside the Grand Am. It was empty except for a pair of black driving gloves on the seat.

The same porch swing hung on the front porch, creaking in the wind. During warmer weather her father spent most of his days there, sitting and watching, waiting, maybe waiting for death.

Phyllis jerked open the door to Ruby's knock, her red lips tight, frowning as if Ruby were an unwelcome solicitor. Ruby pulled open the screen door. "Can you step outside?" she asked her sister. "I'd like to talk to you."

Mary Jean was right. Up close Phyllis looked rough. Her makeup was flawless, thicker than Ruby remembered, smooth as a mask. Her eyes were overbright, intense, with dark circles artfully camouflaged. Tiny lines radiated from her mouth and eyes, everything about her expression drawn and edgy. She was thinner than Ruby recalled, fragile-looking, breakable, yet somehow fierce, as if primed for a fight.

"It's too cold to talk outside," Phyllis said. She was two inches shorter than Ruby, but in her boots they stood eye to eye.

"You had no authority to take Jesse out of school," Ruby said in a low voice.

Phyllis shrugged. "I wanted to see her. She's doing well, don't you think?" she asked as if she'd had a hand in Jesse's long recovery.

Phyllis wore leggings and a blue sweater. When she raised her hand to push back a lock of short hair caught by the wind, Ruby noticed a wide white band on her right wrist as if it had been cut from the cuff of a sweatshirt. An identical band circled her left wrist.

"I know she's doing well."

Phyllis held the door wider. "You might as well come in. We're not finished visiting."

Ruby stepped into her father's house, the plain old man's house devoid of her mother's touch except for the faded furniture she'd chosen forty years ago. A path was worn in the patterned carpet as if he rarely strayed from routes between kitchen and front door, lounge chair and TV. The lights were on, the drapes closed. The air smelled vaguely of onions. Jesse sat at the dining room table across from Ruby's father, a jigsaw puzzle between them. She was the brightest spot in the room, her warm cheeks and gleaming shoulder-length hair, the freshness of youth.

"Hi, Mom," she said, smiling. "Aunt Phyllis brought an underwater puzzle."

"That's good, sweetie." She kissed her daughter's head as Jesse placed two seaweed edges side by side. Ruby's father glanced up and nodded his silver head briefly to Ruby, then turned his attention back to Jesse's careful sorting of puzzle pieces. He was an old man now, his early brutality neutralized by the years, his shoulders bent, his angry eyes gone watery and faded. There was no triumph in seeing him undone by mildness.

Phyllis stood beside the oak hutch, her eyes on Jesse, a slight unguarded smile on her lips.

"Can we sit down?" Ruby asked her, nodding toward the couch in the L-shaped living room. Their father paid no attention to them, picking a corner piece from the box of puzzle pieces and offering it to Jesse. Jesse took it gravely and set it beside other edge pieces of the same color, all laid out in an even square. Ruby knew Jesse would arrange each piece in its proper order and then only when she'd found every edge of the picture would she interlock each with its neighbor, forming a finished frame to build the puzzle inside.

Phyllis looked from Jesse to Ruby and with a delicate sniff of irritation followed Ruby to the end of the living room, choosing the upholstered rocker across from the nubby green couch where Ruby sat, still wearing her jacket. This house had never been warm enough. Behind Phyllis's head hung a print of an old man praying over his daily bread. All Ruby's life that print had hung in exactly the same spot.

"She's better than I expected," Phyllis said, her eyes returning to Jesse.

"It's been eighteen months since the accident," Ruby reminded her.

"Don't get defensive," Phyllis said, crossing one leg over the other and regarding Ruby coolly. "Did you ever figure out what happened?"

Ruby shook her head. "She doesn't even remember the day. The doctors doubt she ever will."

It had been a one-car accident on Highway 1 north of San Francisco. Stan, Ruby's ex-husband, had been killed, but somehow Jesse had been thrown from the car and found beside the road, with a serious head injury. It was a slow and continuing recovery, and Ruby, in desperation, had brought her daughter home to recuperate amid the peace of Blue Lake, to the cabin she'd inherited from her mother.

"You turned out a lot more stylish than I expected," Phyllis said.

"I guess that's a compliment," Ruby said.

Phyllis's toe tapped against a sun-faded rose in the old carpet, pushing the rocker back and forth. She raised her hand to her mouth, briefly inserting her thumbnail between her teeth, then jerking it away as if she'd been reprimanded.

"What's going on, Phyllis?" Ruby asked.

Phyllis's eyes blazed; the jerky rocking stopped. Despite herself, Ruby sat back, feeling the high back of the couch scratch against her neck.

"Does something have to be 'going on' for me to come home?" Phyllis demanded.

Ruby said nothing, silently noting the tic at the corner of Phyllis's right eye. Phyllis stood and jerked open the drapes facing Mrs. Tzesni's clapboard house next door.

"I'll bet that woman's sitting right there behind her blinds trying to get a peek at the excitement over here," Phyllis said.

"There probably hasn't been so much activity since we left home," Ruby said.

"Or since mother's funeral," Phyllis corrected. "Not that you'd know."

Ruby shut her lips tight. Never complain or explain, Gram had always advised her. Nobody cares.

Phyllis gave an exaggerated wave, arcing her arm, toward Mrs. Tzesni's house and primly sat in the rocker again, holding it still, her feet flat on the floor. "Dad says you're a detective now," she said to Ruby, her unblinking eyes watching Ruby's face.

"Not exactly. I'm a forgery specialist. Handwriting. Inks and papers. I work in the loft of the cabin, in the privacy of my own home. I'm not a detective."

"You were hurt last fall," Phyllis said. "Was *that* about forgery?"

"Indirectly." She swallowed, then coughed. Her throat felt raw, rasped. Fever dried her eyes.

"Are you good?"

"Yes," Ruby said without hesitation. "I am."

Phyllis nodded curtly. "I might have a job for you."

"I work through Ron Kilgore, my old boss in California. Call him."

"I don't need a middle man. It's a small job. If you really *are* good, it'll only take you a few minutes."

"I'm not interested, Phyllis," Ruby told her. "I have enough to do here."

"Dad doesn't think you're making much money."

"Some jobs aren't worth the money."

Phyllis shrugged and nonchalantly bobbed the foot of her crossed leg. "Suit yourself. I can afford the best detective alive. I don't need you."

"Exactly," Ruby said. Despite Phyllis's words, the studied ease, Ruby sensed a false, almost childish bravado beneath her sister's claim. *I don't need you.* "If you're willing to pay the world's greatest living detective, you must be in trouble."

But Phyllis was beyond answering Ruby now, beyond giving an inch. Her blue eyes had gone impersonal, her delicate eyebrows arched upward as if waiting for Ruby to perform some gauche act. Ruby had lived with that expression the first seventeen years of her life. She didn't need it now.

She stood and walked toward Jesse, saying as cheerily as she could, "Time to go home, Jesse."

Jesse carefully returned the puzzle piece in her hand to the box, placing it in some indecipherable order, then frowned at the big-numbered watch on her wrist and said, "May I stay another hour?"

Ruby felt the lightest touch of her sister's hand on her arm and turned to see a softened expression on Phyllis's face. "Can she spend the night, Ruby?" she asked. Then, as if it were being forced from her, "Please?"

Jesse stood and said gravely, "I would like that very much. May I?"

"You can sleep in your mother's old room," Ruby's father added, nodding his head in encouragement.

Phyllis moved behind Jesse and touched her hair. The similarities between the two made Ruby swallow: the same intense thinness, the similar hair, pale skin, and fragile features. They were the same height and size. "I'm leaving tomorrow," Phyllis said. "I'm not sure when I can get back again."

The three of them watched Ruby, silently waiting for her answer, their expressions similar across three generations: heads slightly tipped and eyebrows raised. She didn't stand a chance.

"All right," she agreed, "but I'll come by in the morning to take Jesse to school."

Phyllis gave Ruby a thin smile. "Thanks."

Ruby left the house, turning as she closed the front door behind herself and seeing Phyllis's head bent close to Jesse, the light from the overhead lamp shining on their hair.

Hank let himself in, carrying a brown grocery bag in one arm. "Don't get up," he told her as he unbuttoned his jacket, shook off one sleeve, shifted the bag, and shook off the other sleeve, then dropped it over a chair. He brushed his brown hair off his forehead. "Windy out there. I've brought you a bagful of remedies."

He was a consulting forester, and March was the tail end of his slow season, marked by paperwork and a nervous restlessness as if he were a hibernating animal smelling spring on the air, impatient to be poking around in the woods.

He leaned down and kissed her forehead, then sat on the edge of the couch, his hip warm against hers. "Let me show you," he said, and began pulling items from his grocery bag. Spot sat in front of him, eyeing the bag expectantly.

Three lemons, a plastic bear of honey. "And," with a flourish he removed a green bottle of scotch, "the makings of that famous cure-all, the Hank Holliday

Hot Toddy. Fix you right up, or else knock you out until you recover on your own."

Ruby started to thank him, but he held up his hand. "Save yourself. Wait'll you hear the treatment *I* expect when I'm low." He put the scotch and honey back in the bag and juggled the three lemons. "I hear the famous Phyllis is in town."

"Who told you that?" Ruby asked. A lemon landed on her stomach and Hank scooped it up and dropped all three in the bag.

"Who didn't is more like it. The story is she looks a little beaten and tried to kidnap Jesse."

Ruby told him about her two encounters with Phyllis. He shook his head and murmured, "Lucky," when she described Phyllis's walk across the March ice of Blue Lake.

"So there's some truth to both rumors," Hank said when she'd finished. "There usually is. What do you think is going on?"

"I think," Ruby said, remembering the look on Phyllis's face when she offered to hire her, "that she's in some kind of trouble."

"Are you going to help her?"

"*Help* wasn't the term she used; it was *hire*. I told her no."

Hank gazed at her, his hazel eyes intent. He rubbed the sharp line of his jaw shadowed by the day's growth of beard. "From what I've heard about Phyllis, maybe that's as close as she could come to asking."

"We haven't seen each other in thirteen years."

"Has Jesse?"

Ruby nodded. "Phyllis arranged visits through Stan before he was killed. They're close."

"Phyllis hasn't been married?"

"No, but there have always been men."

Hank shrugged and stood. "I'll fill the firebox for you and get cracking on your cure." He shook the paper bag.

Hank was preparing Ruby a second cup of his private version of a hot toddy when her phone rang. She felt warm and slightly muzzy-headed. Blues played on the radio, the fire in the fireplace burned steadily on a bed of red coals. It was nine-thirty, late for anyone to call. Ruby watched Hank reach for the phone, a towel in his hand to protect the receiver; his hot toddies were messy affairs.

He listened, frowning, then beckoned to Ruby. "It's your father," he said, one hand over the mouthpiece, and then he added, correctly guessing Ruby's first concern, "Jesse's fine."

Ruby pushed back the quilt and got up, taking the receiver he'd stretched as far toward her as the cord would allow.

"She's sick," her father said in a raspy, panicked voice.

"Who's sick?" Ruby asked, wondering if he'd lied to Hank, her thinking suddenly coldly clear.

"Phyllis."

"What's wrong with her?" Ruby asked. She couldn't help it; she was so relieved that her voice relaxed, no match to his breathless fear.

"She's on the couch. I can't wake her up."

"Where's Jesse?"

"In bed asleep. I came out to get a drink of water and found Phyllis. What do you think's wrong with her?"

"Call an ambulance," Ruby said.

"No," he blurted. Ruby wiped at her nose and sighed. No ambulance, no doctors until it was too late. Take care of it all in the privacy of your own home. God forbid a public scandal should touch his small life.

"Then I'll call them," Ruby said.

"Can you come here first?"

"I'll be there in ten minutes," Ruby told him.

"Is he coming with you?"

"Yes," Ruby said, glancing over at Hank, who'd turned off the stove burner and was already reaching for their jackets. Here was a bit of scandal her father couldn't control.

"What's happened?" Hank asked as she hung up the phone, holding her jacket open for her.

"He said he can't wake up Phyllis."

"But he won't call an ambulance, right?"

"He's more the kind to call the hearse," Ruby said as she pulled on her boots. "It doesn't make as much noise." Suddenly in her mind she saw the bands around Phyllis's wrists. She paused with her foot halfway into her boot as a chill swept down her arms, wondering what the bands concealed. Whatever her problem, just how desperate did Phyllis believe it to be?

Hank drove fast, weaving around the potholes and

ruts, both hands on the wheel. The Jeep's headlights swept past the bare trees lining the roads.

"Did she seem sick when you saw her today?" Hank asked.

"Tense, but no, not sick."

"Don't be like your dad," he warned. "Call the ambulance."

"If she needs it, I will."

"Want me to stop at the Shell station?"

"The ambulance has to come from Pere. I'll wait and see what's wrong with her. I can't believe . . ." She stopped, uncertain what it was she didn't believe.

As they turned onto her father's street, Ruby hoped Jesse was still in bed, asleep and oblivious to Phyllis's drama. Jesse's response to the unexpected was unpredictable. Too many voices could turn her blank-eyed, causing her to rock herself for hours. Yet Ruby had seen her zero in on a book and remain oblivious to a quarrel in the same room.

Ruby opened her door before Hank turned off the engine, stepping across a frozen puddle. The porch light was on and her father stood in the doorway, fully dressed, even the top button of his shirt done up. He held the door for them, his white hair mussed, his sagging face drawn in worry.

"Where is she?" Ruby asked.

"On the couch."

Ruby pushed past him. "Is Jesse still asleep?"

He nodded.

Lights blazed in the living room: the ceiling light, the floor lamp, and a lamp at either end of the couch burned like candles standing sentinel beside a coffin.

Phyllis lay on the couch on her back with one of Gram's quilts pulled to her neck, her mouth slightly open, her eyes closed but with the narrowest slits of white showing. Moisture shone at the corner of her mouth.

"What's wrong with her?" Ruby's father asked, limping to the couch without his cane, his hands trembling. "Do you know?"

Hank knelt beside Phyllis and touched her throat. Then he frowned and bent close to her face, sniffing at her breath. His body relaxed. He looked up at Ruby and nodded slightly, rising from the floor. "She'll be okay," he told Ruby's father. "Let Ruby sit with her while you and I make a pot of coffee."

As Hank passed Ruby, one hand on her father's elbow, he whispered against her hair, "She's plowed out of her mind."

Ruby gently pulled back the quilt. Phyllis still wore the same stylish clothes, now wrinkled and twisted, one arm beside her body and the other lying across her stomach. Phyllis looked small. Without her sharp eyes and sharp tongue her resemblance to Jesse was even more marked. Plowed out of her mind, Hank had said. Ruby didn't need to place her face as close to Phyllis as Hank had; she could smell the alcohol. Her father hadn't been able to, and the idea that his favorite daughter could drink herself into a stupor hadn't occurred to him.

Ruby glanced at the floor around the couch; there was no sign of a liquor bottle. She pulled the quilt back farther and saw the glint of glass between Phyllis's leg and the couch back. She reached across Phyllis and pulled it out: an empty bottle of Glenlivet. Phyllis had always had expensive tastes.

She knelt on the floor and slid the bottle into the recesses beneath the couch so her father wouldn't see it and then stopped, her fingers still touching the cool glass. Why? Why was she hiding the evidence from him that his daughter drank? Instead, she stood the bottle on the floor beside the head of the couch. Phyllis could explain it to him herself.

The white wristband had slid upward on Phyllis's left wrist. Ruby tentatively touched Phyllis's hand. When her sister didn't move, she turned her hand over, bracing herself for the sight of a thick scar, a sign that Phyllis had attempted suicide.

But what she found shocked her even more. On the inside of Phyllis's wrist was a tattoo: a black dotted line crossing her flesh with the words *CUT HERE* printed above the line.

She roughly grabbed Phyllis's other wrist and pushed up the elastic wristband. The tattoo was identical. *CUT HERE.*

Ruby dropped Phyllis's limp arm and sat back on her heels, gazing at her sister. What in hell was going on? From a great distance she heard Hank's soothing voice as he talked to her father in the kitchen, the clatter of dishes, her own breathing as harsh as if she'd been running. She couldn't take her eyes from Phyllis, glancing again and again at the edge of the black tattoo just visible on her right wrist. *CUT HERE.*

Phyllis was a founding partner of one of the largest engineering firms in Albuquerque, a woman of power and substance. The black cynicism of the tattoo was more what Ruby would expect from a teenager wallowing in self-despair.

She gently pulled the wristbands back over Phyllis's wrists to conceal the tattoos before she rose and tucked the quilt around her sister's shoulders, folding over the seam binding so it wouldn't brush her neck. Phyllis's eyelids fluttered and stilled.

The kitchen was filled with the comforting odor of coffee. Only one light was lit over the sink, and the two men sat in shadow at the Formica table, each with a cup of coffee, another cup sitting in front of an empty plastic and aluminum chair. Hank spoke in a low voice, but Ruby's father paid scant attention, his eyes on the doorway, waiting for Ruby to appear, the dim light deepening the lines in his face.

"How is she?" he asked as Ruby sat down in front of the coffee.

"She'll be fine in the morning," Ruby told him. "I'll stay here tonight," she added, surprised by her own words, wondering when she'd made that decision.

"What's wrong with her?" her father asked. His eyes sagged. His knuckles were knobby with arthritis where he gripped his cup.

Both Ruby and Hank hesitated, and her father picked up a spoon and slapped its bowl against his palm, not looking at either of them. "Has she been drinking?" he asked.

"Yes," Ruby said. "She has. Did she tell you what's wrong?"

He shook his head, still not looking up. "No, but I think it's bad." He set down the spoon and nudged it toward the center of the table, finally raising his eyes to Ruby. "Will you help her?" he asked, his voice catching.

"I don't know," Ruby told him. "It depends on what the problem is and whether she actually wants my help." She thought of Phyllis's offer to hire her and how quickly that conversation had deteriorated.

"Talk to her," her father said again.

"I will in the morning," Ruby told him. She stood without touching her coffee, seeing as she did a shadow pass in front of the light in Mrs. Tzesni's kitchen next door. "Right now I'll check Jesse."

Jesse slept in Ruby's old room. Every vestige of Ruby had been expunged: her posters, her furniture; even the bed was new. The familiar contours of the walls and ceiling were visible in the low light cast by a night-light in the wall socket, but if the room had been pitch-dark, Ruby could have stepped directly to all those missing furnishings, laid a hand on her radio, found her stash behind the dresser, climbed into her missing bed without making a sound.

Jesse slept curled on her side, wearing a pair of Phyllis's silky pajamas, her breath light. Ruby hovered over her for a few seconds, breathing in her daughter's fragrance, then kissed her cheek and left the room.

"Are you sure you want to stay?" Hank asked her as she walked him outside onto the front porch.

"No, but I said I would," Ruby told him, stepping into his arms, clinging to the reason and sanity of his strong body, wishing she could scoop up Jesse and escape to Blue Lake.

"I can leave the Jeep here for you and walk back to my house," he offered.

"No, thanks. Phyllis can take me home tomorrow once she sobers up."

"Do you think she'll recover that fast?"

"I have a feeling this is not an unusual occurrence. I'm betting she recovers by breakfast."

He kissed her on the forehead and said, "Call me, okay? Middle of the night or not."

"I will." She waited on the porch, her hands tucked beneath her arms, until his Jeep disappeared around the corner, listening to the rumble of its engine in the cold night. A dog barked across town as steady as a metronome.

Her father wasn't in the living room when she stepped back into his house. Everything was silent; the kitchen dark. Lying on the recliner chair where Ruby intended to sleep was another of Gram's afghans and a pillow.

Chapter 3

The night passed in a disorienting and scratchy blur, filled with an irritating sense of waiting, of wasting time while she turned from side to side, trying vainly to find a comfortable position for more than ten minutes in her father's extended recliner.

Ruby had left on the lamp that sat on top of the television set: a dusty plastic relic shaped like an upturned cone that glowed and pointed a dim shaft of light straight at the ceiling. Phyllis slept like the unconscious: aside from an occasional muscle twitch, not stirring. Twice Ruby hauled herself from the recliner to check her sister's breathing.

It was still dark outside when she turned over for the zillionth time, hoping to relieve the ache in her shoulder, and saw Phyllis sitting up against the arm of the couch, the quilt wrapped around her and covering her head so that only her pale face was visible. Her eyes glinted in the low light, shadows bagging beneath them. Ruby caught her breath in surprise, then pressed the footrest on the recliner so that the chair raised her upright, its joints creaking. Phyllis didn't move.

"How's your head?" Ruby asked. The house was silent, but in the distance she heard the rumble and clank of trains switching cars in the railroad yard on the south side of town.

"I'll live," Phyllis said. She pulled the edge of the quilt farther forward over her head, covering her forehead so she looked like the icon of an ancient monk, face glowing in the folds. "What are you doing here?"

"Dad called me. He was sure you'd collapsed into a coma from some rare disease."

Phyllis raised her head and cleared her throat. Her eyes glared. "I'm in no condition to listen to that shit, so don't bother."

Ruby leaned forward, resting her elbows on her knees. "Fine with me. Why don't you tell me what's going on?"

"I'm in trouble," Phyllis said simply, her voice flat, no trace of the careful veneer she usually affected. "Big trouble."

"Is that why you came home?" Ruby asked. Hadn't she done the same thing herself? As illogical as it seemed, in times of trouble a person longed for home, no matter what kind of memories it held.

Phyllis nodded. She looked over Ruby's shoulder and said, "I needed help and you were the only person I could think of."

Ruby digested that for a few silent moments, wondering whether it was meant as a compliment and what Phyllis's successful life had become that her only source of hope during "big trouble" was an estranged sister. "How long have you had a drinking problem?" she asked.

"I don't—" Phyllis began, then stopped, pulling herself deeper inside the quilt. "Maybe a year," she said. "Maybe longer."

"And what about the tattoos on your wrists?" Ruby asked.

Phyllis jerked. "You saw them?"

"While you were unconscious." She could tell from the movement beneath the quilt that Phyllis was rubbing her wrists, mentally erasing the marks. *CUT HERE.*

"I don't remember," Phyllis told her in a distant voice. "I woke up one morning a few months ago and there they were, but I can't remember having them done."

"Are you having blackouts?"

She hesitated, then shook her head vigorously in such obvious disavowal that Ruby knew she was lying. She wasn't surprised. Phyllis had always been a liar but a curious kind of liar; she blatantly stretched or altered the truth when it pertained to herself, either to look good or get what she wanted. In all other matters she was scrupulously, even painfully honest.

"It's funny we're here, isn't it?" Phyllis asked. "Like time has warped. We haven't been together in this house since high school, before you dropped out and ran away. Sorry," she added quickly. "Didn't mean to bring that up."

"That's okay. It was the smartest thing I ever did."

"Escaped by the hair of your chinny chin chin," Phyllis commented. "Dad says you hardly ever come inside."

Phyllis was trying to slip away. "You didn't come

back to reminisce about the bad old days," Ruby said, sliding to the edge of the chair seat, closer to Phyllis, waiting.

"All right," Phyllis said in surrender. One thin arm emerged from the quilt and she reached down beside the couch, lifting a slouchy leather purse. She felt inside and pulled out a newspaper clipping. It was laminated the way the local funeral parlor laminated obituaries and mailed them to surviving families. "Here," she said, handing it to Ruby.

Ruby took it and stretched to reach the lamp switch beside her chair.

"Don't," Phyllis said. "Leave it off."

"There isn't enough light in here to read it," Ruby told her.

"I'll tell you what it says. The paper's from two weeks ago. Can you see the picture?"

By turning the clipping toward the TV light she could, enough to distinguish the stiff face of a boy, a teenager with short hair and a sullen broad face, a school photo. The headline was also decipherable: YOUTH KILLED AT BAD DAY, it read in thick black type.

"What does that mean, 'Bad Day'?" Ruby asked.

"It's a park, a picnic area in the mountains by Albuquerque. There's a history to the name."

"What does this have to do with you?" Ruby asked, raising the clipping.

"His name's Eddy Peppermill and they're saying it's my fault he's dead."

"How?"

"He was seventeen, a week from eighteen."

"How are you responsible?" Ruby asked again.

"Eddy," she spoke his name intimately as if in death the teenage boy had become partly hers, "and three other teenagers broke into Bad Day. I designed the park for a mining company trying to improve its image: a gift in the mountains to the public. We were caught by snow last fall and had to shut the job down until spring. And spring came early." Phyllis turned her head so she was in profile, and Ruby understood why she hadn't wanted the room lit; this was a story to be told in the dark, not beneath the bright shine of a lamp.

"These kids had a case of beer and were whooping it up on a section of walkway designed to be wheelchair accessible. The walkway failed and Eddy fell straight down the side of a limestone cliff. He was dead by the time the other kids sobered up enough to go for help."

"Doesn't that make it an accident?" Ruby asked. "If the park wasn't even open to the public? If it was still a construction site, weren't they trespassing?"

Phyllis gave a short laugh. "That's not the way the world works these days. The family hired a hotshot lawyer who's claiming a design flaw. . . ."

"*Is* there a design flaw?" She set the article on her lap, Eddy Peppermill's face blurring to a dark smudge.

"Yes."

"Then . . . ," Ruby began.

"I *didn't* do it," Phyllis said fiercely. "I know I didn't. My plans were changed. I'd never make so gross an error. I need you to come prove it. Eddy's dead. I think about him every day and every night. I will forever, but if they win this suit, I'll lose everything. My career will be over." Her voice went ragged. "What else could I do?"

"Doesn't your company have insurance to cover errors like this?"

"It's more complicated than that. Besides, I *know* my plans were altered. If I can prove it, I may have a chance." She leaned toward Ruby. "You have to come to Albuquerque," Phyllis said and then added hastily, "I'll pay for everything."

"You want me to prove your design plans were forged?" Ruby asked, picturing blueprints and draftsmen's numbers, all as similar at first glance as if they'd been drawn by one person. Disguising numbers was often overlooked by forgers, forgetting that numerals, even punctuation marks, were as individual as handwriting.

The dark room was beginning to lighten as dawn approached, the yellow lamplight fading to a clearer brightness, the furniture emerging from the shadows. Outside, the remaining snow shone white, the morning still too dark to expose its raggedness. Ruby traced her finger over Eddy Peppermill's face, thinking, trying to remember a time when as adults, an association between herself and Phyllis had ended well.

"What do you mean when you say it's more complicated than that?" she asked.

Phyllis shrugged and looked outside, for a moment her face crossed by an expression of surprise as if she'd forgotten where she was, that she'd returned to wintry Michigan. "Isn't everything on this earth more complicated than it looks?" she asked. "Bad Day has been a messy job, politically *and* publicly. There's been infighting in the firm. Nothing to concern you," she added. "Will you come?"

The pain was so apparent on Phyllis's waxy face, the fear so bright in her eyes, that Ruby found herself saying, "I have to think about it."

Phyllis exhaled a deep breath. She almost smiled. "You could probably do it in one day. Just fly in, look at the plans, and fly home again, what do you say?"

"What I already said; that I have to think about it."

Phyllis dropped her quilt and stood. "Why does he always keep it so damn cold in here? I'm going to turn up the heat and take a shower. You stay here and think."

When Ruby heard the shower running, she phoned Hank.

"Yeah?" he answered in that stunned alertness of being startled from a deep sleep.

"It's me," Ruby told him. "Phyllis wants me to fly to New Mexico for a day."

"One single day?"

She explained the tragedy of Eddy Peppermill and Phyllis's conviction that Ruby could prove her design had been tampered with.

"Are you going?" he asked.

"I haven't decided."

"Think about *not* going," Hank advised her. "How will you feel if you *don't* go? That might help you make a decision."

After Ruby hung up, she returned to the recliner. Not going, refusing to help Phyllis, left a sick feeling in her stomach. If she flew in, did the job, and flew out again, surely they could both be civil to one another for that short a time.

Phyllis came out of the shower into the now-warm living room, wearing only her underwear and rubbing her hair with a towel, the bands in place on her wrists. "Well?" she asked Ruby.

"All right," Ruby said, pushing away her reluctance. "Just long enough to do the job. Jesse can stay with my friend Mary Jean. Her daughter's the same age."

"Mary Jean Hannah?"

"Scribner now."

"Mmm. Bring Jesse with you," Phyllis said. "I'll hire someone if we need to." Seeing Ruby's hesitation, she added, "It would be less worry for you."

"That's true," Ruby conceded. "But there's school."

"A couple of days won't hurt." Phyllis's brusque competence had returned. "I leave this afternoon. I'll get tickets for you and Jesse to fly out of Muskegon tomorrow."

"Make it the next day," Ruby said. "I have things to take care of here."

"The sooner—"

"Wednesday," Ruby said firmly.

A frown passed over Phyllis's face and then she gave a quick smile. "Okay, Wednesday it is," she said, leaving the room, the towel wrapped around her head like a turban.

Ruby left her father's house and drove Jesse to school, thinking of everything she had to do before Wednesday. Her thoughts were interrupted by Jesse, who suddenly asked, "Do you know Salina?"

"No. Who is she?" Jesse wore yesterday's slacks with a green sweater of Phyllis's that intensified the color of her hair. Phyllis had offered to loan Ruby clean clothes, too, but she'd declined and wore the jeans and sweater she'd slept in.

"The lady Aunt Phyllis hired to watch out for me when we go to Albuquerque."

Ruby was so surprised, she pulled the car to the side of the street, stopping in front of the Wak 'n Yak beauty parlor. She hadn't mentioned Albuquerque to Jesse yet, and there'd been no time that morning for Phyllis to tell Jesse without Ruby hearing her.

"How did you know we were going to Albuquerque?" Ruby asked. She waved distractedly to Fanny, one of the Wak 'n Yak's beauticians who stood in the plate glass window.

"Aunt Phyllis told me."

Ruby turned sideways in her seat, facing Jesse. "When?"

"Last night, before I went to bed."

"Would you like to visit Albuquerque?" Ruby asked. "You could stay with Barbara and Mary Jean if you wanted to."

Jesse frowned, the two vertical lines appearing between her eyebrows, then nodded. "Aunt Phyllis said there are cactuses—I mean, cacti—and lizards. Can we see them, please?"

"Okay, we'll do it," Ruby said, thinking that once again, her sister Phyllis had managed to manipulate the world to her own desires.

* * *

A representative from United Airlines called that evening to confirm that Phyllis had made reservations for Ruby and Jesse. The departure times were good, with plenty of time to drive to Muskegon and still arrive in Albuquerque in the early afternoon.

"What about the return trip?" Ruby asked.

"It's open."

"Open?" Ruby repeated.

"Paid for, but open. Give us a call from Albuquerque when you decide to leave."

Ruby hung up and called Phyllis. A woman's soft voice answered, definitely not Phyllis. "Who's calling, please?" she asked.

"Is this Salina?" Ruby asked, guessing this was the woman Phyllis had described to Jesse.

There was a long pause. "Yes," she answered cautiously.

Ruby explained who she was and the woman laughed. Ruby caught the timbre of relief in her voice. "Ah," Salina said. "We're waiting for you and your beautiful Jesse."

"How long have you worked for my sister?" Ruby asked.

"Almost a year."

Arrangements were already in place. Ruby pictured the guest room beds made, towels out. This visit was taking on a life of its own, and Ruby felt like a small, unwilling player in Phyllis's drama.

"What's wrong?" Phyllis asked the instant she came on the line.

"Why didn't you make return reservations for us?" Water splashed in the background as if it were being run from a faucet.

"It just made sense, that's all. What if it takes you longer than one day? I'm sure it won't, but then you'd have to go through the hassle of changing flights. There's no problem with the flight down here, is there? Your logger can get you to the airport on time?"

Their father must have told Phyllis about Hank; Ruby hadn't. "He's not a logger," she said, and then bit her lip. Would she ever learn not to respond to Phyllis's barbs?

"As long as he knows how to drive. If I'm late, I'll meet you beside the statue."

"What statue?" Ruby asked.

She could almost feel Phyllis waving her hand in dismissal. "The big one. You'll recognize it. Some guy pulling a bird out of the sky. You can't miss it."

Phyllis wasn't at the gate to meet them, and the statue was titled "Dream of Flight," a breech-clothed Indian with one toe touching the earth, leaping into the sky as he grasped a soaring eagle. It was cordoned off by airport construction, so Ruby and Jesse stood against a pillar beside it, waiting. For such a short trip she'd only brought carry-on luggage and she set it on the floor beside them, away from the bustle of the crowds.

People in every conceivable kind of clothing from every climatic possibility passed by, many of them in shorts. Ruby draped her and Jesse's winter jackets over their carry-ons, thinking of the boots they'd left in their car parked at the Muskegon airport, where the sky had hung low, threatening snow as they'd boarded their plane.

Jesse stared at the statue, mesmerized, oblivious to the passing throngs weaving around the safety tape or the intermittent garbled voices over the P.A. system. She held the denim bag that contained her book and Walkman in front of her, gripped in both hands.

Whenever Jesse met a situation that didn't make sense to her, she studied and puzzled over it until she formulated a logic all her own. Ruby didn't interrupt her.

After fifteen minutes of waiting, a security guard approached Ruby. He was Hispanic, thick-bodied and handsome. "Do you need any help, ma'am?" he asked.

"The person meeting us is late," Ruby told him.

"There are phones down the hall. I'll help you with your bags if you want to make a call."

"Thanks," Ruby said, picking up one of the carry-ons. "Maybe I'd better."

They were interrupted by a lanky man in jeans and a white shirt, who broke away from the press of travelers, a frown on his tanned face. "Ruby Crane?" he asked. Sunglasses perched on his forehead along his receding brown hair.

The security guard stepped back and gave him the once-over, then asked Ruby, "Is this your party?"

"Almost," the man replied for Ruby. "Phyllis sent me." He reached out his hand and shook hers in a strong grasp, bending toward her a little. He was tall and long-faced, with a small V-shaped scar on his left cheek. His dark eyes sloped down at the outer corners. "Welcome to New Mexico. I'm Daniel MacSimon, an engineer in your sister's firm. She got hung up with a problem and for— . . . we lost track of time. Is that Jesse?"

Ruby turned. The security guard had disappeared and Jesse had ducked beneath the construction tape and now stood before the statue, one hand lightly touching its foot.

'I'll get her," Ruby said, and slipped beneath the tape to stand beside her daughter. "Do you like it?" she asked Jesse.

"Is it the man's dream or the eagle's dream?" Jesse asked, glancing from the title, "Dream of Flight," to the Indian's outstretched arms.

"Which do you think?" Ruby asked, knowing from experience not to interject any new ideas or complications into Jesse's ponderings.

Jesse tipped her head. "The man's dream. The eagle can already fly; it wouldn't care."

"Are you ready to go?" Ruby asked gently.

Jesse turned, searching the crowd, her face expectant. "Is Aunt Phyllis here?"

"No, but her friend's come to take us to her."

"All right."

The heat hit them when they stepped out of the airport, bright, shadowless sunshine. Ruby squinted, and Jesse shaded her eyes in the hard light.

"Eighty degrees today," Daniel MacSimon said cheerfully as he led them across the drive to the parking garage, lowering his sunglasses from his forehead to his eyes. "It's early, even for us. You got a cold?"

"Final stages," Ruby told him.

"Shouldn't fly with a cold."

He drove a battered but recent four-wheel-drive vehicle, a beige Jimmy raised high off its tires, steering with one hand and making swift, sure moves through the traffic. A beaded leather string tangled with a pine air freshener on his mirror. Rock music played on the radio and he tapped a finger on the wheel to its beat. Jesse sat in the backseat behind him, silently starting out the window at the scenery.

Ruby had never visited Albuquerque, and as they drove through the city, her impression was of neutral colors. Sand and beiges, whites and pale pastels, as if everyone and everything were trying to camouflage themselves on the vast high desert, to sink into the earth. There were no reds or purples or deep colors in sight. She glanced down at her own dark winter colors, remembering the bulky figures in Michigan still wrestling with winter cold and snow, the gray days of prespring. Here ornamental cherry trees were in blossom, low trees bearing clouds of white or pink. In the distant haze a line of mountains smudged the horizon.

They passed a cemetery without a blade of grass but dotted with statues and fences and complicated structures among wooden crosses and shiny artificial flowers. Daniel MacSimon followed her gaze. "Can't waste water on the dead," he said. "There's a big move here for xeriscaping: gardening with native plants that don't require much water. Desert willow, chamisa, sage, yucca. The city hands out money if you convert." He grinned at her. "You've entered the land of the environmentally conscious."

She gazed at the barren hills, the sandy lots. "It looks like you don't have much choice."

"Adapt or die, you mean? That's about it."

"Where are you taking us?" Ruby asked. The traffic was dominated by four-wheel-drive vehicles, most of them sparkling clean.

"To meet Phyllis at the office." He pointed into the distance. "Can you see those balloons, Jesse? Good calm day for it. We can get some pretty big winds this time of year."

Four colorful hot-air balloons hung in the sky north of the city, slowly moving toward the east. Jesse leaned forward from the backseat, intently watching.

Daniel turned toward Ruby and gave her a long look. "You're a forgery expert, is that right?"

"It is," Ruby told him, still watching the balloons float peacefully above the skyline.

"Phyllis has her hopes pinned on you." He gave his head a slight shake.

"You sound doubtful," she said. The streets they passed had Spanish names, unknown words she wouldn't remember. People here seemed slimmer, or maybe it was just that they weren't swathed in layers of clothing.

"It's not that I don't believe you're good at what you do. But Phyllis . . . well, the last several months have been tough on her."

"How well do you know Phyllis?" she asked.

He braked to let a car switch lanes in front of them and gave an appreciative laugh. "We've been friends for a few years. Nothing serious, if that's what you're thinking. I like her. She's a good engineer."

Ruby was torn between wanting to ask him about Phyllis's situation and feeling she'd be smart to stay out of it. "Are you implying Phyllis *is* at fault and it doesn't matter what I discover?"

Daniel bit his lip. "A kid's dead, and according to the rule of the land, *somebody*'s at fault. Phyllis was responsible for the design."

"When did this accident happen?"

"Almost three weeks ago."

"But you said the last several *months* have been tough on Phyllis?"

"That's right. This latest is the capper, an engineer's worst nightmare." He turned into the parking lot of an office complex where the philosophy of xeriscaping obviously hadn't been embraced. The lawn was as green as a golf course. Cherry trees bloomed white in beds of yellow daffodils.

"Happy days," Daniel said as he competently pulled into a narrow parking space with a wooden sign that read CHOLLA ENGINEERING PARKING ONLY and turned off the engine. "No reporters, no demonstrators to greet you."

"Who's demonstrating?" Ruby asked.

"There's a group claiming we're in devil's league with Southwest Minerals, the ultimate bad guys of mining, a group claiming Phyllis is being singled out because she's a woman. That's all so far. They tend to show up arm in arm with the press. Everyone's very hip to media possibilities." He turned on his seat and looked at Ruby. "Your sister's a very special woman," he said. "I'm sure you'll do your best for her."

Chapter 4

A male receptionist sat behind the desk in the main lobby of Cholla Engineering, wearing a telephone headset. The lobby ceiling soared two stories, the floor was laid with brick-colored tile. Southwest weavings and sand paintings hung on the walls. The receptionist raised his blond head and gave an impersonal welcoming smile until he recognized Daniel MacSimon, then he nodded, the smile collapsed to disinterest, and he returned to a stack of papers on his desk.

"This way," Daniel said, ushering Ruby and Jesse through a double door behind the reception area into a long corridor with offices off either side. The building was air-conditioned, lighted by fluorescent bulbs behind ceiling panels. Somewhere a photocopier whirred, voices blended in earnest discussion. From another part of the office a man's laughter was joined by another's.

Daniel paused at the door of one of the offices where two women were bent over blueprints. "Phyllis still here?" he asked.

"Hi, Daniel," the darker of the two said. She passed

her finger across her throat and grimaced. "She's in Bogart's office talking about the Johnson project. He's—"

"This is Phyllis's sister, Ruby," Daniel interrupted, "and her daughter, Jesse."

A flash of embarrassment crossed the woman's face and then was replaced less by a look of friendliness than one of curiosity. "I'm Paula Abbott," she said, sticking her pencil behind her ear and shaking Ruby's hand. "I work in this insane asylum. Hi, Jesse."

Paula Abbott was striking, tiny and dark, her hair cut into a smooth jaw-length style that gleamed beneath the artificial lights. She wore no makeup on her smooth skin and dark eyes; it would have been superfluous. "You here for long?" she asked, waving her hand between Ruby and Jesse.

"Just a couple of days," Ruby told her. Saying she'd flown over fifteen hundred miles to spend one day with her sister would draw too much curiosity.

"If you're staying with Phyllis, that should be long enough," she said, and laughed, but not unkindly, more with a teasing fondness.

The phone buzzed and Paula Abbott reached for it, mouthing good-bye to Ruby and Jesse. The other woman, who hadn't rated an introduction, continued studying the blueprints.

"I'll take you to Phyllis's office to wait for her," Daniel said, leading Ruby and Jesse onward. Out of hearing of Paula Abbott, he said, "Paula's one of our project managers. She's an ace at what she does."

"Is she a friend of Phyllis's?" Ruby asked.

"One of two in this place, at least right now."

"Who's the other one?"

"Me," Daniel said, standing aside so Ruby and Jesse could enter the door at the end of the hall ahead of him.

Phyllis's office was a corner room. Large windows in adjoining walls overlooked the unnatural green landscaping. The office was scrupulously tidy: a high drawing table on one side of the room, books and binders evenly shelved on oak bookcases, a large desk and comfortable chairs around a conference table. Labeled tubes of blueprints stood upright in a floor stand. Art as pale as the land hung the walls, all of it Southwest and, Ruby noted, all original. A display of Pueblo pottery sat in the center of the conference table. It was an office of affect, of power. Nothing personal marred the impact; no family photos, no funny notes or cartoons. Strictly business.

"How many partners are there in the firm?" Ruby asked Daniel.

"Four, including Phyllis. She and Peter Stern started the business above a taco joint twelve years ago. I heard that the plans for every project they did smelled of salsa."

And obviously the firm was very successful, which Ruby had suspected. She sat in a leather chair and motioned Jesse to the chair beside her, but Jesse stood in the center of Phyllis's office, digesting the room, her blue eyes moving over every object, so Ruby let her be.

"I'll put your bags in Phyllis's Jeep," Daniel told her. "I'm sure I'll see you later."

"Thanks, Daniel," Ruby told him. "I appreciate your coming to get us."

He shrugged, a grin raising one side of his mouth. "Yeah, well, she's distracted right now." And he was gone.

Jesse circled the room, one hand held so it hovered over each object but not touching anything, just looking. She stopped behind Phyllis's desk and said, "I made this."

"What did you make?" Ruby asked, startled.

Jesse pointed to a tiny clay bowl on Phyllis's desk, glazed blue and shaped like an opening buttercup. Jesse had made it in art therapy class last fall.

"I thought you gave that to your grandfather," Ruby said.

"I did."

Had Phyllis taken it from her father's house, or was her father sending Phyllis tokens of Jesse? Her drawings and crafts, class projects?

Ruby sat down again, growing aware of the raised voices coming from down the hall, a man's and a woman's in heated debate. The photocopier ceased its whir, and Ruby leaned back in her chair, trying to hear.

A chill swept down her back. One of the voice's was Phyllis's, and hadn't she heard that icy tone enough in her childhood that she could picture her sister's cold face: disdainful, the belittling lift of the eyebrow, that how-can-you-be-so-stupid glance. But in the past, Phyllis hadn't needed to raise her voice as she was doing now.

The man's voice was marked by a sneer. Ruby

caught the words "the reputation of the firm," and "publicity." Phyllis protested, but Ruby couldn't make out what she was saying. Suddenly the voices silenced and quick footsteps approached the office. Phyllis marched through the doorway, her face flushed. She was dressed for success, in a smart tan suit with a rose blouse that gathered slightly at her neck and buttoned tightly over her wrists. Understated and expensive.

"Ruby," she said, nodding curtly, and then she saw Jesse standing beside the window. Phyllis's tense shoulders relaxed, her mouth curved into a smile. "Hello, sweetheart," she said, crossing the room and gently hugging Jesse, stepping away quickly as if she'd learned in Michigan that Jesse often found physical contact too distracting.

This is why we have families, Ruby thought as she watched Phyllis's face relax as she greeted Jesse; they're the balm of our souls when life goes to hell.

"Trouble?" Ruby asked, nodding in the direction the angry voices had come from.

"The usual," Phyllis told her, dropping into the chair behind her desk. "Bogart Mead is his name, and yes, his mother named him after her favorite movie star. Touching, isn't it?"

"He's one of your partners?"

Phyllis shook her head, her eyes going back to Jesse, who was gazing out the window. "No, but he'd sell his soul—or mine—to become one. Bogart's a man who loves the sound of other people's bones crunching beneath his feet. Where's your luggage?"

"Daniel said he was stowing it in your Jeep."

"You look like winter," Phyllis said, nodding to

Ruby's dark slacks and blue sweater, then Jesse's jeans and long-sleeved sweater.

"That's exactly what we came from," Ruby said. "When can I look at this document?" She glanced around the office. "Is it in here? You said it involved plans?"

"My design notes." Phyllis's eyes shifted away from Ruby. "All eager to go, aren't you? They're in a three-ring binder where I record all the designs and specs for each job before I give it to the CAD person."

"Speak English, please," Ruby said.

"Okay, okay." Phyllis crossed her office to a low set of bookshelves and removed a blue three-ring binder and handed it to Ruby.

"This is it?" Ruby asked, flipping the thick book open to page after page of lists, numbers, and designs, all done in pencil.

"No. That's from another project. I just wanted to show you what design notes look like. These are my preliminary plans, every specification for weight and strengths for all the members we'll use in building, like steel and wood, all the sizes, site slopes and anomalies, that sort of thing."

"In mechanical pencil?" Ruby asked, her confidence faltering a little. Pencil alterations were more difficult to detect on a document than ink. Stroke directions and lifts weren't as obvious, erasures too common. And mechanical pencil was even more difficult than an ordinary lead pencil since the lead didn't wear down, which it did in a standard wood-and-graphite pencil, increasing or decreasing a line's thickness as it wore away and making changes easier to spot.

"Bic throwaways," Phyllis said, pointing to the pencil holder on her drawing table, which held at least twenty black plastic mechanical pencils with various colored clips.

"So what happens after you prepare your design notes?" Ruby asked. Phyllis's handwriting in the binder was as precise as a draftsperson's, excepting a few individualized strokes. There was no chance of confusing her *v*'s and *u*'s or her lowercase *g*'s and *j*'s. That was helpful.

Phyllis strode back and forth across the office, then stopped and leaned against her desk, facing Ruby. "I give it to the CAD person. AutoCAD: Computer Automated Design. And she—that's Monica Toya, she does all my CAD work—creates a set of plans from it, first on Mylar sheets. The blueprints you're used to seeing are made off the Mylars."

"So it was your design notes that were forged?" Ruby asked, flipping through a few more pages.

Phyllis nodded.

"But don't you have to approve the plans once they're created?" Ruby asked, closing the binder, "To catch any errors? Aren't you responsible for their accuracy?"

Phyllis's face darkened in irritation. "Don't get ahead of me on this. I told you it's more complicated than it looks. Just stick to one aspect at a time. Right now all I want you to do is examine my design notes."

"Are they in a binder like this?"

"Right."

"Then why don't you give it to me?" Ruby asked.

"I don't have it." She picked up a piece of black-

and-white geometrically painted pottery, rubbing her hands across its contours as if it were dusty.

Ruby stood and set the three-ring binder on Phyllis's desk. "Where is it?" she asked, trying to keep the irritation from her voice. Phyllis was jerking her around again.

"My lawyer has a photocopy," Phyllis said.

"With something as fragile as pencil forgery, I can't use a photocopy; I have to examine the original. Otherwise, my being here is pointless."

"I can get it," Phyllis said in a sure, almost hearty voice, revolving the fragile-looking pot in her hands.

Ruby knew Phyllis, and she betrayed the uncertainty of her words by her hands: turning the pot in restless motion. "Where *is* the binder with your original design notes?" Ruby asked again.

Phyllis set the pot down with a plunk that made Ruby wince. "The Peppermills' lawyer has it."

"The Peppermills? Isn't that the family of the dead boy?"

Phyllis nodded. "Eddy's parents. But Connie can get it for you."

"Who's Connie?"

"My lawyer."

"Call her and tell her I want to examine it as soon as possible."

"Him," Phyllis said. "Connie's a man. It's a nickname for Conrad. Conrad Tarcher."

When Ruby didn't comment, Phyllis went on as if she needed to convince Ruby that Connie was a legitimate name. "You know, similar to how we called Carl

Joyce 'Carly' to distinguish him from his father, Carl Joyce, Senior?"

"Are you having an affair with Conrad Connie Tarcher?" Ruby asked. It was unusual for Phyllis to defend a point as minor as someone else's nickname.

Phyllis rolled her eyes. "Don't be so provincial. I like Connie. We're good friends. I believe in making my lawyer my friend. Also my accountant, my doctor, and my beautician, anybody who has responsibility for my body."

Ruby picked up the three-ring binder again. "I'm taking this as a standard, to compare your handwriting against. Tell Connie to get the original design notes so I can examine them tomorrow morning. What else do I need to know? What other 'complications'?"

"None," Phyllis told her, raising her chin, her eyes steely. "You don't need to be concerned about any other aspect of this case. Just do one simple little job and you can go home to the back country and dabble your feet in Blue Lake."

"It's too cold," Jesse suddenly said reasonably, still standing by the window, so still that Ruby realized they'd forgotten her. "There's still snow on the ground."

Phyllis's face softened. "You're right, Jesse. I'm being silly." She rounded her desk and reached for her phone. "I have two more phone calls to make and then we can go home. If you want to, there's a picnic table to the left of the front doors. It's in the shade of the building, a nice place to sit. I'll be quick, I promise."

They stepped out of the Cholla Engineering building, pausing to adjust their eyes to the glaring sun. Ruby held her hand above her eyes, feeling like the sunlight ricocheted off every flat surface, assaulting her with light and heat from all directions.

A dark-haired man in casual clothes and sunglasses sat at the picnic table, a pad of graph paper in front of him, a pencil in his hand. His hair was stylishly cut, his skin smooth as if he'd just shaved. He was handsome in a sharp-faced way, broad across his cheekbones and tapering to a small mouth and pointed chin. He rubbed his knuckle against his neck as he studied his paper, reaching for a cup of coffee with his left hand.

Ruby hesitated and he looked up, first frowning, then smiling. "Go ahead, join me," and he pulled his pad of paper closer to himself.

Ruby and Jesse sat side by side across the table from him, their backs to the sun. She was aware of the way the man scrutinized her face and hair, and then Jesse's. "Are you related to Phyllis?" he asked.

"I'm her sister," Ruby told him.

He nodded. "Thought so. That hair. I'm Bogart Mead, one of the engineers."

Here was the man who Phyllis said liked the crunch of bones beneath his feet. She smiled, trying to keep the wariness from her voice. She was *not* getting involved in Phyllis's office politics. "Ruby Crane, this is my daughter, Jesse."

Jesse gazed at him solemnly, not answering his hearty "How are you, Jesse?" which he didn't seem to notice. He turned back to Ruby. "Are you the detective?"

"No, I'm not a detective," Ruby said.

"Just as well. Your sister needs more than a detective to get her out of this mess."

Ruby didn't answer and he went on, "The firm is suffering from her mistake. A dead kid, a pissed-off public. We've already lost business because of the publicity."

"Are you one of the partners?" Ruby asked innocently. "Is that why you're so concerned?"

He flushed. "No, but I have loyalty to this firm. Whatever affects Cholla Engineering affects me."

"You must be concerned for Phyllis, too, since she *is* one of the partners, its founder, I understand."

He snorted and leaned back. "I wish I'd known her then. Her drinking's ruined her talents. Killing kids doesn't enhance her reputation any, either."

"I don't care to listen to any more of this conversation," Ruby said, rising from the bench. "Excuse us."

Bogart Mead stood smoothly, picking up his paper and cup. "No, allow me. Welcome to New Mexico."

"I don't like him," Jesse said, watching Bogart Mead walk briskly toward the office door, rhythmically swatting his pad of graph paper against his leg.

"Me neither," Ruby told her. "But we'll probably never meet him again."

"Good."

Paula Abbott exited the building at the same time Bogart Mead entered. He made an exaggerated bow, holding the door open for the petite woman, who gave him a stiff grin.

"Hey," she said to Ruby, stopping beside them and setting a briefcase on the picnic table. "I see you've met Mr. Charm. Did he give you his our-reputation-is-ruined sob story? Or just his I'm-such-an-asshole act? Sorry, honey," she said to Jesse, winking at her.

"I think we were treated to both," Ruby told her.

"Lucky you. I'd say ignore him and he'll go away, but we've all tried it and he never does."

"*Is* the reputation of the business ruined?" Ruby asked.

Paula's voice turned more serious. "It'll teeter until the suit's settled, and then everything will return to normal. The public's collective memory is about this long." Paula held her thumb and forefinger a quarter inch apart. "Bogart is our Cassandra. He reels in some big-money projects, though, so we have to put up with him."

"Daniel said you're one of Phyllis's friends."

"Yeah, we work well together." She shook her head and made a fist against her heart. "It kills me to see all this happening to her." She glanced at her watch. "I'm on my way to a job site south of town. Too bad you're not staying longer; we could get together. Have a good visit."

Phyllis's promise to be finished quickly stretched into fifteen minutes, then twenty. A white Volvo pulled into a parking space in front of the building and a tall and slender woman with dark blond hair stepped out, pausing to adjust her white linen skirt and touch a pinky finger to each side of her mouth. She was lovely in a tense way, her face blank of expression, her eyes shaded by large sunglasses, but her movements sharp and decisive, concise.

She strode up the sidewalk and was nearly past Ruby and Jesse when she suddenly turned, as if she'd caught sight of them from the corner of her eye. She stopped, one hand raised to a glinting earring, and considered Ruby and Jesse. She raised her sunglasses and exposed artfully made-up eyes. And then the woman gave Ruby such a piercing and venomous glance that she felt chills tingle down her arms in the warm sunshine.

Chapter 5

"Who's the woman with the white Volvo?" Ruby asked as she buckled her seatbelt, nodding toward the white car still parked in front of the building.

Phyllis's Jeep was new, as Ruby had expected, the top of the line, but it was well used, covered by a layer of fine dust and a few long scratches along its sides. Notes on Cholla Engineering memo pads were stacked to overflowing in the console.

Phyllis put the Jeep in reverse and backed out of her slot without glancing at the Volvo. "Charlotte Stern, wife of Peter, one of my partners." She stopped the Jeep and, with her foot on the brake, leaned across Ruby to open the glove compartment and pull out two pairs of new sunglasses, designer labels still stuck to the lenses.

"The red ones are for Jesse," she said, dropping the glasses in Ruby's lap. "I knew you wouldn't think to bring sunglasses, coming from the land of gloom and doom."

Ruby peeled off the labels and handed the red

glasses to Jesse. Both pairs fit perfectly. Donning them was a relief, like cool water over hot skin.

A white sedan entered the parking lot and braked beside the Jeep, driver to driver. A man with a buzz cut rolled down the window, motioning for Phyllis to roll down hers.

"Got time to talk to me?" he asked, leaning his head and shoulders through his open window, squinting into the interior. From the higher vehicle, Ruby could see camera equipment and a brown folder spilling papers on the front passenger seat.

"Not a chance, Joey," Phyllis told him, her voice light. "Scram."

"Who's in the car?"

"Clients. Don't blow the deal," she said, acting at teasing. She waved, raised her window, smiling at the same time she softly cursed him blue.

"Reporter," she told Ruby as she slammed the Jeep into gear, making a quick right turn into traffic and glancing in her rearview mirror as if she suspected he was following them. "Don't talk to any of them," she advised Ruby.

"I don't intend to. Why does Charlotte Stern hate you?" Ruby asked, returning to the blond woman in the Volvo.

Phyllis turned and gave Ruby a long look. Through the lenses of her sunglasses her shadowed eyes were expressionless, masked. "Who told you that?"

"Nobody," Ruby told her.

A tiny smile played on Phyllis's lips. "You're sharp, little sister. Charlotte does hate me, with a passion. It twists her gut into knots and eats her up. She goes purple every time she sees me—and probably anybody who resembles me."

"Why?" Ruby asked again.

Phyllis glanced in the mirror at Jesse, who was deep in a book on cacti she'd found on Phyllis's backseat. "It's not exactly an original story. Her husband, Peter, and I had a brief . . . fling." She flicked her hand and continued casually. "It didn't mean anything to either one of us actually. I liked him before, during, and after, and it wouldn't have interfered with his marriage if Charlotte hadn't found out. But now she's determined he's going to pay for it for the rest of his life. She loves to pop in at the office unannounced, hoping to catch us in a clinch over the photocopier or something." Phyllis shook her head. "Peter and I steer clear of each other now, which is a shame. He's brilliant."

"Didn't you and Peter Stern found Cholla Engineering?"

"That's right. Isn't there a saying about love being ninety-nine percent propinquity?"

Phyllis had turned off the busy thoroughfare onto a wider, less-traveled street through an older, poorer section of Albuquerque. It was shadier here, with unruly cacti and well-grown cottonwood and willow trees clustered around squat golden houses of real, and often crumbling, adobe, with barred windows and recessed doors. Front yards were dirt, fringed with dried speared plants and a few succulents.

"How did Charlotte find out?" Ruby asked.

"An anonymous phone call," Phyllis said tersely.

"We were on a job in the western part of the state, staying at a motel. She found us. Not a good scene."

Ruby felt a wave of sympathy for Charlotte Stern finding her husband in bed with Phyllis. No wonder she hadn't forgiven; Ruby wouldn't either.

They rose into a residential area with real lawns and shrubbery and houses that reflected the tastes of the Midwest more than the Southwest. Phyllis slowed her Jeep near a well-kept tennis court, where a couple in shorts and T-shirts lobbed a tennis ball back and forth. "That's one of our projects," she said, shifting into Park and turning off the engine.

"A tennis court?" Ruby asked. The ball thwacked rhythmically against the rackets, clearly audible. Beyond the tennis court the land sloped away, offering a misty view of the sprawling city. The predominant hues, even in town, were tans and pastels.

Phyllis nodded. "Partly. Beneath the tennis court is a five-million-gallon reservoir tank. Fresh water for the masses. See the controls over there by the fence? You'd never guess the tank was under there, would you?" Phyllis's eyes fondly followed the contours of the disguised reservoir, oblivious to the players.

"No, I wouldn't," Ruby said. "It's very clever."

"Don't be patronizing," Phyllis snapped, turning on the engine and pulling back into the narrow street.

"I wasn't," Ruby told her. "It *is* clever."

"Sorry," Phyllis mumbled. "I'm edgy."

Only when Ruby recognized the same aging adobe houses did she realize that Phyllis had taken her off the route home to show her one of her company's projects.

They passed tile-roofed subdivisions and strip malls with a pinkish pueblo motif, then left Albuquerque behind, driving through barren sandy hills dotted by groups of gray-green junipers gathered like massing troops of soldiers. The sky stretched over them, too big, the land too open. Here and there, pueblo-style houses in sandy hues hugged the earth as if they'd sprouted from the dirt itself. And everywhere the sun shone so bright that soon Ruby's sunglasses felt inadequate. She squinted behind the lenses, feeling an ache at the back of her eyeballs.

"How much do you want to know about Bad Day?" Phyllis asked.

"Only what I need to," Ruby told her. "Jesse and I can't stay long."

"Can't wait to return to the old country, right? Back to your logger and your little hovel in the woods? What a life."

Ruby pursed her lips until they were painful, forbidding herself to respond as she had hundreds of times in the past. She'd make it through the next day or two with as little friction as possible, no matter how much crap she had to take from Phyllis.

"Dear old Sa-ble," Phyllis said, stretching out the word Sable, pronouncing it the way the locals did, like "hobble," not "table."

Phyllis turned the Jeep off the paved road onto a graveled secondary road, and a layer of fine dust swirled behind the vehicle. Here the land rolled and swelled, rising to the foothills and the swath of mountains behind. Pueblo-style houses, stucco not adobe, dotted the hills, each occupying a few acres of empty and sloping land. Ruby didn't know anything about New Mexican architecture, but it was obvious these homes were expensive. Exclusive and expensive.

"There it is," Phyllis said, waving a hand ahead of her. "*My* home sweet home." At the end of a long driveway sat another low home, a shade paler than the sand, all rounded corners and edges, the walls of the courtyard the same stucco as the house, wooden pillars, huge windows with deep overhangs. It had a closed, cool appearance even though there were no trees within sight and very little vegetation.

Phyllis pushed a garage door opener on her dash, and one door in a three-car garage whirred upward. She pulled into the white-walled space next to a white Porsche. Beyond that sat an aging Ford pickup. And in front of the green pickup was parked a chrome-and-yellow motorcycle.

"Are they all yours?" Ruby asked.

"All mine and nobody else's," Phyllis said. "I like to be prepared."

"A vehicle for every reason."

A door opened at the end of the garage and a young Hispanic woman stepped out, smiling. She wore an apron over jeans and a T-shirt, her black hair cut short and slicked back. Earrings shone along the outer curve of her left ear.

"That's Salina," Phyllis said as she pulled the keys out of the ignition. "She does everything. I'd trust her with my life, so *you* can almost trust her with Jesse." She gave a short laugh to show she might have been joking. "She's an illegal alien and doesn't like much attention—or a lot of questions," she warned.

Ruby wondered how difficult it was for Salina to keep a low profile when Phyllis was embroiled in a high-publicity lawsuit. Salina opened Jesse's door and leaned into the Jeep, smiling at Jesse. "You're a bigger girl than I expected," she said in perfect English, her accent not Spanish but more Northeast United States, only the slight melodic rhythm of her words giving away her origins.

Phyllis opened the back of the Jeep and grabbed one of Ruby's carry-ons. "Salina has a boyfriend from New Jersey," she explained. "He taught her English and snuck her across the border."

"Does he live here, too?" Ruby asked, watching Jesse studying Salina before she offered a shy smile. Ruby also smiled, in relief. Jesse was one to contemplate a new face before she made acquaintance. As if personality could be discerned from physical features, she made a usually irrevocable judgment, an analysis that was normally so apt that Ruby had found herself deferring to Jesse's opinions more than once.

"Now and then," Phyllis said, answering Ruby's question. "Salina has her own wing, and Adam works on a ranch down south. He gets up here every few weeks."

"You said he's from New Jersey?" Ruby asked.

"Born and bred. He looks every atom the Southwest ranch hand until he opens his mouth."

Phyllis led the way through a utility room into an entry. The house opened up before Ruby: light and airy. Ten-foot ceilings, white walls, tile and hardwood floors.

"Vigas," Phyllis said when she saw Ruby looking at

the bare beams that crossed the ceilings. The furniture was mission-style. Everything expansive, expensive, and orderly. The decor might have been taken from an architectural magazine. It was as perfect—and impersonal—as Phyllis's office. No photos or cartoons were magneted to the refrigerator, no shaky stacks of mail or magazines like Ruby kept. The effect was of coolness and polite good behavior.

Ruby turned to see Phyllis watching her reaction. "It's a beautiful home," she said. "Did you design it?"

Phyllis nodded.

"Mom would have loved all these plants," Ruby said, pointing to a profusion of green near a north-facing window. A philodendron with gigantic striped leaves nearly touched the ceiling. Cyclamen bloomed, the leaves of succulents glistened.

"She was never here," Phyllis said. "Let me show you your rooms."

As they passed through the kitchen, Ruby noticed a ceramic bowl of Reese's peanut butter cups on the counter, Jesse's favorite candy. "Has Dad seen this house?" she asked.

"No," Phyllis said shortly, leading the way down a tile-floored hall illuminated by skylights. Ruby still wore her sunglasses in the bright house.

Phyllis pushed open a door off the hall. It was obvious that Phyllis had prepared this bedroom for Jesse. A TV and stereo stood on shelves in one corner; posters of insects—Jesse's passion the previous summer—lined the walls, along with pictures of desert animals and plants. A reading light was attached to the bed's headboard, the comforter was a diamond design, rendered in primary colors, still the colors Jesse most responded to. The bookcase held a collection of young people's books: fiction and nature. A framed photograph of Phyllis holding Jesse as a baby sat on the bureau.

Phyllis opened two more doors in the room. "Closet," she said. "Bathroom."

"I'll help you unpack," Salina told Jesse. She pulled open a bureau drawer, and Ruby spotted clothes already neatly folded inside: T-shirts and shorts.

She went back and inspected the closet more closely, fingering dresses and shirts hung on the rack, realizing they were all in Jesse's size, Jesse's favorite colors, more clothes than Jesse could wear during their short visit, more than she could wear in weeks. She turned back to Phyllis, but her sister was already through the door, carrying Ruby's bag.

"You bought clothes for Jesse," Ruby said, catching up to her.

"I didn't want her to look like the poor relation from the Midwest."

"Is that important?" Ruby asked.

"To me it is. She's my niece."

Ruby's room was far less personal than Jesse's. A queen-sized bed sat beneath a window that looked onto a second walled courtyard behind the house. A door led from the bedroom onto a small patio. Here, too, the furniture was heavy mission-style, the polished floors covered with patterned Southwest rugs. The bathroom door stood open, and Ruby stepped into a room the size of Jesse's bedroom in her cabin on Blue Lake. It held a Jacuzzi tub and a separate shower. A window in the shower viewed the juniper-dotted hills.

Two new boxes of tissues sat on the bathroom counter, the kind with aloe, three new bottles of different cold medicines beside them. Thick white towels hung on the towel racks. "Lap of luxury," Ruby commented.

"Then you approve?" Phyllis asked, closely watching Ruby's face.

"It's lovely," Ruby told her. "Where's your room?"

"The other end of the hall. If you continue down this hall, there's a door that leads to Salina's rooms. She'll be close by if Jesse needs her."

"*I'll* be close by," Ruby reminded her.

Phyllis didn't respond but waved a hand toward the courtyard beyond the glass door. "I had to bring in soil," she said, "even for what little grows here. The native soil's too rocky and barren."

A telephone rang and Phyllis stiffened. She tipped her head, listening to the murmur of Salina's voice, her tongue moistening her lips. When Salina's voice ceased, Phyllis turned to the doorway of Ruby's bedroom, waiting expectantly until Salina appeared.

"Who was it?" she asked.

Salina shook her dark head. "I don't know. It was just another of those calls."

Phyllis nodded. "Any other calls today?"

"A KIZ reporter who wanted to interview you, and Mister Haxton of Southwest Minerals wants you to call him."

"Thanks," Phyllis told her.

"Are you receiving anonymous phone calls?" Ruby asked when Salina left the bedroom.

"And you claim you're not a detective," Phyllis said, heading for the door.

"*Are* you?" Ruby asked again. "Threatening calls?"

"Anonymous *and* vaguely threatening," Phyllis said, stopping and leaning against the doorjamb. "Just the generic uninspired stuff with a lot of single-syllable words. Some people get all excited by publicity. Pack instinct."

"Daniel said there's been a lot of publicity," Ruby said.

"What do you think? Dead kid from a trailer park. Parents with limited means and limited brains sue the wealthy engineering firm. David and Goliath. The crowds go wild." Phyllis snorted.

"Any letters?"

Phyllis shrugged. "A few," she admitted, crossing her arms.

"Can I see them?"

"Did you think I'd paste them in a scrapbook? I tossed them out."

"I'm sorry to hear that," Ruby told her. "What did they say?"

"That I'm a murderer who'll rot in hell, that I'm going to pay for the rest of my life."

"Do you remember anything about the handwriting?" Ruby asked.

Phyllis stood away from the jamb. "The *handwriting*? Oh, come on."

"Will I see your design notes in the morning?"

"Connie will get them for you." Phyllis took a step

through the door. "We're eating in tonight, do you mind? You probably expected Mexican food, but Salina's made a pot roast. Influence of the boyfriend again."

"That sounds fine."

"It's a clear night," Phyllis told Jesse after they'd finished slices of frozen carrot cake. "I set up a telescope in the back courtyard so you can see Hale-Bopp."

She couldn't have said anything to endear her more to Jesse, who'd been longing to view the comet through a telescope ever since it first appeared in the sky. They sat in Phyllis's dining room, candles on the table, the overhead chandelier off, and the glass door to the rear courtyard open to the night. Ruby and Phyllis sat across from each other, Jesse beside Phyllis. Salina had taken her dinner to her rooms. "Usually we eat together," Phyllis said.

They'd eaten late, after darkness had fallen, and once Phyllis had raised her head. "Hear that?" she asked Jesse. "Coyote."

They paused, forks poised, listening to the eerie lone voice waver and rise, holding its note and then dropping to a series of yips.

"I hope they don't keep you awake."

We are being so polite, Ruby thought, treading on spun glass, biting back words, trying to remain impersonal. Only one more day, she told herself. She could keep it up for one more day.

* * *

Ruby awakened in the night, disoriented for a moment, hearing the coyote's wavering cry. She sat up, rubbing her arms in the cool bedroom. The waxing moon had already set.

No, it wasn't a coyote. The slap of footsteps hurried past her room and she jumped from bed, thinking it was Jesse, her arms out in front of her, searching for the light switch. She spotted the sliver of light beneath her bedroom door and jerked it open in time to see Salina running to the other end of the hall, a pale robe billowing behind her.

Ruby slipped inside Jesse's room long enough to be sure her daughter was asleep, her hair glowing in the yellow cast of the night-light, before she crept down the hallway to Phyllis's room.

Ruby stopped in the doorway of the softly lit room. *Here* was where Phyllis lived. The room was a jumble of books and papers strewn over the furniture. And the furniture: not the mission-style Ruby had expected but the shabby furniture from their old home in Sable: Gram's rocker, the cheap pine dresser from Phyllis's bedroom, an armed cherrywood chair that had once sat at the head of the dining room table.

On the bed Phyllis sobbed in Salina's arms. Salina rocked her, saying over and over, "Shhh, shhh," as if she were comforting a child. Salina glanced up at Ruby and, barely perceptible, shook her head.

Ruby turned and left the doorway but not before she smelled the odor of alcohol.

Chapter 6

It was barely light when Ruby woke up the next morning. She stretched, closed her eyes, and when she opened them again, just that quickly, dawn had arrived. Instantaneous, the air bright and crisp, every feature at that altitude distinct as an etching. She turned on her side and glanced out the window that was only a few inches above the bed. The desert plants in the courtyard were still, dusky green and pale yellow against the sandy stucco wall. A hollowed-out rock, like a dry birdbath, sat on the ground next to a pot filled with exotic cacti that hung over its sides like a tangle of studded snakes, their barbed spines evident even from Ruby's distance.

Walled courtyards jutted off the front and rear of Phyllis's house. It was a necessity, Ruby supposed, to wall off a space in the midst of this open land, to contain yourself so that you weren't lost in its vastness. Or had Phyllis tried to create walls around her private life as Ruby had attempted when she'd returned to Sable, vainly hoping to lock out the world?

Indistinct voices reached her from another part of Phyllis's house, laughter. Too muffled to identify, but

Ruby glanced at her clock—6:15 A.M.—and guessed it was Salina and Jesse.

She pulled on a pair of shorts and opened her bedroom door, sniffing the rich brown odor of coffee. At the other end of the hall Phyllis's door stood firmly closed.

Jesse's bed was empty, already made. Before Jesse's accident eighteen months ago, making her bed wouldn't have entered Jesse's head. But this new, slightly modified Jesse had a compulsion for order, as if her recovering mind couldn't move beyond her surroundings unless they were uncluttered, without distraction.

When Ruby got to the kitchen, she stopped and blinked. The voices didn't belong to Salina and Jesse but to Jesse and Phyllis. They sat at the oak dining table next to each other, their similar heads bent over an open magazine, milk and cereal on the table, orange juice sparkling in crystal glasses, a black ceramic mug in Phyllis's hand. Jesse wore white cotton shorts and a striped shirt that Ruby had never seen before. Her hair was tied back by a coordinating length of ribbon. The morning shadows were sharp, every juniper bush defined, the west-facing mountainside still in blue shadow.

"Hello, Mom," Jesse said, looking up at Ruby and giving her the slow, thoughtful smile that transformed her face. "We're looking at desert plants. This is a cholla. When it dries up, it only leaves an exoskeleton, like an insect."

Her finger was held to a color photograph of a gray-green plant of many-spined branches growing out of bare dirt. "Maybe we can find a piece to take home," Ruby told her.

"There's coffee," Phyllis said, pointing to the electric coffeemaker on the counter, a third full. "Cups in the cupboard above."

Shadows sagged beneath Phyllis's eyes but only as if she hadn't slept well, not as if she'd been on a bender. Ruby wondered if this was how she got away with it: some capacity to hold her liquor, to drink herself into oblivion when she was alone and to recover quickly, thinking nobody knew. But that only worked for so long. People caught on to the cleverest of deceptions and then the news traveled like wildfire. We can't even keep our own secrets, she thought as she poured coffee into a blue mug. "You look nice, Jesse."

Jesse fingered the fabric of her shirt. "Thank you. Aunt Phyllis said I look like a native."

"Well," Phyllis told Ruby as if she sensed Ruby was about to bring up the new clothes again, "this morning I'll take you up to Bad Day so you can get a feel for the site."

"I don't need to see the site itself," Ruby told her, "just your design notes, remember?"

Phyllis shrugged and stood to pour herself more coffee. "Connie can't get ahold of the binder this morning. Some lawyer thing."

"You already talked to him?" Ruby asked, glancing at the wall clock that read 6:23.

"Last night. He keeps late hours. But you may as well know what my notes are referring to. Or aren't you normally that thorough?"

"What about Jesse?" Ruby asked.

"Salina is taking Jesse on a walk over the hills to delve into the secret world of cacti. It may be a little early in the year for lizards, but who knows."

"Is that okay, Jesse?" Ruby asked.

"I'd like that," Jesse said, tapping the picture of the cholla in her book.

"I have to stop by a project south of here before we go up to Bad Day," Phyllis said as they drove the gravel road out of the hills. The paved road lay below them, a sleek black ribbon that cut across rather than wound around the landscape like the gravel road they traveled in Phyllis's Jeep. Phyllis drove fast, one hand on the wheel, the other on the armrest of her door. She wore jeans and a pale lavender button-up shirt open at her throat, the sleeves rolled up to her elbows. The hems of her jeans hung over soft leather boots worn so much that they showed the outline of her feet, creasing across her toes.

"What kind of a project is it?" Ruby asked. Ruby wore jeans and the only short-sleeved shirt she'd brought with her, her hair fastened in a knot low at the back of her neck.

"An arroyo." She gave Ruby a quick glance, anticipating her next question. "A ditch to carry rainwater to the river. You wouldn't believe it now, looking at these dry hills, but when the rains come in July and August, the land can't soak up the water and it has to go somewhere, so we try to control its path to the nearest stream or river. There's an arroyo coming up here to our right."

Phyllis slowed, and Ruby looked down into a concrete ditch that paralleled the road, twenty feet across. Two boys rode bicycles down its center, snaking past one another. Dust and sand lay in its bottom, a tumbleweed caught against a pile of empty beer bottles.

"Every year, just as sure as the seasons," Phyllis said, "somebody drowns in one of these things. They just can't believe a wall of water can come racing down unannounced. Hell of a lot of force."

Phyllis's arroyo curved across the land, a huge swath of excavated dirt as wide as a country road. "This is a soft-channel arroyo," Phyllis said, pointing to the track of the arroyo, which twisted in lazy bends through a low area that crossed beneath the highway and into distant trees where Phyllis said the river flowed. "A site-specific design. No straight lines or definite slopes. We don't try to change its path but follow the lay of the land so it won't look artificial. Well, not overly artificial, anyway."

Above the excavation the construction yard was surrounded by a chain-link fence and contained heavy machinery: dump trucks, graders and excavators, construction trailers.

She turned the Jeep off the road and drove through an open steel gate, passing men in hard hats, their faces solemn in concentration.

"We took that out of the excavation," Phyllis said as they passed a mountain of sand. "We'll use it to make finished-soil cement: ninety percent sand and ten percent cement so it matches the surrounding earth. You'll hardly be able to tell." There was a timbre of excitement in Phyllis's voice. She glanced lovingly at the sand mountain and flashed possessively across the heavy yellow machinery. Ruby had never seen her sister so animated, so . . . unguarded.

Phyllis waved to a man backing up a front loader and drove directly down into the trough of dirt, the future arroyo. The sides towered above the Jeep as they drove along its bottom, and Ruby shifted uncomfortably in her seat, glancing at the walls of dirt on either side of them, the deep cut in front and behind, all of it the same pale sand. Clods of dirt had rolled down the freshly dug slopes, leaving long trails, and from above came the clank and rumble of machinery she couldn't see. She imagined a wall of muddy water racing down this tunnel at her, rolling dirt and debris in front of it, as she tried frantically to scramble up the arroyo's sloped sides.

"We have to build for the hundred-year storms," Phyllis told her. She raised her voice, pushing buttons to electronically lower all the Jeep's windows. "The walls will be eight feet thick to prevent erosion, the base eighteen inches."

A rill of redder unexcavated dirt lay across the bottom of the arroyo in front of them, and Phyllis stopped her Jeep. "Here's the problem," she said. Phyllis wasn't speaking to Ruby, only to herself. She grabbed a hard hat from behind her seat and jumped out of the Jeep, leaving the driver's door open. Ruby climbed out and walked around the front of the Jeep, uncertain what the "problem" was. It looked like plain dirt to her.

Phyllis bent down and scooped up a clump of dirt in her hand, squeezed it, and dropped it to the ground. It retained its shape, still holding her handprint. "Clay," she said. "Who'd have expected it here?"

A man in a blue hard hat walked heel first down a cut in the side of the arroyo, which was more compacted than Ruby had realized. A few trails of dirt slid beneath his feet. "What do you think?" he asked. His eyes were only on Phyllis; he didn't even acknowledge Ruby's presence.

"We'll have to dig it out and replace it with sand," Phyllis told him, gazing at the rill, her hands on her hips.

"Yeah, that's what I figured you'd say. I've got a six-twenty-three Cat waiting to get down here." They paused while a water truck sprinkling water on the dry earth drove past above them, shaking loose more trails of sand.

"Good job," Phyllis told him. She waved briefly and got back into her Jeep.

"Why can't you just leave the clay where it is?" Ruby asked. "Wouldn't clay be more solid than dirt?"

"When clay gets wet, it expands and weakens the soil-cement. Cracks it."

They drove downhill, following the slope of the arroyo toward the unseen river. Phyllis steered between the wider tracks made by another, heavier vehicle.

"What are those blue tufts in the dirt," Ruby asked, "sticking up like paintbrushes?" The bright blue tufts were positioned every few yards, close to the sloped walls.

"Blue-tops," Phyllis explained. "They indicate the level the grade has to be brought up to."

Ahead of them Ruby spotted the tops of tall cottonwoods just leafing out and through the open windows caught a whiff of the damp odor of fresh water.

Suddenly a man stepped from behind a yellow grader into their path, and Phyllis braked, a smile on her face. "Cesar," she called, opening her door and getting out.

The man was in his late forties, dark with broad shoulders, and as Phyllis spontaneously hugged him, Ruby watched through the windshield. His smile wasn't as broad as Phyllis's, but it was just as warm. He was dressed like most of the other men Ruby had seen around the construction site: in jeans and a light shirt, wearing sunglasses and a hard hat. A thick scar snaked up the outside of his right arm, puckered like an old burn.

"When did you get back?" Phyllis asked him, stepping away from their brief embrace.

"Yesterday afternoon," he told her. "I heard about Bad Day."

Phyllis brushed both hands through her hair, side to back. Her shoulders sagged and the openness in her face was replaced by a pained expression. "Yeah," was all she said.

"I'm going out there," Cesar said casually, but he glanced once toward Ruby and then to either side as if he were on the lookout for eavesdroppers. "Think we could talk this afternoon?"

"I'm taking my sister up to see it as soon as we're finished here," Phyllis told him.

"How about if I meet you there?" He glanced at his

bare wrist as if there should have been a watch circling it. "Maybe in an hour?"

"Did you . . . ?" Phyllis began, but he shook his head. "We can go over it at the site." He smiled toward Ruby. "So your sister has come to visit. Can I meet her?"

"Of course, I'm sorry." Phyllis walked with him to Ruby's side of the Jeep. "This is Ruby."

Ruby opened her door and shook Cesar's hand as he removed his sunglasses, smiling at her, the skin around his dark eyes crinkling. "Ruby," he said. "It's good you're here. A person needs family during a time like this."

Behind him, Phyllis shrugged as if to say she couldn't be blamed for anything he said, no matter how outrageous. Cesar put his sunglasses on again and said, "I'll see you at Bad Day, then."

Phyllis climbed back into the Jeep, her expression lighter, as if a burden had been lifted. She waved again to Cesar and they drove onward.

"Is he an engineer?" Ruby asked.

Phyllis shook her head and put her Jeep in gear. "No, but he should be."

"Where's he been?"

"On a job in southern Nevada. He's a contractor and goes where the construction isn't shut down by weather."

"Then he worked on Bad Day?"

"No. If he had, Eddy Peppermill would still be alive." She said Eddy's name solemnly, reminding Ruby of a reading of names of dead soldiers she'd once attended. "Cesar helped me with the design in the first place. Some contractors never question what's on the plans; in fact you wonder sometimes if they even read them. But Cesar *knows*. He's everybody's contractor of choice."

Phyllis pointed out a deeper excavation to the side of the arroyo, still a raw hole in the ground. "That'll be a desilting pond. It's a drop structure so the sediment will filter out of the arroyo water before it flows into the river. We can't let the dirt and debris dump into the river."

"Were the other kids with Eddy Peppermill injured?" she asked her sister as they continued down the arroyo bottom, the air changing, moistening, the light less glaring.

Phyllis turned to her and said earnestly, "Let's not talk about that here. This is a good place; don't taint it."

Despite Phyllis's superstitious words, Ruby knew what she meant and didn't say any more about the death at Bad Day. Instead she eagerly glanced through the windshield at the upcoming vegetation, feeling it had been much longer than twenty-four hours since she'd left Michigan, where there were at least skeletons of verdant seasonal growth.

"This is the bosque," Phyllis said as the arroyo grew more shallow, motioning toward the dark water that moved sluggishly through shrubbery and wetlands, "the river bottoms." She stopped and turned off the Jeep's engine. "I like this spot," she said, resting both hands on top of the steering wheel and leaning her chin against them, gazing through the windshield at the willows and cottonwoods, the thick brush. "It reminds me of home."

To Ruby it was a tangle of unrecognizable vegetation, even its green too pale, drained of color by the sun, nothing like the lush greens of Michigan.

"There's an endangered bird that lives in here," Phyllis said, still gazing at the scene. "It's called a willow flycatcher and it nests in May so if we don't have this portion of the arroyo finished by May first we'll be fined and shut down until October."

They sat for a few more minutes, and then Phyllis started the engine and turned around. They drove back up the arroyo in silence.

Ruby spotted a dense planting of trees and cacti, some tied with orange plastic ribbons and the whole grove surrounded by a line of plastic ribbon like a crime scene. "What's that?" she asked Phyllis.

"Plants or trees that were here before the excavation. We do that on all our jobs now: try and save them so we can replant when the job's finished. Sustainability. It's more expensive and sometimes it works; sometimes it doesn't."

A man in a hard hat waved them through the gate between dump trucks, and Ruby glanced at her watch. "It's already eleven," she told Phyllis. "Do we have time to visit Bad Day? Didn't you say it was in the mountains?" She glanced up at the rounded mountains to the east. "Maybe your lawyer has your design notes by now."

"He doesn't," Phyllis said, pressing her foot on the accelerator and pulling onto the highway, throwing up a cloud of dust behind them. Phyllis's jaw was tense; she didn't turn to look at Ruby.

"Is he getting it today?" Ruby asked.

"Nope." Phyllis passed a van and cut in sharply in front of it, ignoring the bleet of its horn.

"I see," Ruby said. "You've known he wouldn't have it today ever since I came to town, haven't you?"

Phyllis adjusted her sunglasses. "You'll just have to stay a couple more days."

Ruby felt a hot wash of anger; she'd been manipulated once again. "Is that why you brought me down here to see the arroyo project?" she demanded. "You're trying to involve me in your life until I agree to help?"

"I thought you already *had* agreed," Phyllis said calmly.

"You know what I mean. Beyond the forgery detection." She burned, wondering if Phyllis had pretended to show her softer side, playing on Ruby's sympathies, claiming with false nostalgia that the bosque reminded her of "home."

Phyllis tightened both hands on the steering wheel. "Don't make me beg, Ruby. Is that what you want? Would that gratify your years of jealousy? Of living on the edge of life while the rest of us slogged away building lives you'll never have?"

"Jealousy?" Ruby spat out. "Jealous of what? My sister who lives alone and drinks . . . ?"

Phyllis was coming up too fast on the car in front of her. She slammed on the brakes and the Jeep slewed, rocking sideways, tires squealing. For one breathless moment Ruby was positive the Jeep was going to roll;

she felt it tip up on two wheels and grabbed for the dashboard. Cars and trucks whizzed past; other brakes squealed, horns honked, and the world twisted in on itself. Ruby closed her eyes, thinking "Jesse."

"Are you okay?" Phyllis asked, her hand tight on Ruby's arm. "Ruby?"

Another voice, a man's, asked, "Everybody all right?"

"We're fine, thanks," Phyllis told him.

"Better pull out of the road, then."

Ruby opened her eyes. There was no mistaking the fear on Phyllis's face. "That was stupid of me. I'm sorry," she said.

"I knew there was a reason Dad yelled at us for fighting in the car."

"Okay," Phyllis said, pulling her seatbelt snugger. "Any more fighting has to be done on dry land, agreed?" She held out her hand to Ruby.

"Agreed," Ruby said, shaking Phyllis's thin hand.

While she still held Ruby's hand, Phyllis asked, "Will you stay a couple of days longer?"

"I'll think about it," Ruby said, knowing full well she'd just agreed.

Chapter 7

"Bad Day was originally intended to be a gold mine," Phyllis told her as they turned onto a two-lane road that headed up into the mountains. The land changed at once, rockier, with thin brown grasses left from the previous year lying low to the ground. Ahead of them Ruby could see pines and thicker vegetation. The air was already cooler, fragrant.

"Gold was mined northeast of here in the Cerrillos in the eighteen hundreds," Phyllis went on. "The fever heated everybody up back east, and one optimistic prospector was positive the Sandia Mountains were rich in the stuff, so he decided to get the jump on everybody. He was *way* off the mark. Legend is he said, 'It was a bad day when I laid eyes on this place.'" Phyllis shrugged. "It's probably a lie, but it makes a good tale. The site's in the Sandia National Forest."

"The national forest?" Ruby asked. "I thought you said Bad Day was a project you were doing for a mining company."

"It is. Southwest Minerals did some pretty devastating stuff while they were mining gypsum and pumice, and they're hot to improve their public image."

"And?" Ruby asked, not understanding what that had to do with the national forest. They passed a small store with two gas pumps and a sign that read LAST CHANCE!

"Well, they wanted the most bang for their bucks, so they ran their numbers and figured it was more cost-effective to create a public park closer to Albuquerque than on mountain land they'd already wasted."

"More publicity, you mean?"

"Publicity, goodwill, whatever. Government budgets are being hacked left and right. In fact, this weekend the Forest Service starts charging picnickers to park at picnic grounds. The public is screaming for more park land, more facilities and services. For years the Forest Service has been aching to develop this area, but they lacked the funding."

"Enter Southwest Minerals," Ruby provided.

Phyllis nodded, then pointed out her window at tall pine trees with blue-gray needles. "You know piñon nuts? Those are piñon trees: *Pinus edulis*, the New Mexico state tree." Then she continued, "Southwest offered to develop Bad Day with their money, their engineers and crews, then fund its upkeep for two years and pass it back to the national forest."

"And what does Southwest Minerals get in return?" Ruby asked. The piñon trees, gray-barked and sprawly, had replaced the junipers of the lower elevation.

"A good public image. It was a novel way to get more public recreation areas, cooperation between corporate and government interests, et cetera, et cetera. Believe me, the newspapers jumped on this story from day one." She paused and gave a single shake of her head. "Unfortunately."

"So Bad Day was already in the news before the accident," Ruby guessed. "And not only is Southwest Minerals interested in the outcome of the suit, but so is the Forest Service."

"You said it."

The higher they drove, the more remnants of winter snow they encountered in the deepest shade of the northern slopes—heavy, wet snow with rivulets of water melting from beneath it. Now *this* looked familiar.

"Gorgeous picnic grounds along here," Phyllis said, slowing down and pointing to the locked gates of a Forest Service picnic area called Cienega. "See what I mean about the public wanting access?"

Five cars were parked outside the chain-link gate and through it Ruby could see picnic tables tucked beneath pines she recognized as ponderosa, a bridge across a small stream, sun dappling the earth and melting tongues of snow. She opened her window and breathed deeply the heady odor of living pine, gulping it in. In Michigan it was too early for smells except for the subtle icy odor before a fresh snowfall.

Few vehicles traveled the road and most of those were four-wheel drive: Jeeps, Explorers, Broncos, and Jimmys. "We turn off just past the next picnic ground," Phyllis told her.

"Why are these guardrails rusted?" Ruby asked, pointing to the dulled reddish guardrails along a curve.

"That's called self-weathering steel," Phyllis explained. "It corrodes to red but doesn't lose any strength. Blends in with the surroundings better than bright steel."

Ruby looked away, thinking a rusty-appearing guardrail was more alarming than steel, when she spotted a pickup barreling down the mountain toward them. She had time to notice the dark figure at the wheel, the swaying mirror ornament, the wide hood that didn't match the blue body color before she realized the pickup was weaving, crossing the lane and heading straight toward them.

She reached across the seat and jerked the steering wheel to the right, and Phyllis's Jeep bumped onto the rocky shoulder. They weren't traveling fast and the vehicle merely stopped instead of careening off the road into the ditch and trees, but the pickup flew past them, swerving back into its own lane and on down the mountain without slowing.

"Asshole," Phyllis snarled after it. "He could have killed us." She tipped her head. "At least that would have ended my problems."

"Not mine," Ruby told her, gazing after the disappearing vehicle.

"That's right; you have family who'd miss you."

"So do you," Ruby said.

Phyllis made a *pfft* sound with her lips and then pulled back into the road, continuing their journey upward.

After the next Forest Service picnic area Phyllis turned onto an unmarked narrow road, paved but pitted and heaved by weather, and within a hundred yards stopped in front of a locked chain-link gate. The land behind the fence was heavily treed, tender spring growth greening up in the sunnier spots. A rough wooden sign was crookedly attached to the gate, hand painted in red lettering that warned BAD DAY, ENTER AND DIE. Here the remnants of yellow tape still tied to the gate post fluttered in the light breeze. The letters POLICE L were visible from the phrase POLICE LINE. DO NOT CROSS.

"Shit," Phyllis said, her mouth tight, staring at the rough sign. "Now what?"

To the left of the gate a green pickup was parked, empty. "That's Cesar's," Phyllis said. "Good. He's probably already poking around. If only he'd been working with me . . ." She jumped out of the Jeep, tore the wooden sign off the gate, and tried to break it over her knee. When that failed, she tossed it through the Jeep's open door into the backseat and told Ruby, "Grab one of those sweaters and come on. I'll show you the scene."

There was only silence when Phyllis turned off the engine. A bird tweaked and a breeze huffed in the pine treetops. The gravel crunched overloud beneath their feet. Phyllis ducked beneath the chain holding the gate closed and squeezed through the gap. Ruby did the same, catching the sweater on protruding wire and tearing a hole in the sleeve.

"Never mind," Phyllis said. "They're just throwaway clothes."

Ruby had seen the label at the sweater's neck. Throwaway clothes *she* couldn't afford. Phyllis walked in a tight stride, her arms close to her body. Ruby followed her across a paved parking lot, which Phyllis eyed critically, stopping once to toe a crack and say, "He'll have to redo that."

Bad Day was designed to be a picnic area, a day park. Concrete pads and seated pipes marked where picnic tables and grills would be placed. Finished rest rooms stood locked. Curbings hadn't been completed, a boarded-up construction trailer sat on blocks at the edge of the parking lot.

The music of falling water sounded through the trees, splashing and hissing, although Ruby couldn't see its source. Phyllis led the way along a wide, gently-sloping path that entered the trees toward the sound of the water.

"It's cement," Ruby said as she stepped onto the path that held firm beneath her feet yet appeared to be packed dirt.

"Concrete," Phyllis corrected. "Cement is the powder, concrete is the finished product. This is colored concrete." She spoke like a teacher giving a lesson she'd taught so many times she said it without thinking, all the while glancing around her, searching for signs of Cesar. They walked side by side on the wide path.

"You should give Jesse a little more room," Phyllis suddenly said. "You hover."

"I give her as much room as she can handle," Ruby told her, keeping her voice neutral. "She has a long way to go yet."

"She's farther along than you give her credit for. Maybe it's too comfortable for you if she's dependent on you."

Ruby didn't answer, and after a few seconds Phyllis

began to hum a song their mother used to sing: "When the red, red robin . . ." It had never been a happy tune for their mother, more of a "trouble song," accompanying tension and frustration. Hearing Phyllis hum it, Ruby felt the same discomfort as when she'd heard her mother sing it.

The gently sloping path continued to ascend toward the face of the limestone cliff in front of them, traveling closer and closer to the falling water. Sun shone through the ponderosa pines, but even here it was too bright, the greens bleached and the shade not dark enough.

"I designed a broader section into the walkway, a landing wide enough for wheelchairs to pass and where people could stand out of the way of the traffic and view the spillway," Phyllis said. "That section of the walkway was cantilevered." She stopped and pointed ahead of them where the curve of the cliff and the continuation of the walkway were more visible. The walkway sloped up the side of the cliff, unfinished, a minimal structure that clung to the escarpment overlooking a stream of water that tumbled down the side of the cliff and into a rocky bed.

"I expected it to be built of wood," Ruby said, studying the elegant steel and green structure.

"Wood requires too much maintenance," Phyllis told her. "That's a big issue these days. The decking is recycled plastic, the supports steel."

A bird chattered in the trees above them, scolding, and Phyllis took two steps closer to the cliff.

"That's where it happened," she said, and Ruby stepped nearer in order to hear her low voice. "On the broader landing. Four kids, two of them football players. Eddy played defense."

She didn't have to point it out. In front of them a section of the walkway hung collapsed against the cliff, as if too much weight had been set on a hinged shelf. Ruby imagined it: four drunk teenagers, maybe dancing on the wide landing to a boom box, whooping it up not worrying about trespassing, danger, or mortality. The sight of the dangling structure was desperately forlorn, potent with tragedy, a sight she wanted to turn from as Phyllis just had.

On the ground beneath the walkway, where Ruby could see a tiny patch of white spring flowers, lay broken beer bottles. Beside her, Phyllis looked to the site again, her faced closed of all emotion, absently rubbing the flesh of her wrists beneath the bands.

"It's coming down next week," Phyllis told her. "We had to wait until the investigation was finished."

"Why did it collapse?" Ruby asked.

Phyllis sighed. She broke a cluster of needles from a nearby pine bough and absently began breaking them into pieces, sniffing their bruised fragrance. "That's the whole crux of the problem, isn't it? The landing's cantilevered. Structural steel tubing is embedded into the cliff the same length as the cantilevered walkway's width. I'd specified A36 steel tubing, but what was used on the broader section—the portion of the walkway destined to receive the most weight—was A91100 aluminum alloy. Nowhere near the strength in that grade."

"What does A36 steel mean?" Ruby asked.

"It's an ASTM standard, with a stress factor of

thirty-six thousand psi, that's pounds per square inch. The aluminum had an H12 temper, only eleven thousand psi."

"Wouldn't aluminum alert somebody?" Ruby asked. "That sounds like an unusual building material to me. Remember those webbed-lawn-chair legs?"

"Not that unusual. It's lightweight, strong, good to use around water since it doesn't corrode. It's used more often near seawater, not so much here. It's expensive." She tossed down the cluster of needles. "And it's brittle. After a winter of heavy snow . . ."

"This grade of aluminum wasn't strong enough?" Ruby asked.

"Definitely not. It was bound to fail. I wouldn't have specified H12 aluminum even on . . . my worst days."

"Then maybe it was a problem during construction, not in your design," Ruby offered.

"Haven't you been paying attention, Rubina?" Phyllis asked, turning cold eyes on Ruby. "My specifications were changed. What the plans say ain't what *I* said." She turned in an irritated circle. "Where's Cesar?"

This was a beautiful place, Ruby thought, removing the image of death from her mind and looking at the walkway itself, the way it seemed to grow from the ground beneath the trees and curve gradually up the side of the cliff. The water in the spillway beside it fell in frothy curtains and then gathered in the rushing stream at the foot of the cliff. It appeared untouched by humans, although Ruby realized the spillway had been designed to keep the water contained. The paths and walkways completed the setting instead of intruding upon it. She wondered if now it would be forever branded as a place of death.

Suddenly Phyllis gasped and ran to the shallow stream beneath the spillway. She splashed into the water, slipping on the rounded wet rocks, falling once and then rising to her hands and knees and continuing onward, making frantic birdlike sounds in her throat. Ruby ran behind her, not understanding what was happening until she saw Phyllis frantically pulling at something in the water.

It was a man, lying facedown, his dark hair swirling in the stream's currents.

"Cesar, Cesar," Phyllis cried. She pulled at him, turning him over and pulling his head onto her lap. A pair of sunglasses, one earpiece still looped over his ear, slid from his face and splashed into the water. "Help me, Ruby," she cried.

But Ruby could see that it was already too late.

Chapter 8

Phyllis turned Cesar's body, wrenching him by the shoulder, and Ruby caught sight of a deep slash on the side of his neck, bloodless, washed clean by the icy water. All seen in an instant because she was already in the stream pulling Phyllis away, repeating, "He's dead, Phyllis. We can't help him."

Phyllis turned on Ruby as if Ruby had struck her. Her eyes blazed. "How do you know?" she demanded, her words tangled. "Why? Have you made yourself God?"

Water poured over their feet and numbed their legs. So recently had it been snow that it was a bitter shock of reality. Phyllis raised her hand, swinging it at Ruby and Ruby grabbed her wrist, shouting, "Look at him, Phyllis. He's dead."

Phyllis threw back her head and instead of looking at Cesar, raised her eyes to the piney treetops, her face in full sun. Her jaws worked as if she might howl and then she lowered her head and looked at Ruby and said, her voice eerily reasonable and controlled, "I know he is." She dropped to her knees in the icy clear water beside the body, the flow of water parting around her.

Ruby waited for a few moments and then said, "Come out of the water, Phyllis. We have to call the police."

"You go do it," Phyllis told her without looking up. "I'll wait here."

Ruby hesitated, reluctant to leave her sister in this remote place with a body. "Where's the closest phone?"

"In my glove compartment."

Phyllis refused to leave the stream to dry off in the warmth of her Jeep, and now she and Ruby sat on the rocky bank, keeping vigil. Ruby had finally convinced Phyllis to leave the body where it lay for the police to examine, and Phyllis had complied, drawing into herself and obeying Ruby without question.

Ruby found a picnic blanket and another jacket in the back of Phyllis's Jeep and carried those to the stream.

"For Cesar?" Phyllis asked numbly, shivering now.

"For us," Ruby told her, wrapping the blanket around Phyllis's wet legs and tucking it beneath her. And there they sat in the dappled sunlight beneath the pines without speaking, waiting, hearing only the splashing water and a few birds.

A green Forest Service pickup and a police vehicle arrived together, their engines straining over the uneven terrain. The Forest Service truck led the way, with a navy blue sedan following close behind the cruiser. Ruby stood and waved her arms and the three vehicles drove as close as they could to the rushing water. An ambulance arrived last, driven slowly, its lights off. Phyllis stood and wrapped the blanket around her waist.

Two policemen in uniforms and a man in dress slacks and white shirt with a tan cotton jacket approached them, the uniforms as raw a note in this setting as the body. The man in the jacket showed them picture ID and said, "I'm Detective Nick Powell, with the sheriff's department." He was tall and lean, with shockingly slender hips and legs that slightly bowed. A cowboy's body with a smooth city face and manner.

"You found him?" he asked.

Ruby nodded. One of the policemen circled the body, snapping photographs.

"Do you know who he is?" he asked, pointing to the stream.

"Cesar Peron," Phyllis said, her gaze steady, her voice completely under control. "He's a contractor."

"On this job?" the detective asked, and from his voice Ruby knew he was well aware of the death of Eddy Peppermill here and the controversy that surrounded it. He removed a notebook from his pocket.

"No," Phyllis told him, pulling the blanket tighter and tying the ends together. "A friend. He's done other jobs for our firm."

"You're with Cholla Engineering?" he asked.

"Yes, I'm Phyllis Crane." His eyebrows raised, and Phyllis nodded to Ruby. "This is my sister, Ruby Crane."

The policemen wore rubber boots. Ruby couldn't remember telling them Cesar was in the water, but she must have. One of them waded into the stream and squatted beside the body, taking notes.

"Then you were together?" Detective Powell asked.

"No," Phyllis said, "but he planned to meet us here."

"Have you touched the body?" he asked Phyllis.

Phyllis faltered and Ruby answered for her, "Only when we found him, when we thought he might still be alive."

The detective nodded and joined the policeman in the shallow water. The driver of the Forest Service truck, a big man wearing a green uniform, leaned against the hood of the pickup and crossed his arms, his eyes invisible behind mirrored sunglasses, but Ruby felt him scrutinizing the scene. He said nothing.

"Do you know if that's his pickup parked outside the gate?" the detective asked from the stream, raising his voice over the sound of the water.

Phyllis nodded and Ruby added, "It was there when we arrived." He went back to jotting in his notebook. The two women EMTs stayed in the ambulance, amiably chatting with each other. Sunlight flashed from their glasses. Sunglasses, everyone wore sunglasses, even the body.

A red Chevy drove up behind the ambulance, and three young men peered out rolled-down windows, heads craning for a better look.

"What's going on?" the driver asked, trying to see

around the vehicles. He was pimply-faced and dark-haired, with the overgrown face of a teenager.

The Forest Service employee stepped away from his truck and approached the car, flexing his shoulders as he walked. "You got any business here?" he asked.

The kid shrugged and the man pointed his finger and turned it in a circle, motioning for them to turn around and leave.

"I'm going down to lock the gate," he said to no one in particular, and headed down, already unpocketing his keys and following the Chevy as it backed up and turned around, spinning a defiant spray of gravel.

Detective Powell joined Phyllis and Ruby on the bank. "Anything else you can tell me?" he asked them. "Why was he planning to meet you here?"

"To talk about the accident," Phyllis told him.

The detective nodded, glancing up toward the collapsed walkway. "He didn't fall from up there," he said.

"His sunglasses were still looped over one ear when we found him," Ruby said, "so he probably didn't fall any distance."

For the first time Detective Powell gave Ruby a considering glance, more than just the professional attention normally given to a witness.

"What else did you notice?" he asked her, leaning toward her slightly. He swatted away a long black insect that landed on his sleeve.

"The wound on the side of his neck. The water has washed it clean, but it must have bled a lot."

"Are you in law enforcement?" he asked, and she

saw through his blue lenses the way he narrowed his eyes.

"She's a private detective," Phyllis offered, "in Michigan."

"I'm a forgery specialist," Ruby said, "*not* a detective."

"But you notice the details," he said.

"Sometimes." Ruby told him. "About ten feet from his body on the opposite side of the stream, there's a rock out of place."

He raised his eyebrows and looked at the tumble of rocks along both sides of the stream. "A rock out of place?" he asked.

"I'll show you," Ruby said. She left Phyllis and led the detective across the stream on a timber that stretched from bank to bank. Left by the construction workers last fall? she wondered. Or by Eddy Peppermill and his friends?

She'd noticed the smooth rock while she waited with Phyllis for the authorities. Under any other circumstances she wouldn't have paid any attention to the upturned stone, its sides still dark with dampness. In another hour it would be dry, the dirt falling from it, no different than the other rocks along the stream.

"See," she said, pointing to the round rock among the other pale stones. "The dirt still clinging to it is damp, as if it had been recently kicked over."

"Did you and your sister walk on this side of the stream?" Detective Powell asked Ruby.

"No, I noticed it while we were waiting for you to arrive."

He bent lower and studied the ground. Another

rock a foot closer to the stream was also upturned, its wet underside nearly dry. And at the very edge of the stream, the gravel-sized rocks were parted at the water. "Looks like he might have skidded here," he said, pointing to the scuff in the dirt.

"Or maybe whoever killed him was scrambling to get away."

Powell looked up at Ruby. "You've been thinking about this. I don't remember mentioning murder."

"Someone could have stabbed him from behind and he fell dead into the stream; that's why he was still wearing his sunglasses. Or if he was hit and knocked unconscious and *then* stabbed."

He straightened and gravely considered Ruby. "Do you know a reason anybody might want to kill"—he glanced down at his notebook—"Cesar Peron?"

"Robbery? Was his wallet stolen?"

He shook his head. "Still had thirty bucks in it."

"I didn't know him, but he was a friend of my sister's."

"And she's involved with that kid's death up here. What's his involvement?" He unconsciously nodded toward the body that still lay in the babbling water. His eyes had gone steely, his face that impersonal mask Ruby had seen so many times on policemen and investigators. Tending to business.

"I told you I didn't know him. You'd have to ask Phyllis."

"I'll do that," he said, and took a step back toward the timber across the creek.

"But not now," Ruby told him. "I'm taking her home."

"Wait a minute," he said. "I'm not finished."

"But we are. She'll be able to answer your questions better tomorrow. She'll be more coherent. You have her phone number in there, right?" Ruby asked, nodding toward his notebook.

"Yeah, I've got it. You're staying with her, that right?"

"For a day or two," Ruby told him.

"Have you come to help her out in this lawsuit?" he asked. "Maybe with those sharp eyes of yours?"

"Just to visit," Ruby said. "If you'll excuse me." Ruby turned and stepped across the timber, hearing the detective's irritated grunt behind her, feeling him so close at her back that if she tripped, he'd stumble across her body.

Phyllis stood where Ruby had left her, still staring into the stream. The two EMTs had climbed from the ambulance and were opening the back doors.

"Let's go," Ruby told her sister.

"Shouldn't we stay until . . . ?" Phyllis untied the ends of the blanket around her waist and looked from the stream to the ambulance. "I guess there's no reason, is there? We may as well go home."

"Why don't we stop somewhere for lunch and a talk?" Ruby suggested.

"Should I call Donna, his wife?" Phyllis asked. She moistened her lips. "There's a little boy."

"Let the police do it." Ruby picked up the jacket she'd sat on and shook it off. Phyllis watched her dully, not moving until Ruby did and then silently following after her.

"Do you want me to drive?" Ruby asked her when they reached the Jeep.

Phyllis glanced over at Cesar's pickup and said angrily, suddenly awakening, "I can drive. Worse things have happened to me and my driving hasn't been impaired. Stop with the protective-sister act, all right?"

But Phyllis drove more slowly down the mountain, more carefully. Brushes with death do that to us, Ruby thought, reminding us how easily, how randomly it all ends. The heat was turned on high, their windows open all the way; the warm air blew on their wet legs and feet.

They stopped at a café that reminded Ruby of California, a lot of light and plants and tables with white tablecloths, specials jotted on a blackboard in colored chalk, bland music. She glanced around at the two other occupied tables. No locals here.

When the waiter had served them each a beer with sections of lime perched on the lips of the glasses, Ruby asked, "Who has a reason to kill Cesar?"

Phyllis didn't even flinch. "Maybe whoever forged my design notes," she said. "Cesar knew the truth."

"And what's the truth?" Ruby asked. She squeezed the juice from the lime into the glass and dropped the rind inside.

"That my design was forged, I already told you that. Cesar helped me with the details. We were sitting in a bar in Old Town. He'd been to the site and we worked on the walkway, including the cantilevered landing."

"What's Old Town?" Ruby asked.

"The oldest section of Albuquerque. Expensive shops. It's touristy, but you should visit it, I guess."

"Do you have notes or drawings from that meeting?"

Phyllis picked at the label of her beer bottle. It was obvious to Ruby that Phyllis was struggling to remember the evening with Cesar. Finally she sighed. "I brought home a napkin," she said, and in a smaller voice, "I threw it away."

"Then you're saying that Cesar was the only one who knew what you'd planned for the support? The steel size?"

"A36 steel, not aluminum," Phyllis supplied. Half the label curled off the bottle. "He could have testified for me. He could have said we'd talked about structural-steel tubing sizes."

"But Phyllis, aluminum was specified in your design notes. If that was the forgery, shouldn't you have caught the mistake on the plans themselves?"

"I did," Phyllis said, still concentrating on the label.

"You did?" Ruby asked. "You didn't tell me that. What happened?"

The face Phyllis raised to Ruby was tortured, uncertain. Her reddish gold hair was uncombed and feathered, a childish cowlick on top of her head. "I put in a work order to change it."

"Then why wasn't the design changed?"

Phyllis bit her lip so hard, Ruby could see the outline of her teeth through her flesh. "There's no record of the order and I can't really . . ."

"Remember whether you did it or not," Ruby supplied.

"No, I *know* I did. But . . ." She stopped in frustration, closing her eyes for a moment. "See, if Cesar could have testified that my original plans specified A36 steel, and you could prove my design notes were forged, it would give credence to my having issued the work order that disappeared. Somebody's trying to sabotage me and ruin my career."

"Who?"

"I don't know. That's why I need you."

Ruby felt like she was surrounded by writhing snakes, none of which she could get a handle on, none of which she wanted to touch. "Why can't your lawyer get the design notes for me?" Ruby asked. "Tell me the truth."

"I haven't asked Connie yet," Phyllis said, raising her chin and meeting Ruby's eyes without apology. "I wanted you and Jesse to stay longer."

Ruby clasped her hands together beneath the table until they ached. Her heart whooshed in her ears. She counted to ten and said carefully, "Call him. I want to see the notes today. Now."

Chapter 9

Conrad "Connie" Tarcher's office was on the north end of Albuquerque in a bland two-story stucco building that could have passed as a group dental practice. Around the building xeriscaping had given way to zeroscaping: scattered tufts of gray-green vegetation hugging the ground, a few scraggly cacti, rough sand, and gravel.

"How did you meet this lawyer?" Ruby asked as she and Phyllis approached a plate glass door with smears and fingerprints around the handle and a set of small lip prints at knee level.

"Don't let the building fool you," Phyllis said. "This is where he opened his office ten years ago and he's too busy to move." She spoke in a distracted voice, and every once in a while she licked her lips as if she were thirsty. Their jeans were dry but not their shoes. Ruby's socks and sneakers rubbed against her feet, cold in the warm day.

Tarcher's office was on the second floor. His was a solitary practice and three secretaries worked in the front office in an air of industry, each in front of a computer. An air conditioner hummed, accompanying the soft *tic tic* of computer keys. The silver-haired woman at the desk closest to the door looked up and removed a headset. Her hands were youthful, with dark red nails squared at the tips. "Go on in, Phyllis," she said. "He has a meeting in twenty minutes."

"Thanks, Rachel," Phyllis said. "We'll be finished by then." Rachel looked curiously at Ruby, but Phyllis didn't introduce her. Phyllis pushed the wide oak door open without knocking, but Conrad Tarcher sat at his desk, his concerned face turned expectantly toward the door, as if he'd been warned by his secretary out front.

Unlike the industrious front office, the lawyer's inner office was a refuge: Bach played faintly in the background though Ruby couldn't spot a stereo. The carpet was plush green, the art on his walls of undefined soothing colors. The chairs were comfortable wingbacks, expensive and inviting. It might be the office of a highly paid psychiatrist: Step right in and we'll solve your neuroses together.

"This is my sister, Ruby," Phyllis said. "Give her whatever she wants. I'll be back in a few minutes." With that she turned and walked out of the office.

"Phyllis," Conrad Tarcher called, but the door closed softly behind her. He shook his head, then rose and held his hand out to Ruby. "Good to meet you, Ruby. What is it that I should be giving you?"

He was a compact man, not short or small, just compact, the contained type who rarely moved without a reason, and when he did, Ruby bet it was in quick, effective bursts. She couldn't picture him wasting his own or anyone else's time. He might be forty;

it was difficult to tell; his hair was prematurely silver, cut big-city short, and Ruby imagined him keeping it that way so he didn't have to comb it between showers. He had sharp blue eyes and wrinkles beside his eyes as if he'd squinted too much from forgetting his sunglasses. She felt him zeroing in on her. He was not a person who'd appreciate wasted words.

"I'd like to examine Phyllis's design notes from the Bad Day project," Ruby told him, matching him glance for glance. "Did she explain that I'm a documents examiner, a forgery specialist?"

He looked at her quizzically. "Actually she hasn't mentioned you at all."

"Phyllis claims somebody altered her designs and she's asked me to discover if that's true."

"Can you?"

Ruby sat down in the chair beside his desk. "Yes," she told him. "I can."

He came around from behind his desk, still holding the pencil and pad of paper, and sat in the chair opposite her. "I'll provide Phyllis with the best possible defense in this case," he said, tapping the worn pencil eraser against his paper. "But even if you can prove Phyllis's design notes were tampered with, if every page in the whole damn binder has been forged, it isn't going to get her off the hook. Ultimately the design is her responsibility, start to finish."

"But if somebody forged her specifications . . ."

He leaned back. "She should have caught it; that's her job."

"She said she did catch the error, but the work order disappeared."

Connie flipped to a clean page on his yellow pad of paper. "Disappeared," he repeated, and Ruby couldn't read what he meant.

"Can you get her design notes for me?"

"How about a photocopy?" he asked.

"It won't do. I need the original."

He shifted on his seat and scribbled something at the top of the clean page. Ruby tried to read his handwriting, but it was a series of slashes, a personal style of shorthand. She wasn't surprised.

"The Peppermills' lawyer has the original." He looked into the air above Ruby's shoulder, frowning, then a smile lifted one corner of his mouth. He reached across his desk and picked up the phone, pushed a button, and asked, "Rachel, when's that hospice benefit tournament?" After a few moments' silence he said, "Thanks," and hung up.

"I can get it," he said to Ruby.

"By tomorrow?" Ruby asked. "I'd like to examine it in the morning. Early."

"Can do. Come here to look at it, okay?"

"That's fine."

"What do you need?" Connie asked her, his pen poised to write.

"A bright light. I have my equipment with me. Depending on what I find, I may need other lab tools. I'll tell you when I see the notes."

"I can arrange it," he said, adding a few more slashes to his yellow pad.

"If there *has* been tampering," she said. "wouldn't that be a mitigating circumstance in the suit?"

He gazed at the ceiling. "Possibly. If you found the

person who did the tampering and we could prove criminal intent. It's a touchy issue."

"Did Phyllis ever mention Cesar Peron to you?"

"The man who helped her with the design? Yes. He's scheduled to return from Nevada today. Phyllis said he'd remember the particulars of the design."

"Actually," Ruby said quietly, hating to be in this position, the one who gave the bad news and was then associated with it, tainted by it, "he arrived yesterday. But we just came from Bad Day and we found his body in the stream there."

"Damn," Connie whispered. "Damn." His pencil stilled. "Murdered?"

"It looks like it."

"Damn," he said again. "You two found him? The Crane sisters. Anybody else there? Kids? Tourists? Anybody at all?"

"No."

He shook his head once and then glanced toward the door. "If I were you, I'd go catch up with Phyllis."

"What do you mean, catch up with her?" Ruby asked.

"She'll be at the Boston Bar, about a block south. I told her no more public drinking until this case is over, and when Cesar's death gets out, every step she takes will be suspect. The press will be all over her."

"Thanks," Ruby said, standing, realizing he was sending her on a mission of damage control more than one of personal concern. "Can you have the binder with her design notes by eight o'clock in the morning?"

"Eight o'clock. We'll talk more about Cesar's death

then. I'll see what I can find out." He was already reaching for his telephone.

"Will you give me the details of the case itself tomorrow?"

"Your sister said to give you whatever you wanted," he said, raising his pencil to his forehead in a brief salute.

The interior of the Boston Bar was dark wood and low lights, without windows, a darkness antithetical to the Southwest brightness. All the better to hide, Ruby thought as she noticed *ristras*, strings of chili peppers, hanging above the bar, a reminder that this *was* New Mexico, not Boston. She stepped around a table and headed for a row of shadowy padded booths near the wall. Phyllis sat alone, a double whiskey in front of her.

"You're quick," Ruby said, pointing to the empty glass near Phyllis's elbow.

"I have only just begun," Phyllis said. "Times like these I wish I smoked."

"It's not too late to light up," Ruby told her. "As long as you're dissolving your liver, you might as well take a shot at your lungs too."

"Cute," Phyllis said. "Did Connie tell you the whole sordid story?"

"He told me you'd never mentioned me in connection with your design notes or why I was here."

"Careless of me. So can he get my binder for you?"

"Tomorrow morning. But he didn't sound optimistic even if . . ."

Phyllis glanced toward the door and her shoulders slumped, relaxing. "Here they are," she said.

Ruby turned to see Daniel MacSimon and Paula Abbott enter the bar. Daniel removed his sunglasses, glanced around the room, and then nodded grimly as he saw Ruby and Phyllis. He came directly toward their table, Paula behind him, his eyes only on Phyllis. She slid over on her seat and he sat down beside her while Paula sat next to Ruby.

"I can't believe it," Daniel said, putting his arm around Phyllis in a quick hug before he let her go. "Cesar. My God, what happened?"

The bartender stopped beside their booth. "Bourbon," Daniel told him. Paula ordered a diet Coke, and Ruby paused before she said, "Gin and tonic."

"That's a summer drink," Phyllis said.

"This feels like summer to me," Ruby told her.

"Hello, Ruby," Daniel said as if he'd just noticed her. "Were you with Phyllis at Bad Day?"

"Yes."

"He was lying in the water," Phyllis said, her voice flat like a recitation. "Facedown. His neck was cut."

Daniel swallowed, his eyes going distant as he raised his hand to his own throat and then jerked it away.

"From a fall, or inflicted?" Daniel asked.

"We don't know officially yet," Ruby told him. "But my guess is that it was inflicted."

Paula listened, her dark eyes moving to each speaker's face. Tears slid down her cheeks and she didn't bother to wipe them away.

Daniel rubbed his hands around each other, frowning. "Maybe it was a robbery. Bad Day's pretty remote. Some ghoulish kids checking it out, buddies of Eddy Peppermill, maybe. They see a lone guy and think, what the hell . . ."

"He still had his wallet, cash, and car keys," Ruby told him.

"We just saw him this morning," Daniel said, sounding as if that made it impossible for Cesar to be dead, as if he had a responsibility to argue the point.

"Where?" Ruby asked.

"He came by the office looking for Phyllis. Chatted with everybody like he always does . . . did. He said he was glad to be out of Nevada. Didn't you see him, Paula?"

Paula nodded. "For about five minutes. He played five dollars for me in Vegas and dropped off twenty-three dollars." She looked down and shook her head as if she'd said something stupid.

"Did he talk about Bad Day?" Ruby asked.

Daniel glanced apologetically at Phyllis, briefly touching her arm. "It's the main topic of conversation around the firm."

"But he didn't offer any opinions of his own?" Ruby asked.

"None that I heard. When it came to serious subjects, Cesar was one to listen more than to talk. The deliberate type, you know the kind?"

"He was tense," Paula added. "He said people were just standing around with their thumbs up their butts watching, that nobody was trying to help Phyllis and change the direction of the investigation."

"Change it toward what?" Ruby asked.

"He didn't say," Paula told her, shaking her dark head regretfully.

"Did he tell you he was on his way to Bad Day?"

The bartender delivered their drinks, and Daniel took a hefty swallow from his glass before he answered. "He implied that. I can't remember him using the exact words, but I had the impression that Phyllis and Bad Day were the two major subjects on his mind. Or maybe it's just that I *expected* him to go to Bad Day to look over the situation. It was no secret he helped Phyllis design the park, and he was conscientious."

Phyllis suddenly leaned toward him, her hand clenched around her glass. "Are you saying I wasn't?"

"No, I'm not saying that at all," Daniel assured her, touching the white band that encircled her wrist, but Ruby thought she heard the slightest hesitation.

"So your whole office knew he was on his way to Bad Day," Ruby said, ticking off her fingers. "Someone at the arroyo site might have heard him arranging to meet us there. He might have been followed. Is there anybody with a grudge against Cesar?"

Daniel and Paula exchanged quick glances, and Ruby asked. "Who?"

"Well, there *was* trouble on a job last fall," Daniel told her. "Cesar caught some guys on his crew dealing drugs from the site. He had a hot temper. There were words and fists and then he was harassed for a few weeks. Threats."

"At the same time we had vandalism outside the office," Paula offered. "Garbage spilled in front of the doors, spray-paint graffiti on the glass, kid stuff, even though the firings wouldn't have had anything to do with Cholla. The contractors hire, pay, and fire their own workers."

"He didn't turn these crewmembers in to the police?" Ruby asked. The gin and tonic *did* taste like summer, and she suddenly wished she had ordered something stronger and more appropriate to the occasion.

Daniel shook his head. "Cesar didn't trust the law much."

"Anybody else who might be an enemy?"

"Not that I'm aware of," Phyllis told her. "But I don't know much about his personal life beyond his wife." Phyllis stopped and took another drink, then said, "And his son. I've seen pictures."

The liquid in Phyllis's glass was low and the vigilant bartender appeared beside their table. "Get you another one?" he asked. Phyllis opened her mouth, but Daniel answered, "No, thanks, we're fine."

"Maybe *you* are," she mumbled under her breath, but Daniel ignored her and gave Ruby a long look.

"Are you going to stay a few days longer?" Paula asked.

"It looks that way," Ruby told her.

Daniel smiled at her. "Good. That's very good. Anything you need, call me. I'd better get back." He touched Phyllis's wrist again. "I'll call you again, just to see how you're doing."

"You don't have to," Phyllis told him. She nodded at Ruby. "I've got my sister here to keep me straight."

It was out of Ruby's mouth before she thought: "I'm not interested in baby-sitting you."

"My my, touchy," Phyllis said, raising her empty glass and tipping it as if she were looking for one swallowable drop.

"I'll call," Daniel said.

After Daniel and Paula left, Ruby said to Phyllis, "He's in love with you."

"Marginally," Phyllis agreed. "But luckily we progressed beyond it to becoming good friends. Daniel's basically lazy. He culls his dates from women in the office so he doesn't have to waste time looking out in the real world." She nudged Ruby's gin-and-tonic glass, which held only melting ice. "Sure you don't want another one?"

Ruby knew that Phyllis wasn't asking for Ruby's sake but for her own. "I'd rather go back to your house and see how Jesse's getting along with Salina. You can tell me more about Bad Day and Cholla Engineering on the way."

"Are you trying to divert my attention from another drink?" Phyllis asked.

"Yes," Ruby told her.

Chapter 10

"The Peppermills?" Phyllis asked in response to Ruby's question. "I haven't met them. I've seen the father on television, vowing revenge. He doesn't blink when he's in front of a camera, just stares bug-eyed. The news has painted them as a poor struggling couple with health problems. Eddy was a delinquent, I guess. Not that that's such a big deal, but the press played it down and focused on his one redeeming quality: He was a football star with the nickname Mincemeat—can you picture it? He would have been thrown out of school if it wasn't for his coach. Bad grades, bad rep, a police record. But what's the harm in that if you can charge down a football field and knock heads?"

"He was eighteen?" Ruby asked. Phyllis sped toward home, barefoot, her boots in the backseat and her body more relaxed the closer they got to her house. Ruby knew that feeling. She felt the same way when she was almost home to her cabin on Blue Lake. Refuge, safety, a world she had at least some control over.

"Almost eighteen," Phyllis said tersely. "He was

celebrating his birthday at Bad Day. The four kids lugged a case of beer up the walkway, and who knows how much they drank before they got there."

"And the other three weren't hurt?"

"Not at all. Eddy's the only one who tipped over the edge. He'd been living on his own for the past year. His parents had washed their hands of him until this happened. The dead are so much more congenial to live with."

"But he *was* their child," Ruby pointed out.

"I know," Phyllis said. She swallowed, and hit her fist against the rim of the steering wheel. "I don't forget that, never, not for a single second." She gazed at the road in front of her and passed a motor home before she continued, "The Peppermills are claiming Eddy could have played football professionally and he was such a good boy, such a decent son, that he surely would have shared the fruits of his promising career with his beloved parents."

She snorted in disgust. "If I lost my child, I'd go mad, not run pell-mell for my lawyer. I'm the first step on the Peppermills' grief-filled road to riches. If they win this lawsuit, they've got their very own gold mine. They can stick it to Southwest Minerals, the Forest Service, maybe the company that didn't build an Eddy-proof fence around the site. The sky's the limit."

Ruby thought about what Connie had said, that no matter whether there was forgery or not, Phyllis was still responsible for the design of the walkway, start to finish. "What would you do if you were forced to leave engineering?" she asked.

Phyllis was silent. Her jaws tensed. She stared at

the desolate landscape and then she said, "I couldn't run home to Michigan to lick my wounds like you did. Nobody willed me the family cabin for a hideout."

"Mom didn't will it to me as a hideout; she knew how much I loved the place."

"So much so that you didn't see her again after you ran away. You were seventeen years old, Ruby. For nineteen years you didn't come home, not even for her funeral. Why in hell she left it to you, I'll never be able to figure out. You never visited her; you never wrote. It's like some bad Prodigal Daughter joke."

"That's not true," Ruby said.

"Which part? The Prodigal Daughter?"

"That I never wrote."

"She didn't say so. So what happened, the letters all got lost in the mail? Tsk tsk."

"She kept a post office box in Pere," Ruby told Phyllis. "I wrote to her there." Every week. Ruby had seen their mother, too, but that wasn't something she was about to share with Phyllis. Brief, clandestine meetings, once in Chicago, twice in Detroit, watching her mother's final fading away under her father's thumb, too timid to fight back, their meetings probably the most defiant acts she'd ever committed. A woman of another era, overrun until she was broken.

"I see," Phyllis said, sounding more angry than relieved that Ruby *had* kept in contact with their mother. "Family secrets."

"It looks like you have company," Ruby said as Phyllis turned in to the long driveway to her house. A dusty blue pickup with a dented passenger door sat beside the garage, and parked in the driveway was a white Lexus.

"The pickup belongs to Salina's Adam and the Lexus belongs to Peter Stern, one of my partners," Phyllis told her.

"Husband of Charlotte who hates you?" Ruby asked.

"The very same."

Inside the bright but cool house a man sat with Jesse and Salina at the dining room table, a stack of books opened and unopened in their midst. It took no time at all to discern that he was Peter Stern and not Salina's cowboy boyfriend.

He radiated self-confidence. Not brashness but a friendly certainty that he knew what he was about, knew his roles and his capabilities, and wasn't interested in proving them to anyone. Peter Stern wasn't handsome; his jaw was too long; his eyebrows met over his nose, his cheekbones too prominent. He rose when Ruby and Phyllis entered, and Ruby caught the spark that lit up Phyllis's eyes and then passed between them. The affair might be over, but the feelings obviously lingered.

Jesse glanced up and smiled, her finger to the color illustration of a cactus, her mind on the wonders of desert plants. Ruby and Phyllis were secondary.

"So you're Phyllis's sister," Peter Stern said, shaking Ruby's hand warmly, glancing from Phyllis to Ruby as if confirming their likeness.

"Peter, this is Ruby, Ruby, Peter," Phyllis said quickly.

"Good to meet you," Ruby told him, meeting those

warm eyes and wondering why he was here. Was Charlotte far behind?

They stood awkwardly, smiling, players without a script. The heat coming from Phyllis and Peter Stern turned the others into outsiders, until Salina said, "Jesse and I will sit in the front courtyard for a while. It's shady there now."

Salina and Jesse each carried an armload of books with them through the glass doors. There was no sign of Adam's presence, other than the pickup out front.

"I'll be back in a few minutes," Ruby told Phyllis.

"Okay," Phyllis said, her attention on Peter Stern.

Ruby went to her room, wondering if Peter had heard about Cesar's death and if that was why he'd driven to Phyllis's house so openly, risking his wife's rage.

She changed her damp shoes and socks and then traded her jeans for the only pair of shorts she'd brought with her. From her suitcase she pulled out the zippered plastic bag that held her magnifying glass, clear plastic templates and rulers, along with disposable gloves and evaluation forms. These and a bright light were usually all she needed to evaluate a document's handwriting.

She'd also brought a handheld ultraviolet light which, when used in a dark room, could enhance faded writing. It worked best with ink but could also expose pencil alterations on paper, such as erasures and corrections.

The skill came in experience and close examination, normally not in any high-tech equipment. Ruby used little else in her lab at home except occasionally her stereoptic microscope and a light table.

She rearranged her forms and added a second pen from her purse, putting it all together for the morning. Ruby *was* good; she'd been trained by Barker Thompson, one of the best in the business. A document waiting to be examined filled her with the same hunger as a book she longed to read: the eagerness to touch the pages and begin puzzling out the nuances of another person's loops and lifts and slant, to discover the weaknesses of a forger or the truth of an honest person. Because as surely as the soul couldn't be kept hidden forever, neither could deception in handwriting. There was always a slipup, the minutest mistake that could only be detected by the most diligent.

But still, she wished Phyllis's design notes were in ink rather than in pencil. And what if she *did* discover the notes were tampered with? What difference would it make?

She sat on the bed and glanced at her watch; it was two hours later in Michigan. She reached for the telephone on her bed table and dialed Hank's number, listening to the phone ringing in his rented house in Sable, four times before his machine picked up. He hadn't bothered recording a message. "This is Ruby," she said into the silence after the beep. "It looks like we might be staying a few extra days. I'll call you tonight, or you can call me." She paused. "Or you could just drop by."

After Ruby hung up, she lay back on the bed, bunching the pillow beneath her head and looking out the window to the west. A jet trail crossed the sky: a smear that tapered to a point, still lengthening from an invisible airplane. Aside from the jet trail, the sky was perfectly clear, featureless.

Phyllis's house was silent, the murmur of voices ceased. Ruby dabbed lotion on her tender nose before she left her bedroom and walked down the hall. The dining room was empty. In the living room Phyllis sat in a wide chair, her legs pulled up and her arms wrapped around her knees. Her face was partially hidden against her legs.

Across from Phyllis, Peter Stern sat forward on the edge of the couch, his elbows on his knees and hands clasped, his face solemn. He looked up at Ruby and nodded.

"Excuse me," Ruby said. "I'll join the others in the courtyard."

Phyllis raised her head and swiped her hand through her hair. "That's okay. Peter was just leaving. You can walk him to his car."

He frowned, but he was too much the gentleman to disagree and he stood, then leaned forward and kissed the top of Phyllis's head, his hand lingering overlong on her shoulder. "I'll talk to you tomorrow."

Phyllis nodded and laid her head back on her knees, her face turned away.

Ruby and Peter didn't speak until they were outside, then he removed a pair of sunglasses from his jacket pocket, put them on, and said, "Phyllis said you're staying a few days longer?"

Ruby nodded. "I'm examining her design notes tomorrow morning." She waited for him to reiterate what Daniel had said, how good it was, what a comfort she'd be for her prickly sister, but instead he reached for the door handle of his Lexus and said, "This isn't Michigan."

Ruby took an involuntary step back. "That's obvious," she agreed. "Are you trying to tell me something?"

He opened the car door and the trapped heat spilled out, and along with it the expensive odor of a new vehicle and hot leather. "Your being here might help your sister weather this mess, but don't get involved." He spoke in a casual voice, like a friend giving requested advice. "The easier and sooner this ends, the better it'll be for everyone." He leaned inside and turned on the engine and air conditioner, then stood in the open door. The engine purred; they didn't even have to raise their voices.

"Is this damage control?" Ruby asked. "You're afraid that if I ask any questions, I might rile up the locals, maybe toss bones to the press, and add another black mark to Cholla Engineering?"

"I'm saying that you should concentrate on being a comfort to your sister, that's all. Leave any detecting to the law."

"And this isn't Michigan, so I'm out of my league, right?"

He slid behind the wheel and smiled a thin smile. She couldn't see his eyes. "Every region of the country operates differently, that's all I'm saying. I know you don't want to add any more grief to your sister's life."

Ruby thought of Peter Stern's affair with Phyllis. What kind of damage had *he* done? "I think two deaths require that *somebody* asks a few questions," she told him.

His hand froze, inches from the gearshift. "Two deaths?" he asked. "What two deaths?"

Ruby stared at him and saw in his slack expression that he didn't know. Once again she found herself explaining the worst news in the world: death.

"Cesar?" Peter Stern asked. He stepped out of his car, looking back at Phyllis's house. "She didn't tell me. Why didn't she tell me?" He kneaded his forehead. "Do you know what I just did to her? In the middle of this . . ." He took a step back toward the house. "I have to talk to her," he said in a rush, "to explain I was in that damn meeting; I hadn't heard."

Ruby grabbed his arm. A puff of sand rose between them. "No," she told him. "Whatever you've done, leave it alone for now. Don't complicate it."

"But . . ." He tried to shrug her hand from his arm, but Ruby held tight.

"Leave her alone," Ruby said again, "please."

He removed his sunglasses and looked down at Ruby. "All right," he conceded. "Tell her . . . hell, I don't know."

"Tell her yourself in a day or two," Ruby said. She let go of his arm and he climbed back in his car, glancing back once more at the house as if Phyllis might step through the door and motion for him to come back.

Ruby stood in the driveway and watched his white car coast down the driveway. He drove slowly, sedately, and, Ruby hoped, with some remorse.

Chapter 11

Ruby left the driveway and returned to Phyllis's living room, hearing the engine of Peter Stern's car rev up as he pulled from the driveway onto the road. She found Phyllis sitting exactly as she'd left her, huddled in the chair, her arms around her legs.

"He's gone," Ruby told Phyllis, and sat down opposite her.

"Did he tell you the chilling but true story of why he drove all the way out here?" Phyllis asked.

"Other than to warn me not to stir up more bad publicity by snooping around, I gathered it was concern for you."

Phyllis laughed shortly. "Hardly. He brought me an offer from my partners in the firm."

"An offer for what?"

"To buy out my partnership." She waved her hand toward a large brown envelope sitting on her end table. There was no writing on the outside, and somehow Ruby found that simple lack of acknowledgment—not even a scrawl—ominous, an unspoken threat. "They all got together in a cozy little meeting and drafted a very generous offer. Peter obviously drew the shortest straw and had to play messenger boy." She frowned. "Or else they thought he was the most likely choice to soften me up."

"What reasons did they give you for the offer?" Ruby asked. So this was what Peter meant when he spoke of what he'd "done" to Phyllis.

"What do you think?" Phyllis asked. Her voice was hard, pitched high, and her words came fast. "I'm sure they're not listed on the paperwork, only offered verbally. The scandal is hurting the business. Oh, they'd kindly keep it confidential until after the trial so it wouldn't look like they've abandoned me. If I announce I've reached my own decision to leave the firm, the offer becomes even more generous. How could a girl refuse?"

"Did you?" Ruby asked.

"Did I what?"

"Refuse their offer."

Phyllis flicked the brown envelope with her finger. "I said I'd look it over, but that's all I intend to do. I started Cholla from a one-room office in a bad part of town; I'm not inclined to take a few bucks and walk away from it."

Ruby glanced out at Salina hunkered with Jesse at the border of the sparse garden in Phyllis's courtyard. They were studying a pale green plant that looked to Ruby like one she'd dig *out* of her garden, not plant on purpose. Jesse held an open book and was pointing from the illustration to the plant's ragged leaves.

"Chamisa," Phyllis said, following Ruby's glance. "Native shrub once considered an outcast, now politically correct. If we wait long enough, even weeds come into their own. Have their heyday, so to speak."

Ruby chose her words carefully. "Connie didn't sound completely confident about defending the suit."

"He's cautious," Phyllis said. "It makes him look better when he wins." She unwrapped her arms from around her legs and stretched them out in front of her.

"What is there to win?"

"My reputation." She turned her head away. "That's all I care about."

Ruby wondered if Phyllis believed that was all she had in her life: her reputation. She wanted to say more: words of caution, of warning that Phyllis's life might be about to change forever; she should begin to prepare herself. She opened her mouth to speak, then closed it again. When had Phyllis ever accepted advice from Ruby? When had Ruby ever *offered* it?

"I need to order flowers for Cesar's funeral," Phyllis said. She reached for a pencil sitting on the coffee table as if she were about to make a list, although the only paper Ruby could see was the brown envelope Peter Stern had brought. "And Masses. He's Catholic. Do Catholics still buy Masses for the dead?"

"I don't know," Ruby told her.

"You left that Catholic mumbo jumbo behind when you left Sable, too?" Phyllis asked.

"Didn't you?"

Phyllis kissed the tips of her fingers and threw open her hand, then placed her bare feet flat on the floor and stretched her shoulders, first in one direction, then in the other. "At times like these, though, you wish it could all be true." She collapsed back into the chair. "I also wish I had the power to offer up somebody else in Cesar's place. I could name a few likely candidates. Cesar shouldn't have died."

"Why didn't you tell Peter Stern about Cesar's death?" Ruby asked. The afternoon sun reflected off a mirror into her eyes and she shifted away from its glare.

"He didn't give me a chance. He was on a single-minded mission to zap me with the results of their meeting and get the hell out of here."

Ruby looked out the window and saw a lean and wiry young man join Salina and Jesse. He carried a beige cowboy hat with a fluff of a green feather in its band.

"That's Adam," Phyllis said.

Phyllis was right: He looked the part of a cowboy, his face sunburned and his hands hardened. His blond hair was pressed close to his skull, marked by a crease all the way around his head as if he'd just removed his hat during a break from sweaty work on the range. A budding Marlboro man with early lines and wrinkles in his young skin. His eyes were half closed in a permanent squint, his thin, sharply defined lips formed a laconic grin.

Salina stood, smiling, and he put his arm around her and then squatted beside Jesse, flipping his hat onto his head and peering at her book.

"Who gains from Cesar's death?" Ruby asked, half thinking aloud. "If it was a revenge killing, why follow him all the way up the mountain to do it? Are the crewmembers he fired still around?"

"How would I know? I don't keep track of guys on the construction crews. They don't have anything to do with me. Besides, the problem doesn't pertain to the actual construction of the walkway. We're not talking another Kansas City here."

"What's Kansas City?"

"When the walkways collapsed at the Hyatt in the early eighties and a hundred and fourteen people were crushed to death. It's a murky case, but basically a contractor tried to save money by using a cheaper form of connector."

"I didn't know that."

"Now you do. An engineer's demon nightmare. But we're off the subject of Cesar."

"We already know the motive wasn't robbery because his wallet still held money. He came back to town after being gone on another job how long?"

"Four months."

"Four months," Ruby repeated. "The first thing he does is find you and arrange to meet you at Bad Day, where he's immediately killed before you can even speak to each other."

"Because he knew how I'd originally designed the walkway and the landing that failed," Phyllis said. "Somebody wanted to make sure he didn't testify. Maybe Cesar even had an idea who forged my design notes."

"Exactly what was his role in the design?"

"I told you," Phyllis said impatiently. "I was having

trouble with the access and the slope of the mountains. It needed a rise of no more than eight point three percent, but the incline was too steep, so we met for a drink to talk about it."

"Did you have calculations with you? Your design notes?"

"No." Outside, Salina and Adam sat on either side of Jesse, and Ruby heard their muffled laughter.

"Then how could you discuss the walkway? Did Cesar have the numbers?"

Phyllis looked at Ruby as if she were as dense as concrete. "I *knew* the figures, that's all."

"You *remembered* them?"

"Yes."

"I'm impressed. But still, you two must have sketched out the design at the table."

"We did. I told you I brought home a paper napkin."

"Which you threw out."

"That's right," Phyllis said, raising her chin. She glanced out the window to the south and said wearily, "Here comes somebody else. Maybe it's another emissary from the office. Since Peter couldn't soften me up, now they're sending a big stick."

"Which one of your partners would be the big stick?" Ruby asked.

Phyllis didn't answer her question but said, squinting at the approaching navy blue car, "It's that cop, the detective or whatever he is. Must be to see you. A courtesy call, maybe, since you're in the same profession. Would you mind? Run interference if you can."

Ruby stood and watched the blue car pull into the driveway, recognizing the long narrow face of Detective Nick Powell behind the wheel. He was alone.

She opened Phyllis's door as the thin detective got out, shaking his body a little as if he'd been folded up too tightly in the driver's seat. He waved briefly to Ruby and turned beside the car, looking at the hills, the distant low houses, the even more distant mountains. "Nice views," he said. Then he turned and glanced at Phyllis's house. "It looks like engineering is a good business to get into." He wore a white shirt with the sleeves rolled up, the collar undone as if his workday was finished.

"Are you here regarding Cesar Peron's death?" Ruby asked.

"I don't know you well enough yet to be here for any other reason," he told her, grinning. "Is your sister home?"

"Inside. Come on in."

The first thing Ruby noticed when she stepped inside and glanced through the big picture window onto the courtyard was that Salina and Jesse and Adam were gone. She started to say something and then remembered that Salina was an illegal alien, and instead led him into the main room, where Phyllis sat.

Phyllis rose from her chair and offered the detective her hand as if he were an honored, or at least expected, guest. "Detective Powell, would you like a glass of iced tea?"

"No, thanks." He removed a notebook from his jacket pocket and sat down, glancing around the room, and Ruby would bet he didn't miss a thing, not even the plain brown envelope on the end table. Without his sunglasses his eyes were light blue, as if the sun had bleached them.

Ruby sat down on the sofa next to him, just close enough to see the writing in his notebook: a modified print of rounded letters, easily readable. At the top of the clean page he'd written their names and the date.

"I'd like to ask you two a couple of questions about this morning."

Phyllis's face paled, but she didn't falter. "It's not solved yet?" she asked lightly.

"Not quite. You said the body was in the water when you arrived at Bad Day, is that right?"

"The body?" Phyllis asked. "It wasn't a body, like a slab of beef; the body had a name and it was Cesar Peron."

"Sorry," he said mildly, and repeated the question, using Cesar's name. Ruby recognized the patient response of a man who'd had to deal with every kind of reaction to his questioning, whose calm wouldn't be ruffled by rage or hysteria.

"We already established that," Ruby said. "What's the real reason you're here?"

He drew a star above the date in his notebook, retracing it until it was filled in. "Last fall he fired three members of his crew who he believed were dealing drugs on the job. Do you know their names?"

Phyllis shook her head. "How did you know that?"

"I stopped by your engineering office on my way here," Detective Powell told her.

"Did you speak to Daniel MacSimon?"

The detective nodded. "Among others. He told me about the incident."

"I don't know who they were," Phyllis said.

"But you must already have their names," Ruby interjected. "It would have been simple enough to check employment records."

He shrugged and flipped to another page. "I was only asking whether your sister knew. Daniel also mentioned an Allen Kentzner; I understand you fired him?"

"That's right. He was an overenthusiastic draftsman. Good at what he did but too independent."

"He worked in the office while you were designing Bad Day?"

Phyllis nodded. "Did Daniel tell you that after Kentzner was fired, he worked as a laborer at Bad Day?"

"There's a comedown," Nick Powell commented. "Do you know where he is now?"

"Laborers come and go. I don't keep track of them."

"So his association was with you, not Cesar?"

"As far as I know."

The detective took a few moments to scribble in his notebook. Ruby watched him clearly write what Phyllis had said, then she stood and looked out the window, searching for a sign of Salina, Adam, and Jesse but only seeing the surrounding land. A flock of tiny birds rose up from one juniper and disappeared into another.

"Did you see Cesar Peron between the time he left

Albuquerque last fall until he returned yesterday?" Nick Powell asked Phyllis.

"No," Phyllis said. "And we didn't exchange phone calls or letters, either."

"That right?" he asked, crossing his ankle over his knee. "He helped you design Bad Day and you never spoke to him during the construction phase?"

"He wasn't part of the construction. He was very knowledgeable about designing, generous with his ideas. A social relationship wasn't part of our association."

"Because he was Hispanic?" the detective asked casually.

"Because I'm a partner in the firm and he was frequently one of our employees."

"If he wasn't part of the Bad Day construction, why did he want to meet you there?"

A wave of sorrow crossed Phyllis's face. "Presumably to go over the design failure with me."

"How did other people in the firm feel about Cesar?"

"Everybody liked him, as far as I know. We all definitely respected his ideas and we listened to any comments he made if he was our contractor."

"Beloved by all," the detective commented.

"There *are* people like that," Phyllis said.

"How did he die?" Ruby asked, leaving the window and standing beside Phyllis's chair.

"The autopsy hasn't been completed."

"But you must have an idea."

He glanced at Phyllis, then at Ruby, and seemed to

be making a mental decision. "This is only from observation, nothing official yet."

"I understand," Ruby said.

"My opinion is that he was hit in the back of the head and knocked unconscious into the stream."

"And the cut on his neck was insurance, in case he didn't drown?" Ruby asked.

"That's my opinion. The artery was severed too neatly for it to have been a fall on a rock."

"Are you going to question the men who were fired?"

He rose from his chair. "That's next on my list. I'll want to talk to you two again." He gave Ruby a business card. "Call me if you remember any other details about the death scene or anything else about Cesar."

The telephone rang and the detective glanced at it. "The media will be hot on this, you can bet. Reasonable or not, they're going to connect Cesar Peron's death with Eddy Peppermill's. You might let somebody else answer your phone once the news breaks."

"And because we found the body . . ."

"That's right. It's bad enough he was killed at Bad Day, but to have you two find the body. Anybody else . . ." He shook his head.

After another ring Ruby heard the recorded voice of an answering machine, probably from Phyllis's bedroom. "Are feelings running that high?" she asked.

"Stick around a couple of days and you'll find out," he told her. "Southwest Minerals has a reputation for trashing any area it mines, so the company was already a hotbed of controversy. Some people feel the government sold out by allowing Southwest Minerals to develop a park on federal land. Other people thought Bad Day shouldn't be developed at all. It was already a deadly subject before Eddy Peppermill's death. And now this. Go down to the public library and check out the back papers. Your sister"—and here he nodded to Phyllis—"is at the very heart of the controversy."

Chapter 12

Once the detective left, not only did Salina and Jesse return to the house, but Salina's boyfriend, Adam, appeared from around the side of the courtyard and sauntered inside.

"Glad to meet you, Ruby," he said, touching an invisible hat brim when Phyllis introduced them, his words cowboyish and his accent shockingly New Jersey. Ruby couldn't suppress a smile when he went on to say, "You girls look like three peas in a pod. A couple more years and everybody will swear you're sisters," sounding like a man who'd been handed the wrong movie role.

"Thanks," Ruby said. "Phyllis said you work on a ranch in the southern part of the state."

"Yes, ma'am. I come up to see Salina when I get a few days off."

He sat at the dining room table with Salina and Jesse, lounging in his chair, his hat on the table beside him, occasionally rocking backward so the front legs lifted off the floor.

"Somebody left a message on your answering machine," Ruby reminded Phyllis. "It might have been Hank returning my call."

"Will you listen to it for me?" Phyllis asked her. "I don't think I can bear any crank calls today."

Ruby followed Phyllis to her bedroom. On the threshold she turned to Ruby, her hand on the doorknob, and said, "I don't want any comments about my room, okay?"

"Okay," Ruby agreed, not mentioning that she'd already seen Phyllis's bedroom the night before when Phyllis had been sobbing on Salina's shoulder.

By daylight the room was equally . . . well, eerie. The furniture of their Michigan past, the nest of blankets and pillows on the bed, the teetering piles of books and papers. Dust had settled on the flat surfaces.

"Just push the button," Phyllis said, pointing to the gray answering machine on the bedside table, a low-tech version that held a tape. "I'll wait in the living room."

Phyllis closed the door behind her, and Ruby glanced around the room, looking for hints of her sister's personal life. The rest of the house was comfortable, tasteful, expensive, and impersonal. This was obviously where Phyllis lived when she was home alone.

Two framed color photographs sat on Phyllis's dresser. One that looked vaguely familiar and that Ruby finally recognized as their mother's garden in Sable: vibrant and wild, a jungle of color and greenery. "A green thumb," everybody had said in praise and wonder, not realizing that plants were their mother's escape: The more desperate she became the more vibrant her garden grew. No one knew how to read the frantic messages in its beauty.

The other photo, smaller, sat beside it: Phyllis and Ruby as children. They were dressed for Halloween, their faces concealed by masks, their bodies by costumes: a skeleton for Ruby, a princess for Phyllis. Their heads were covered by hats and their hands by mittens. They could have been any two children in the world.

Looking around at the old dresser and familiar rugs, one of Gram's quilts, Ruby sensed that whatever lovers Phyllis took, they weren't invited into this room but into the less personal bedroom where Ruby slept.

Finally she turned her attention to the answering machine. The red light pulsed twice. Two messages. Beside the machine sat a pile of newspaper articles, laminated the same as the article Phyllis had brought to Michigan. Ruby picked them up and sorted through them, glancing at the headlines.

There wasn't any need to go to the library as Detective Powell had suggested; here was the history of Bad Day from the first small mention of Southwest Minerals' negotiations with the Forest Service, through the local suspicions of Southwest's motives, to construction reports, and finally, most abundantly, to Eddy Peppermill's death. Each article after the accident carried a picture of Eddy, the same sullen and grainy school photo.

Ruby smoothed the pile flat, wondering if Phyllis tortured herself by reading the articles at night before she went to sleep. With one hand still on the cool plastic, she pushed the play button and listened to the answering machine whir to the beginning of the tape. To collect the stories as well as laminate each one . . . why?

The machine beeped and the message began. "Well, bitch," a voice burst into the room with such vehemence that Ruby took a step back from the machine. "You've killed somebody else at Bad Day. You're going to pay for this just like you'll pay for the last one. I'm watching you."

Then there followed a howl, like a tortured cat, and the sound of the receiver being crashed back onto the cradle. Ruby stood stunned by the rage in the caller's voice, uncertain whether it had been a man or a woman or whether the voice had been altered.

The machine beeped a second time and a familiar voice said, "Phyllis, it's Daniel. There was a Detective Powell here at the office. Can you call me as soon as you get a chance?"

Daniel's voice brought her back to herself; she frantically pushed the Save button and with fumbling fingers flipped open the plastic flap that covered the tape compartment.

At first the tape stuck when she tried to lift it out. She grabbed a nail file from the bedside table and pried the tape out of its holder, then slipped it into her pocket, leaving the plastic lid raised.

Adam and Salina were gone, but Phyllis sat on the sofa in the living room beside Jesse, one arm across the girl's shoulder. Jesse still didn't initiate affection, but she accepted it when it was offered. It wasn't that she rejected intimacy, not at all, but it was as if it never crossed her mind.

Phyllis looked up, her face questioning. "Daniel wants you to call him," Ruby told her. "It sounds like he phoned before the detective arrived."

"Who else called?"

"He, or she, didn't say."

"I've had those calls before," Phyllis said, keeping her voice neutral as Ruby often did in Jesse's presence. Often it was the tone more than the words that disturbed Jesse.

"For how long?"

"Six months maybe."

"Have you let anyone else listen to the tapes?"

Phyllis shook her head. "Salina's heard them, but I haven't mentioned them outside the house."

"Did you save any of the tapes?" Ruby asked hopefully. "Or write down the messages?"

"I'd rather forget about them."

"I removed the tape," Ruby told her, patting her pocket where it rested. "Do you have a blank to put in the machine?"

"Maybe I'd just as soon not hear any more at all."

"No. Now it's time to gather every bit of evidence we can."

"But the messages have been going on a long time. They don't have anything to do with Eddy's—" She glanced at Jesse and left the sentence unfinished.

"The publicity over Bad Day began when, about a year ago?"

"Yeah, about the time the agreement was negotiated," Phyllis said, conceding the connection, "but it didn't really heat up until the construction began last June."

"That's nine months ago," Ruby said, counting off on her fingers.

Phyllis shuddered and tightened her arm around Jesse. "I don't answer the phone very often anymore."

Jesse looked up at her, frowning.

"I can't blame you," Ruby told her.

"Mom doesn't even have an answering machine," Jesse offered.

"I know," Phyllis said, and Ruby wondered how many times Phyllis had called her the summer before.

"You could get a dog like Spot," Jesse said. "He'd guard you."

The phone rang again, and Ruby couldn't help it; she went as tense as Phyllis. "I'll get it," she said, and walked to the kitchen wall phone. She braced herself before she lifted the receiver, expecting a string of vituperations or the slamming of the receiver in her ear.

"Ruby?" a man's voice asked. "This is Daniel MacSimon. Did Phyllis get my message about the detective?"

Ruby silently mouthed "Daniel" to Phyllis, who nodded. "After the fact," Ruby told him. "He's already been here."

"Is Phyllis okay?"

"She's fine. Would you like to speak to her?" she asked before she saw Phyllis shaking her head no.

He hesitated. "Tell her . . . she can call me if she needs anything. This isn't much of an introduction to New Mexico, Land of Enchantment, is it?"

"It's not what I expected. Do you know if Cesar's death is on the news yet?"

"One of the TV stations called the office around four o'clock wanting to verify who had died, so it probably is."

Ruby calculated the time. Daniel had called about three-thirty while Detective Powell was at the house, so the other call had come before that, before Cesar's death was picked up by the media.

As Ruby replaced the phone, Jesse stiffened beside Phyllis and pointed out the window. "Look!" she cried.

Walking along the top of the courtyard wall was a sleek brown and white bird, its head forward on its long neck, its long legs swiftly moving.

"It's a roadrunner," Phyllis said.

"Like in the cartoons?" Jesse asked, not taking her eyes from the nervously moving bird.

"The very same, only a little more serious-minded."

They watched the long-tailed bird until it suddenly flapped its wings and was gone, flying low toward a line of junipers.

"On the bookshelf in your room," Phyllis told her, "there's a book describing birds that live in the Southwest."

"I'll go read about it," Jesse said, her attention slipping away, zeroing in on this new project.

"You thought of everything," Ruby said when Jesse left the room. "Clothes, books, her favorite posters."

"I tried to," Phyllis told her. "I haven't read some of those books since I was a kid. Good stuff." She settled into the couch, pulling a pillow behind her back. "Sit down. What's your plan of attack now? How are you going to investigate this? And don't give me any I'm-not-really-a-detective crap."

"I'll examine your design notes tomorrow morning and decide whether they've been forged."

Phyllis waved her hand in irritation. "They *were* forged. Then what?"

Ruby picked up a black-and-white clay pot from the coffee table and turned it over. *Acoma,* it read on the bottom. She wondered whom she should talk to first: Connie the lawyer? Detective Powell? There was a whole city filled with law enforcement people, official organizations with rules, policies, and procedures, not a Michigan rural county where things got done by whoever was capable or whoever got to it first.

"So let's say your design notes were forged," Ruby said, putting down the pot. "Who had access to the binder? Are we limiting the criminal to someone in your office?"

Phyllis thought. "People who had access," she said aloud. "My office is unlocked most of the time; somebody's always needing a manual or paper. I lock it when I leave for the day."

"Did you ever take the binder home with you?"

"A couple of times, near the deadline. But only home. Nowhere else and this isn't exactly society central."

"But it had to be forged before it went to your computer person, what do you call her?"

"The CAD designer, or the engineering technician, or more familiarly: Monica. And Monica worked directly from the book; she's good with AutoCAD but she cares more about last week's boyfriend than she does about engineering. She works strictly without creativity—and I mean that as a compliment in the type of work she's doing."

"So you're saying anybody in the office could have slipped in and altered your design notes?"

"Technically, yes."

"Anybody outside the office?"

Phyllis thought, chewing on her nail. The right wrist band had slipped, and Ruby glanced away from the dark dotted line. "Janitors maybe. Spouses come and go. The landscape architect's wife brings him a hot lunch every day."

"What about Peter Stern's wife?" Ruby asked, seeing again the hate-filled glance of the blond woman.

"Charlotte, you mean? She comes and goes like the queen bee."

"Does she have any engineering experience?"

Phyllis laughed. "Peter plucked her from the ranks of engineering students when he was a guest lecturer at the university. She spread her legs, dropped engineering like a hot iron, and took up Chinese cooking and flower arranging."

"That's a little harsh, isn't it?" Ruby asked.

"That's my mild version. Put an *X* beside her name for motive and opportunity." She drew an *X* in the air.

"If we're talking motive, Phyllis, who else would like to end your career?"

Phyllis turned her head. "I don't know about wanting to end my career, but this past year has been tough. There have been a few—" She stopped.

"Complaints," Ruby provided. "Warnings?"

"Something like that."

"Why's the past year been tough?"

"Just one of those years. Ever have one? Oh, yeah, I forgot, you went through yours when you were seventeen. Well, I never did. I played by the rules, obeyed all the laws, changed my underwear every day, paid off my student loan, honored our father and mother—up to a point. And here I am." Phyllis waved toward herself in her designer clothes, dismissing her beautiful home and successful career. It all looked good to Ruby.

"You were never a goody-goody, Phyllis," she said. "Don't kid yourself on that score."

"I *looked* good, though, didn't I?"

"A paragon," Ruby said.

Without warning, Salina's cowboy friend, Adam, entered the living room, slouching into a chair with such ease and comfort that Ruby expected Phyllis to bristle.

"Howdy, girls," he said, sounding like a comical imitation of a grade-B Western. He zeroed in on Phyllis. "You doing okay?"

"Just fine," Phyllis said.

Ruby watched the glance exchanged between Phyllis and Adam, the easy smiles on both their faces, and felt her stomach sink. Whatever Adam had been to Salina, it was apparent that now he was having an affair with Phyllis.

Chapter 13

After Jesse went to bed, Ruby and Phyllis sat at either end of the sofa in the living room and waited for the ten o'clock news to come on.

Light shone from a single floor lamp beside the sofa, and along with the TV screen—where a comedy series unfolded with its sound turned off—there was enough illumination to see but not to read, reminding Ruby of the night they'd spent in their father's house in Sable.

Phyllis drank hot chocolate, but she'd already sloshed it onto her hands twice because she kept shifting on the sofa, moving in jerking motions.

"Tell me about Daniel," Ruby asked, trying to fill the long minutes of waiting.

"He's from California," Phyllis answered eagerly, as if she too longed for a diversion from the upcoming news. "Good engineer, one of those strong in detail. There's an ex-wife somewhere, painful divorce. The usual story." She licked the hot chocolate off her hand and laughed shortly. "If he takes a liking to you, don't share your passions with him."

"Why not?" Ruby asked.

"He's one of those men who likes to 'help.'" She made quotation marks in the air. "I told him I was interested in Acoma pottery and he printed reams of stuff off the Internet for me, bought a book on it as a gift, gave me that pot for Christmas, things like that. It's sweet unless you like to figure things out for yourself."

"And Paula Abbott?"

"A dynamo. She can juggle fifty things at once; that's why she's such a good project manager. She has a stay-at-home husband and two toddlers, twins. Just like Paula to do it all at once. She's probably an indifferent mother, maybe even lousy, but she shines otherwise."

Ruby was beginning to understand that in the world of engineering, personal lives had a tendency to take second place.

"Why do you want to know?" Phyllis asked. She set her cup, half full, on the coffee table and left it.

"I'm trying to get a more complete picture of your office, that's all."

Phyllis nodded, satisfied with the explanation.

"What about your other two partners?" Ruby asked, but Phyllis raised her hand and grabbed the remote as the color logo of the ten o'clock news filled the screen.

"Shhh," she warned, unnecessarily since she'd turned up the sound loud enough to drown out any conversation.

"Our top story," a grim-faced young woman said. "Another death at Bad Day park, where only two weeks ago young Eddy Peppermill fell to his death in an accident his father claims was caused by a gross error in design."

Phyllis stared at the screen, the remote still held at the end of her outstretched arm.

The scene flicked to a reporter, a man in a blue windbreaker holding a microphone, standing outside the chain-link gate of Bad Day in early evening. "At this point police aren't disclosing the cause of Cesar Peron's death," he said, "although unidentified sources are calling it"—he paused for effect—"murder. An unconfirmed report claims the body was discovered by an employee of Cholla Engineering, the firm that's being sued by the Peppermill family."

The cameras cut back to the news desk, catching the anchorwoman shaking her head in simulated dismay. "More on the story on tomorrow morning's six A.M. report. Now, a look at today's—"

Phyllis stabbed at the remote and the screen went black. "They don't know yet that I'm the 'employee of Cholla Engineering' who found him." She dropped back against the sofa. "This is going to get very bad," she said, and Ruby had no response to give her.

There was no sobbing to awaken Ruby that night, no howling of coyotes or mysterious movements in Phyllis's house. But still she couldn't sleep. She lay awake in her bed beneath the window, her pillow wadded beneath her neck, watching the Hale-Bopp comet, its tail a gauzy blur that disappeared if she stared at it too long. The sky was clear, deceptively close but a nearly full moon had just risen, and the stars retreated in its milky glow.

If she craned her neck, she could see a corner of the window of Salina's room. A low light shone there, like a night-light. Was Adam with Salina or Phyllis? Had he been allowed into Phyllis's nest? Ruby sighed and returned to gazing at the comet; it wasn't any of her business, but an affair with a man like Adam wasn't something she'd expected from her sister.

She rose to check Jesse one more time and at last fell into a fitful sleep, waking every hour or so and glancing at the red digital numbers on the bedside clock. Finally, when she opened her eyes, it was to bright sunlight.

The house was silent, the silence of absence. Ruby got up and, wearing just her T-shirt, checked Jesse's room. It was empty, the bed made, her shorty pajamas folded at the foot, slippers Phyllis had bought for her tucked neatly beneath the dust ruffle, nothing out of place. Phyllis's bedroom door stood closed as usual, and on the kitchen counter lay a note written on Cholla Engineering notepaper. *We've gone for a hike. Take the Porsche.* It was signed *P.*

Ruby picked up the car keys beside the note and jingled them, studying Phyllis's handwriting, which was curiously similar to her own, as if penmanship were hereditary, like hair color and cheekbones. Phyllis's handwriting showed more evidence of speed: briefer or absent connections between letters, half print, the *P* of her signature formed by one stroke beginning at the bottom of the shaft, a characteristic she could identify by the weight of the tail, the feathered ending at the lower end of the *P*'s bowl.

She didn't like to leave without seeing Jesse, but it was already seven o'clock and her appointment at Connie's office was scheduled for eight.

As she returned to her room, the door to Salina's room opened and Adam exited, bare-chested and barefoot, wearing faded jeans. His hair was tangled and his face flushed from sleep.

"The little sister," he said.

"My name's Ruby," she told him. "Why aren't you hiking with the others?"

He grinned at her. "Late night." He leaned against the wall in the hallway and regarded Ruby, rubbing one hand across his bare chest. "You don't know me well enough to look at me like that," he said.

"How am I looking at you?" Ruby asked.

"As if I'd crawled out of a drainpipe."

"You're saying if I knew you better, the look would be justified?"

His grin widened. "You're Phyllis's sister, all right."

"Excuse me," Ruby said, reaching for the doorknob of her room.

"Care to have a cup of coffee with me?" he asked.

"No, thanks. I have an appointment."

"That's right, I forgot. With the megabucks megalawyer."

"Does Phyllis discuss her personal affairs with you? Or does Salina pass on the intimate details of this household?" She stood taller, realizing the absurdity of standing in the hallway challenging this man, wearing only a T-shirt.

"Salina doesn't blabber," he said, his face darkening. "What I know I've been told by the principals themselves," he added, sounding like an East Coast lawyer.

"And you know the details of Bad Day?" Ruby said, then asked, not expecting a serious answer, "Have you formed an opinion?"

The arrogant look slipped from his face. He frowned and tightened his lips, suddenly appearing earnest and thoughtful and several years younger. "Either Phyllis made a major mistake at Bad Day and Cesar coincidentally got himself killed on the site, or whoever hates Phyllis messed up her design and killed Cesar. Maybe if somebody solves one, they'll solve the other."

"Who hates Phyllis?" Ruby asked him.

"Couldn't say. I'm just the hired help."

Ruby studied his face. "Hired to do what?"

"You figure it out," he told her, and sauntered past her toward the kitchen.

By the time Ruby left Phyllis's house, Adam had made himself scarce. His pickup was still parked beside the house, so she left the door unlocked and drove away in Phyllis's vintage Porsche, which was slung low to the ground and smelled of leather. The little white car leapt forward at a touch on the gas, and Ruby felt the delicious possibility of dangerous speed. A white layer of clouds, like a smear, hung to the southwest, and the morning was cooler than it had been the day before.

Twice she took the wrong street before she found

Connie Tarcher's office, pulling in between a Ford Explorer—Eddie Bauer model—and a BMW. The lock button on the driver's door of Phyllis's Porsche was broken, and Ruby checked the car to be sure nothing valuable was in sight.

Rachel, the gray-haired secretary, glanced up at Ruby and smiled. "He's waiting for you." A photograph of a set of dark-haired twins filled a gold frame beside her computer.

Connie looked up from his desk. Brown and blue law books were piled to either side of him, all open like wings to mark his place. Lawyers used computer services now and, barring that availability, paralegals. Obviously, Ruby thought, Connie liked a more hands-on approach. Nondescript instrumental music played softly from hidden speakers.

"I called a friend who works for the FBI and he faxed me a list of equipment for you," he said, skipping any greetings. "But you name it and I'll send out for it." He waved his hand toward a corner table in his office. "Make yourself comfortable. I'll keep on working, if you don't mind."

Two lamps sat on the table, one of them a mercury arc lamp, positioned next to a stereoptic microscope with a high-intensity light attached to it: new, not beat-up like Ruby's at home in her loft. There was also an assortment of plastic rulers and fine-scale test plates. In the center of the table next to pencils and paper sat an object in a plastic evidence bag. It was a worn blue three-ring binder, its fabric cover soiled and resembling a school notebook at the end of the academic year.

"I could have left my own equipment at home," Ruby said, sliding her fingertips across the cool metal of the microscope's arm. "This is perfect. Thanks."

"There's bottled water and diet soda in that cabinet," he said, smiling, all his attention on Ruby, but probably eager to be back to his research, and she imagined that once he turned his attention to his own business, he'd be completely oblivious to her presence. She could identify; all her life she'd been teased for her own ability to zero in on a subject, to the detriment of all else, whether it was to her benefit or not. "Self-centered," her father had called her. "Intent," her mother had said with more astuteness. As he returned to his desk, Ruby knew that in a few minutes she'd be no more aware of Connie Tarcher than he would be of her.

Ruby removed her own meager equipment from her bag and pulled on a pair of disposable plastic gloves. "Isn't there a chain-of-evidence form to fill out, showing I've handled this binder?" she asked Connie.

He focused on her, one finger still on a line of text. "Guess not. Just jot the info on a slip of paper, would you?"

She paused, considering the lawyer. "My examination of these notes *is* legal, isn't it?"

"Definitely," he said, too heartily.

"Are you humoring me by allowing me access to Phyllis's design book?"

"If you find evidence of tampering in there," he told her, pointing to the binder, "I assure you it'll be used in court. Have you testified in court before?"

"Several times," Ruby assured him. "But you're not optimistic I'll find anything."

He shrugged, one side of his mouth rising. "You said you were good. So prove me wrong."

And they both proceeded with their work. A yellow Post-It marked the page Phyllis claimed had been altered. Ruby gently opened the binder.

There it was, in the middle of the page: aluminum. She pulled out the specification Phyllis had jotted down for her, the notation she claimed she'd written: *ASTM A36,* and beneath it the description, *Corrosion-Resistant Alloy Steel.*

Instead the specification written here was: *ASTM B313 A91100 H12* and beneath it, *Corrosion-Resistant Aluminum.*

The handwriting was draftsmanlike, learned for accuracy, not style, although less rigid than most penmanship of its type: a half-print, half-cursive style. That was good.

First Ruby did an oblique-light examination, pulling the lamp down and shining it at a low angle across the page.

The roughened page showed definite signs of erasure, but that in itself wasn't unusual. She concentrated on the letters first, studying the capital *A* in *Aluminum,* which was set slightly apart from the rest of the word, measuring its style and angles with other capital *A*'s in the binder, finding it consistent with Phyllis's *A.*

She felt discouraged until she realized that it made perfect sense for a forger to make use of Phyllis's *A* in the word *Alloy* for the *A* in *Aluminum.*

For the next two hours she used her own test plates and those Connie had provided to measure and remeasure every slant, connection, and height relationships of the seven remaining letters in *Aluminum.* Then she used the microscope to study the lifts and starts, always referring to the design notes in the binder Phyllis had given her the day before as a standard. She carefully filled out her usual report as she worked.

Finally she sat back, rotating her cramped shoulders, and found Connie leaning back in his own chair watching her. "You look satisfied. Good news?"

"There's been tampering," she said. Whoever had altered Phyllis's handwriting had been good, but not good enough. "It's more apparent in the letters than the numbers. I'd be less sure if the forgery had only been executed in numbers and capital letters. The B in B313 is suspect, but every writer is more precise in forming their capitals, and a forger is most careful copying a prominent letter. It's in the body of words where a writer is most natural—and where a forger is most likely to slip up and revert to his or her own writing style."

"What about the numbers?" Connie asked as he rose from his chair.

"In normal penmanship," Ruby told him, "forgers frequently overlook careful reproduction of numbers; it's one of my favorite places to catch them out. But numbers are so standardized in the engineering profession that there's very little individualization."

"So if there *was* tampering," Connie said, standing

beside her and peering down at the binder, "it was done by someone familiar with engineering."

"I'd say so," Ruby agreed. She pulled the lamp down so that it shone laterally across the page. "See the evidence of erasure here? Probably a gum eraser because it roughed up the paper so little."

"Phyllis could have erased it herself."

"Definitely. But here's the good part." She showed him how the initial *A*'s in the words *Alloy* and *Aluminum* were both Phyllis's, but the connection and spacing, the relationship between letters of the rest of the word were unlike her sister's handwriting.

She gave him a magnifying glass. "See how the connection between the *l* and *u* in *Aluminum* is made with a single stroke? If you look at this sample of *l* and *u* in *flue* in Phyllis's genuine hand, and here, in *plus*, you'll see she doesn't actually connect the letters; it's a two-stroke process that *appears* to be a connection."

She turned the binder toward him. "Now look at the *m*. Phyllis's *m*'s—and I examined twenty-three of them—all begin with an upstroke that has a slight tail at the top she strokes over. This *m* begins with a down stroke, so at first glance it appears identical. There's also more pressure brought on the construction of the word; the forger pressed harder than Phyllis normally does, commonly indicating concentration, leaving an imprint on the reverse of the page that actually extends through two more pages. There's more." She tapped her report. "I detailed it in here."

"But you can't swear to it?" Connie asked, straightening and setting the magnifying glass beside the binder.

"No documents investigator could—or should. We only testify to the likelihood."

He chewed his lip, staring at the page. "As I said before, it was still Phyllis's responsibility to discover any design flaws before the walkway was built. This may not make any difference in the lawsuit. Besides, you're—."

"Her sister," Ruby provided. "Not exactly a disinterested party. I can give you the names of other highly respected experts in the field who will reach the same conclusion. This *is* evidence of criminal intent. According to Phyllis, any qualified engineer would know not to substitute this grade of aluminum for A36 steel in a cantilevered design like this. Whoever did this was plotting sabotage. They *knew* the landing would fail when there was substantial weight on it."

"At this point the police aren't involved in the lawsuit," Connie told her. "It's a case of negligence, not a criminal case. There isn't any investigation for sabotage."

"But they *are* involved in investigating Cesar Peron's death. That is a criminal matter."

"Do you believe Cesar's death is connected to this?" He pointed to the binder. Ruby sensed he'd already made up his mind about the connection, that he was only asking to reinforce his own beliefs.

"I'd say it's more than a curious coincidence, wouldn't you?"

He sat down in the chair opposite Ruby. "I do. What's your theory about the connection?"

"Cesar knew the original design of the walkway and

the landing. Whoever altered Phyllis's notes didn't want him to testify."

Connie made an imaginary gun with his hand and playacted at shooting the wall. "Bang," he said softly.

"No, a concussion and gashed throat."

"Does it look accidental enough to confuse the issue?"

Ruby nodded and began repacking her equipment in her zippered bag. "Barely. Tell me about the dead boy's parents, the Peppermills. Have you met them?"

"Briefly." He remained in his chair, watching Ruby put together her bag. "Mister Leon Peppermill is a piece of work. He was investigated by Protective Services eight years ago for beating Eddy. He threw the boy out of the house when he was sixteen and hadn't spoken to him in a year. Leon's chronically out of work; he was investigated for Welfare fraud, but that went nowhere. He smells big money. Talks to the press a lot to keep the fires flamed."

"And the mother?"

Connie tapped the arm of his chair. "She's the bewildered type, under her husband's thumb so much she hardly speaks without glancing at him first. Do you know the kind?"

"Yes," Ruby assured him. "I do."

His face saddened. "She's truly broken up over the boy's death. I had the feeling she finds the whole suit distasteful, not that she'd ever have the courage to say so."

Ruby made a mental note of that tidbit and asked, "Is there a court date?"

"Not yet." The stiffness with which he said it was a

clear indication that he hoped the case didn't go to court.

"What's your plan?" she asked.

He sighed. "I'm recommending Phyllis and the firm settle out of court with the family. Mistakes happen, the public forgets. This is what errors and omissions insurance is all about."

"Phyllis will never agree to that. Her career's at stake." And maybe her life, too, Ruby thought.

"She risks losing more by fighting this," Connie said. "She could lose her engineering license. She makes herself a target."

"Are you saying she's in physical danger?" Ruby asked.

"No." He stood and paced between his desk and the window. "At least I hope not. But the media loves this case. Beautiful female engineer screws up. Federal land and private money. Southwest Minerals is thwarted trying to clean up their act. A kid is dead; there are rumors of lovers and alcohol abuse. Feminists believe it's a gender issue. Everybody has an opinion; they're eating up the details."

"She's received threatening phone calls," Ruby told him. "She got another one yesterday."

"Talk her into changing her number."

Ruby stood and returned the binder holding the Bad Day design notes to the evidence bag, carefully resealing it. "I'll make a copy of my report for myself," she said as she stripped off her gloves and dropped them into an oak trash basket. "You can send a copy to the Peppermills' lawyer if you want."

"Thanks. Are you going home now?" he asked. "I mean, to Phyllis's."

"I think I'll stop at Cholla Engineering first."

"Good luck," he said, but Ruby knew his words were only a formality.

Chapter 14

At the edge of Cholla Engineering's parking lot, amid all the expensive vehicles, a battered blue pickup with a missing tailgate crookedly filled a slot. Through the cab's rear window Ruby could see the shape of a man sitting behind the wheel, his movements those of a man eating. She parked closer to the office door, grabbed her notebook, and went inside.

The young man at the reception desk glanced beyond her as if he remembered her and expected Phyllis to walk in next. "Can I help you?" he asked.

Until that moment Ruby hadn't thought of the excuse she'd use to get into Cholla Engineering. In her mind it had seemed reason enough that she *needed* to.

"I'd like to see Peter Stern," she said, choosing the name of the highest power she knew.

"And you are?" he asked. Ruby could tell by his eyes that he knew damn well who she was.

"Ruby Crane," she told him.

"You can wait over there," he said, pointing to the arrangement of comfortable chairs surrounding a coffee table with magazines fanned neatly across the top.

"Thank you," Ruby told him. She moved to the

waiting area but didn't sit down. Trying to rise from a chair with deep padding created an awkward movement when there was serious business at hand. Maybe that was why offices had chairs that visitors sunk into up to their necks; it disarmed them.

Peter Stern didn't keep her waiting long. A frown of consternation dissolved into a smile on his face as he shook Ruby's hand. "Phyllis isn't with you?" he asked.

"No. I'd like to talk to you for a few minutes if I may."

"Sure. Come on back to my office."

Ruby followed him down the hallway hung with enlarged photographs of Cholla projects: arroyos, roads, subdivisions.

"Is Phyllis all right?" he asked.

The question was so ridiculous that at first Ruby wasn't going to answer. "She's upset," she finally said.

She didn't understand corporate hierarchy, so she was uncertain what it meant, if anything, that Peter's office was the first one along the hallway, as large as Phyllis's but more cluttered. A haphazard collection of rolled blueprints stood on end in the corner. There was evidence of a woman's touch here beneath the stacks of papers and engineering books: lampshades that matched the drapes, a landscape hanging behind the desk. Three framed photos sat on the table behind Peter, watchful like those childhood pictures of saints who never took their eyes off you. All were of the blond woman who'd given Ruby such a scathing glance. Charlotte, the wife.

Peter sat down in front of a set of plans spread

across his desktop, one side weighted with an onyx paperweight. Ruby chose a chair to the side. "I plan to ask your employees a few questions," Ruby told him.

"In what capacity?" he asked. He lifted the paperweight off the plans, his eyes on Ruby.

"As background for my work with Phyllis's design notes."

"And you're asking my permission?"

"I already have Phyllis's," she said. "But I wanted you to know I was here."

"Do you think your questions will do Phyllis—or the firm—any good?" he asked as he rolled up the blueprints and rubber-banded them.

"I hope so. I'd like to establish which people handled the binder that held her design notes and in what order." She shifted in her chair so that the lamp on his desk blocked the most piercing set of Charlotte's eyes.

He tapped the roll of plans against his hand. "Ask away, then. Do you have questions for me?"

"Not at the moment," she said, and was surprised to catch a look of disappointment on his face.

"Well, I'll be here if you do. What did you discover when you examined the design notes?" he asked.

"It wasn't totally conclusive," Ruby said. She'd already decided on this tack, realizing how rapidly the news would spread if she said yes, she definitely did believe that Phyllis's specifications had been purposely altered.

"Did Phyllis tell you about our offer?" he asked as he leaned back his chair and inserted the rolled blueprints into a slotted case beside his desk.

"She did. Is that what they call 'cut and run'?"

His eyes narrowed and he worked a second rubber band around and around his index fingers. "Yeah, maybe so," he said, his expression troubled. "It wasn't a decision that was made lightly, and not just by the partners, either. We included representatives from both our employees and our clients."

"Such as Southwest Minerals?" Ruby asked.

"They were represented, yes," he admitted.

"And was Bogart Mead one of your representatives?" Ruby asked.

"One of several," he said. He looked up at Ruby. "Nobody enjoys making a decision like this. If Phyllis were in our place, she would have come to the same conclusion—reluctantly, but her first concern has always been for the business."

"You may be right," Ruby said. "How many years does she have invested in this business? It probably hasn't given her much time for a personal life." She held Peter Stern's gaze. "At least not outside the firm."

He snapped the rubber band and winced in pain. "I care about your sister's welfare," he said through tense jaws. He placed his hand on the telephone. "I'll let you proceed with your questioning now. This is a busy day."

"I agree, it is," Ruby said. She opened her notebook and removed the pencil from inside the spiral binding, feeling like she now carried the trappings of Sable's Sheriff Carly or Detective Powell. "Thank you. I'll be in touch."

When she left Peter Stern's office, the first person she saw was Daniel MacSimon thumbtacking a notice for softball tryouts onto the bulletin board. He turned and smiled. "Hi, Ruby. I heard you were here. How's Phyllis?"

"I didn't see her this morning, but she seemed a little better last night. I'm here to ask a few questions. Do you have a minute?"

"Come into my sanctum," he said, pointing to a door across the hall that stood open to a crammed office without windows. "You should have seen my first space," he told her as he removed file folders from a chair for her. "What do they call it, interior landscape? Three wobbly movable walls next to a copy machine. I'm definitely moving up." He sat on the edge of his desk. "Any luck with Phyllis's design notes?"

"Maybe."

"That's good news." He nodded, bobbing his whole upper body. "What can I do to help?"

"Tell me who had access to Phyllis's notes between the time she finished her calculations and when she gave the binder to the CAD designer."

He pinched his lips together. "Just about anybody who has access to the office," he said, repeating what Phyllis had already told her. "We're a pretty open bunch around here. You can talk to Monica, Phyllis's CAD designer. I can show you where she hangs out."

"Good. Who benefits if Phyllis is out of the firm?"

He shrugged. "Well, there'd be more room at the top, for sure. The company's been moving toward big corporate jobs: dams, roads, government contracts. But Phyllis still likes the smaller contracts that don't bring in as much money."

"Like Bad Day?"

"It was bigger than some, but yes. She believes the firm owes its success to smaller contracts, so she has a level of loyalty."

A man stepped into Daniel's office and Daniel stiffened. Ruby recognized Bogart Mead. He wore a gray suit and looked more like a stockbroker than an engineer. She smelled aftershave.

"I thought I heard Phyllis's voice," he said, nodding to Ruby and giving a short laugh. "Pleasant surprise. She's smart to stay home with the publicity coming down after yesterday."

"Do you believe she's responsible for Cesar Peron's death?" Ruby asked.

His face was bland, without expression. "No, but disaster seems to sit on her shoulders lately."

Ruby said nothing, feeling herself being baited. Bogart glanced at his watch. "Have to catch a big meeting: prospective client. Take it easy, Dan-O."

Daniel waited until Bogart was gone, and said quietly, "Man on the move."

"He doesn't get along with Phyllis," Ruby commented.

Daniel shaped his hands into fists and butted them together. "Nope. He's into manly men ripping up the earth with big machines. No place for a little lady."

"I see." Ruby made a note to talk to Bogart. "Does he get along with the other partners?"

"He brings in some lucrative jobs, and money *is* the great persuader." Daniel lifted a yellow pad from his desk. "Forgery detection sounds like a pretty interesting career. Can you peek into a guy's personality from his handwriting?" He held out the yellow pad, and Ruby glimpsed a half page of handwriting in the style of a young schoolboy: graceless round letters crabbed together without shortcuts, each letter connected solidly to the next.

"You're talking about graphology," Ruby told him. "That's a different field altogether."

He laughed, and returned the yellow pad to his desk. "You say 'graphology' like it's a form of fortune-telling."

"Not really. I've examined enough handwriting that I recognize probable personality traits. I just don't believe it's an exact science."

"Yeah, if you can't prove it with numbers, it isn't science." He stood. "I'll take you to Monica. She's one of the best."

Ruby had heard every employee described as the "best" at some form of engineering. Where did the merely "good" fit in?

Monica's corner was in a climate-controlled windowless computer room in the center of the building, which she shared with three other CAD operators, each with his or her own station. Only two operators were in the room at the moment. A machine four feet long and three feet high filled the farthest corner.

"Design plotter," Daniel supplied. "It creates the Mylar sheets blueprints are made from."

A child's mobile of colorful animals hung from the ceiling over Monica's computer, turning slowly in the circulating air currents. Monica sat before her blue screen, intent on moving a triangular shape between a confusing array of lines. Daniel waited until she clicked her mouse before he said, "Monica, this is Phyllis's sister, Ruby."

Monica turned, removing a pair of red glasses. She was plain with straight short brown hair and heavy makeup. Black liner swept upward at the corners of her eyes, emphasizing their size. "Ruby," she said, shaking Ruby's hand in a firm grip. "You look like Phyllis."

"Thank you," Ruby said without thinking. Phyllis had always been referred to as the more beautiful, "the pretty one."

"Ruby's asking a few questions about the Bad Day project," Daniel told Monica. "I'll be in my office if you need anything else, Ruby."

"Thanks," Ruby told him, noting the way Monica's eyes softened as they followed Daniel's retreating figure.

The other CAD operator leaned back from his computer and stretched his arms over his head. He stood, a man as tall as a professional basketball player. "I'm taking a break," he told Monica. "Want anything from the machine?"

"No, thanks, Jim."

Ruby pulled a wheeled office chair next to Monica's station. "I've been examining Phyllis's design notes," she said.

Before she could finish, Monica nodded, and said with a defensive edge, "I know. She claims they were changed, but I only made the plans using her figures."

"That's not an issue," Ruby assured her. "If her specifications were changed, we know it was done before you did the CAD work. Where do you keep the design notes while you're drafting plans?"

Monica pointed to a low shelf beside her computer. Two binders similar to Phyllis's sat next to CAD manuals. "Right there."

"And is this room locked?" Ruby asked.

"Now it is." Monica kept glancing uncomfortably at Ruby's notebook, and Ruby closed it, setting it on the table beside Monica's computer.

"Because Phyllis claimed her design notes were altered?"

Monica nodded. "We should have been locking it all along, anyway. All this expensive hardware, but . . ."

"Phyllis said you're the best CAD person she's ever had."

Monica smiled, and absently turned her chair back and forth. "I like what I do," she said.

"You're lucky. Did you notice anything unusual about the Bad Day design?"

"You mean the aluminum instead of the A36? I know about it now because everybody's talking about it, but at the time . . ." She shrugged. "I don't know enough about engineering, and I'd never change anything an engineer specified in design notes."

"So if anybody *really* wanted to tamper with a design, they could have removed the binder from your shelf, made the alterations, and returned it without you ever being aware."

Monica nodded. "I guess that's true."

"Do you remember anyone asking to see Phyllis's designs for Bad Day?"

Monica shook her head.

"Then, you do believe Phyllis?"

Monica pondered the question for so long that Ruby was about to repeat it when she finally said, "Phyllis is very thorough, very careful."

"But?" Ruby asked, hearing the unspoken word.

"Lately . . ." Monica blushed as if she were being disloyal. "She's made a few mistakes. Not big ones, just simple things that aren't as careful as she usually is, simple stuff like blurring the numbers 4 and 9."

"Anything as momentous as switching aluminum for steel?"

"I told you. I don't know enough about engineering to claim that."

"Were there any simple mistakes on the notes for the landing design at Bad Day?"

"Not really," Monica said. She frowned, and turned in her chair again. "I mean, not a mistake. I looked at the notes again before the lawyers took them."

"And?" Ruby encouraged her.

"It doesn't mean anything, but aluminum *is* corrosion resistant."

"I'm not sure what you're getting at," Ruby told her.

"Phyllis specified 'corrosion-resistant aluminum.' "

"And that's redundant," Ruby supplied. "So it would be more likely that she would specify 'corrosion-resistant alloy steel,' is that right? And just let the word *aluminum* stand by itself?"

"Either *aluminum*," Monica agreed, "or aluminum alloy."

Ruby reached for her notebook in order to write this down. "Did you know Cesar?"

Monica's eyes moistened. "Yes. I can't believe . . ." She lowered her head, not finishing her thought.

"Did he ever discuss Bad Day with you?"

"No, not ever," Monica said with certainty, firmly shaking her head.

"Thanks, Monica," Ruby told her as she stood and pushed the office chair back to its place. "I appreciate it."

"I hope you can help Phyllis," Monica said before she turned back to her computer screen.

As Ruby left the computer room, she nearly bumped into Bogart Mead, who was carrying a briefcase and heading toward the rear of the building.

"The press is gathering out front like a pack of the proverbial," he told Ruby, rubbing a hand across his sharp chin. "You look enough like your sister that if I were you, I'd head out the back door."

"They're looking for Phyllis?" Ruby asked.

"In their dreams. They like to use our building as a backdrop for their news stories. Very dramatic. Come on," he said, gesturing as if he were about to tuck Ruby beneath his arm. "I'll protect you."

It was the way he said it that irritated Ruby. The slight leer, the condescension. "My car's out front and I don't have any reason to hide," she told him.

"You'll regret it," he warned her. "Or are you looking for publicity, a sympathy scene for Phyllis?" He made motions of quoting words in the air, intoning:

"Beautiful little sister rushes across country to save alcoholic sister's"—he winked—"career."

Jesse's words of yesterday came back to Ruby, and they seemed the most logical response. She looked at Bogart steadily and said, "I don't like you."

"I'm crushed," he said lightly, clutching his chest, but Ruby caught the narrowing of his eyes. "Maybe I'll grow on you."

"I doubt if there'll be an opportunity."

He laughed, and reached out to touch her shoulder, but Ruby sidestepped his hand and, without looking back, headed down the hallway toward the front door.

"Ruby," Daniel MacSimon called as she passed his office. She stopped, and he rose from his chair to meet her at his doorway. "You look a little hot under the collar." He glanced down the hallway as Bogart Mead turned the corner beneath the Exit sign. "Ah, I see. I just talked to Phyllis and she wants you to bring home another half gallon of milk and two green peppers."

"She tracked me down here?" Ruby asked.

"No. I called her to invite you all out to dinner tonight, but she invited me instead." He hesitated. "I don't think she's eager for public exposure right now."

"I hear the press is outside," Ruby told him.

"Yeah, they've been favoring us lately. You're not planning to run the gauntlet, are you?"

"Are they dangerous?"

"Matter of opinion."

A white television van was parked in the lot, and standing in front of Cholla Engineering, but not on their sidewalk, was a TV crew clustered around a well-dressed woman holding a microphone close to a heavyset man in a short-sleeved white shirt. He wore his jet-black hair, which was so flat and black and nonreflective that it shouted dye, greased back. His face was flushed, his shirt too tight beneath his arms.

A man standing next to a cameraman spotted Ruby and intercepted her. "Are you Phyllis Crane?" he asked.

"No," she told him, and kept on walking.

He kept pace with her, walking in a sideways gait, facing her. "Then, do you work for Cholla Engineering?" he asked, his face avid, hungry on hers.

"No," Ruby said again, and that quickly he lost interest in her, drifting back to the TV interview.

That was easy, Ruby thought. It was as if she'd suddenly thrown on a cloak of invisibility.

She passed along the line of vehicles facing the office, her eyes suddenly caught by the front end of the blue pickup she'd noticed in the parking lot earlier.

She paused. The hood was green, a replacement hood that didn't quite fit right. It was familiar. Where had she seen it before? Religious medals hung from the rearview mirror. A Sacred Heart statue was balanced on the dashboard.

She stood on the sidewalk until she remembered, reliving the sharp fear at the sight of the pickup racing down the mountain, coming straight at Phyllis's Jeep as they drove toward Bad Day and Cesar's body.

It was the same truck, she was certain. Perceived in a second on the road but with the clarity of vision that frequently accompanied terror.

She turned and looked at the office building, intending to go back inside and hunt down the truck's owner, and then saw the phalanx of reporters. Rather than call attention to herself by walking past them again, she decided instead to wait in her car until they gathered up their equipment and left.

Phyllis's Porsche now sat in the shade of a scraggly tree. She rolled down the windows and took advantage of the time to jot notes from her conversation with Monica.

A light suddenly flashed in front of Ruby and she jumped, gasping and looking up to see the same reporter she'd talked to earlier standing by the tree with a camera aimed at her. "This is Phyllis Crane's Porsche, though, isn't it?" he asked, stepping closer and bending down at her window. He wore a baseball cap and mirrored sunglasses.

"Very similar," she said calmly.

"But you're not Phyllis."

Ruby gazed at the reporter, deciding that wasn't a question worth answering.

"You her sister?"

"What's the press doing here?" Ruby asked, closing her notebook and setting it on the passenger seat.

"You know," he said. "The Bad Day deaths."

"Who's being interviewed?"

"You either don't have a TV or you're not from here. Everybody knows Leon."

"Peppermill?" Ruby asked, craning to see the cluster of reporters, but her view of the heavy black-haired man was blocked.

"Yeah, Peppermill. He's always looking for a new

angle to keep us interested." His voice dropped to an intimate level. "So give me a break, what's your story?"

"I don't have one," Ruby told him, and rolled up her window. He tapped his knuckle against the glass once, then snapped another photo that Ruby suspected was out of aggravation, and finally walked back to the reporters.

She immediately rolled down both windows, her eyes on the TV crew, watching for another view of Leon Peppermill. She'd only had a glimpse of him, not enough to form an impression. And now her curiosity kept her waiting in Phyllis's hot car until she could get a good look at Eddy's father.

The shade was moving away from the Porsche when the reporters broke down their props, the interview finally ended. They were surprisingly fast. Here was a crew that knew its business.

She opened the car door and got out, standing next to the Porsche and watching the big man who'd been interviewed separate from the group and walk in a lumbering gait down the sidewalk. He was shaped like a child's toy top, wide-girthed and narrow-shouldered. He unbuttoned the second button of his shirt and stopped beside the blue pickup with the green hood.

Even while his hand was on the door handle, Ruby made her decision and pulled her pencil and notebook from the front seat and ran to his truck, holding her notebook open as if she were in the midst of scribbling a news story.

"Excuse me," she said as she reached the pickup.

His door stood open, one hand on the steering wheel to help hoist himself inside.

"Yeah?" He turned, fastening his gaze on Ruby. He had a wide nose and padded cheeks that pushed his eyes upward, squeezing them smaller. An upper front tooth was chipped, matching a thin scar on his lower lip. He was in his forties, as pale-skinned as Michiganders in winter.

She raised the notebook, drawing attention to it, and asked, "Do you have time for one more question, please?"

He let go of the steering wheel and turned, standing flat-footed on the pavement, squaring his shoulders as if photographers were present. "What is it?" he asked. His voice was high-pitched, a contrast to his bulk.

"Why were you seen at Bad Day the day Cesar Peron was killed?"

He stood completely still, not even breathing. Then his face reddened, he leaned closer to Ruby. "Who are you?" he asked in a low voice. He looked over her shoulder as if the answer were behind her.

"Could you answer the question, please?"

He unbuttoned a third button on his shirt. "You made a mistake."

"Why's that?"

"Why did you make a mistake?" he asked, his lips tugging upward as if he were being clever. "Don't ask me." He grabbed the steering wheel again and hauled himself inside. The cab rocked beneath his weight. Then he waved toward the Cholla Engineering building. "By the time this is over, they'll have to pull down the building and sell the scrap to pay for what they did to my boy."

He slammed the door and turned on his engine, revving it up until it roared.

Ruby watched him pull away, ignoring the friendly wave of one of the reporters closing up his TV van, before he roared into the street, tires squealing.

Chapter 15

From a pay phone outside a grocery store a block from Cholla Engineering, Ruby phoned Detective Nick Powell, holding his card between her thumb and forefinger, tapping and turning it against the change box while she waited for the receptionist to transfer her call. A toddler being pushed past in a grocery cart began screaming, "But I wanted *chocolate!*" and Ruby missed hearing the detective answer his phone.

"Anybody there?" he asked, impatience edging his voice.

Ruby covered one ear with her hand. "It's Ruby Crane," she said. "We met at—"

"Bad Day, for starts," he interrupted. "Did you remember something about Cesar Peron's death?"

"No, but I have a tape I'd like to give you. It's from my sister's answering machine."

"Regarding Cesar Peron?" he asked, following one track only.

"Indirectly. It's the tape of a crank call that she received within a few hours of his death, definitely before the press got ahold of the story."

"I don't know," he said. "You'd be surprised how fast word gets around."

"No," Ruby assured him. "I wouldn't. Will you listen to this tape?" Two teenage girls stopped a few feet from the phone booth, looking at her in stances of exaggerated waiting.

"What do you want me to do with it?" the detective asked.

"Make a record that it exists. Don't you have a standard procedure for threatening phone calls?"

"Depends on the case." Ruby remained silent, and the detective said, "Yeah, okay. Where are you?"

"A block from Cholla Engineering. "By the Sunny Pueblo grocery store."

"I know the place. Across the street there's a strip mall, see it? Built in the seventies."

Ruby glanced at the one-story row of shops. Six or seven stores, all in tawny pueblo style. She wondered what made it obviously from the seventies. "Yes."

"Behind it there's a little café called Mama Linda's. I'll meet you there in ten minutes."

Ruby left her car parked in the grocery store lot and walked across the street to the shops. A craft store occupied the end space, its windows filled with an array of images of the Anasazi flute player, fashioned from unlikely materials: yarns, ceramic, tin, bangles, stained glass. "The dearly maligned Kokopelli," Phyllis had told her. "As common as a smiley face, and now just as meaningful."

Mama Linda's had once been a house, a half block behind the busier street. Low to the ground, small windows, crumbling adobe walls. A locust tree and a cactus taller than Ruby stood in the grassless front yard.

The inside was as battered as the outside. Still, every booth but one was occupied. Elvis Presley sang from the speakers; a dusty and faded yellow donkey piñata hung in a ceiling corner. There was no air-conditioning, only fans whirring in the ceiling. The green walls were badly painted.

"Just an iced tea," Ruby told the waitress, who approached her booth carrying ice water and a hand-printed menu that had been around awhile.

"You can't keep a booth unless you spend two-fifty," the girl told her, pointing to a sign on the wall that said the same thing. "How about a nice burrito or some nachos?"

"Nachos," Ruby told her. Her stomach wasn't ready for lunch yet.

While she waited for Nick Powell to join her, she thought of Leon Peppermill, guessing that he and not the television crew had chosen the setting for his interview, thrilling to the drama of standing in front of the engineering firm he intended to bring down, enriching himself in the process.

Then she chided herself; after all, the man's son was *dead*. She remembered those first touch-and-go days after Jesse's accident, when she'd been warned Jesse might die or that she might remain in a catatonic state all her life. She couldn't think of any disaster more horrible than losing your child, not anything. And if you were estranged, all that grief would be compounded by crushing guilt.

The tortilla chips were warm and so thin they were

as breakable as potato chips, and the green salsa had a bite that began after she swallowed. She was draining her glass of iced tea when Nick Powell slid into the booth seat opposite her. He wore a gray suit and tie and cowboy boots. "Looks innocent enough, doesn't it?" he said, pointing toward the bowl of salsa. "Sneaks up on you."

"Like a bomb," Ruby said, using her napkin to dab at the sudden perspiration on her brow.

"Some people swear jalapeño peppers are an aphrodisiac. But then they say that about oysters, too."

"I can't feature either one of them," Ruby said around the ice cube she was sucking. She removed an envelope from her purse that held the tiny tape from Phyllis's answering machine and set it on the table.

"Ah, the evidence," he said, studying it without touching it. "Tell me again what you want me to do with it."

"Listen to it. It's the first call on the tape, made some time between Cesar's death and the second call, which was made while you were at Phyllis's, a friend saying you'd been asking questions at Cholla Engineering." Ruby paused. "Did you really expect her to be at her office after having just discovered Cesar's body?" The waitress came by and poured more iced tea into Ruby's glass.

He finally picked up the envelope, tore off the edge, and blew inside. "No, but I wanted to ask about the employees your sister said Cesar fired, remember?" He shook the envelope, peering in at the tape. "And to see what the place looked like, get a feel, you know what I mean?"

Ruby nodded at the thin man. "You said you were involved in the investigation of Eddy Peppermill's death; didn't you get inside Cholla then?"

He shook his head. "I wasn't as involved. Cranston, who was, is in Hawaii for a month. This is the best time of year to be *here,* why go to Hawaii now?"

"Is it cheaper now?" Ruby offered. She ate more chips, skipping the salsa.

He laughed. "That fits Cranston." He folded the envelope around the tape and slipped it inside his jacket. "I'll listen to this. If it's relevant, I'll send it out to be analyzed, but like I told you, word gets around fast. Some crank who's been following the case might have heard about the death on his CB radio and called Phyllis."

Elvis Presley had been replaced by rock and roll performed in Spanish. "That's Tejano," the detective said, nodding to the speaker hanging close to the ceiling. "It grows on you. Did the voice of the anonymous caller sound familiar to your sister?"

"This isn't the first threatening call she's received and she wasn't up to listening to it," Ruby told him.

"Too bad. She might recognize the voice. Well, she can come to the office and hear it if we need her to. She's been getting a lot of calls?"

"Maybe not a lot, but definitely memorable ones."

"Even an unlisted number doesn't help these days." He shrugged. "It used to, but now, if they're halfway to smart, they'll find the number on some computer somewhere."

"I ran into Leon Peppermill an hour ago."

He leaned forward. "Yeah? Where?"

"Giving a television interview in front of Cholla Engineering."

The detective shook his head and grinned. "He should have been a promoter. He even did one in front of the juvenile detention center, fondly remembering how Eddy spent six months there when he was fifteen after his tenth arrest for shoplifting. He's desperate to hold the public's attention. The press was easing off until . . ."

"Until Cesar died."

"That's right."

"When Phyllis took me up to Bad Day, when we found Cesar's body, we met a pickup racing erratically down the mountain. It nearly hit us head on."

"Yeah?" Nick asked, his eyes intent on Ruby's, hand pausing in its reach for a tortilla chip, then pulling back to drum his fingers on the edge of the table.

"I'm sure it was the same pickup I just saw Leon Peppermill driving: blue with a green hood as if he'd replaced it."

"Did you ask him about it? No offense, but you strike me as the type who'd take on a crook before you even thought of calling the police."

"He said I was mistaken."

For the first time, the detective pulled a notebook from his pocket and jotted notes. "What model?"

"An older Chevrolet, maybe mid seventies."

He raised his head. "When did you recognize it was a Chevy, when you met it on the road or when you saw Leon Peppermill getting into it an hour ago?"

"When I saw Leon open the pickup door, but it was

the same size and shape. That's pretty coincidental, don't you think?"

"Might be. I'll check it." He closed the notebook, then hesitated. "Anything else?"

"Isn't that enough? A tape and seeing Leon Peppermill at the scene of the crime?"

"Not at the scene of the crime. You said you saw a *similar* truck on the road *miles* before Bad Day."

"How many other places could he have been coming from?"

"Plenty. There are four picnic grounds up there, a ski area, a road down the other side of the mountain." Seeing Ruby's face, he held up his hand. "I'm not saying I disbelieve you. I'm just being realistic, thinking like a judge and jury."

"Has the autopsy report come back on Cesar?" Ruby asked.

He hesitated, watching a young man and woman enter the restaurant holding hands, and Ruby assured him, "I won't mention it."

"It's probably already out. Maybe it's even on your sister's answering machine. Sorry." He piled a generous dollop of salsa on a sturdier chip, and Ruby winced as he swallowed it whole and kept right on talking, not even reaching for his glass of water. "Good hunch on your part. He was hit on the head hard enough to crack his skull, then probably fell, or was pushed, into the stream. The cause of death was drowning, but without aid he would have succumbed to the neck wound."

"Was he hit from behind?" Ruby asked. She absently stacked three chips, one on top of the other, matching sides.

"Yes. He might not have seen it coming."

"Do you really believe that people 'don't see it coming'? That they 'never knew what hit them'?" Ruby asked.

Nick was silent for a few moments. He slowly shook his head. "No, I don't. In some little corner I think everybody knows. But in a lot of cases we'd rather believe they didn't."

Ruby nodded, agreeing.

Nick Powell drove her back to the grocery store parking lot and stopped behind Phyllis's Porsche, blocking the aisle. He glanced with longing at the little white car. "Cops don't make that kind of bucks," he said.

"Neither do document examiners," Ruby told him.

"I forgot about that. What did you discover when you studied your sister's designs?"

"How did you know that?" Ruby asked. She took her hand off the door handle.

"I talked to Connie yesterday. I figured you didn't come down here to vacation with your sister in the midst of this mess."

"My opinion is that yes, Phyllis's design specifications were tampered with." Behind them a car honked.

"Hold your shirt," Nick said over his shoulder. "But she didn't catch the alteration?"

"She claims she did, but there's no record of her issuing an order to correct it." She made a move to open the door, and Nick smiled. "I'll be in touch. Call me anytime. I mean it."

Ruby stepped out of the car and waved, watching the detective pull his car out of the parking lot and casually enter traffic, forcing a van driver to slam on his brakes and give him the finger out the window.

"You make friends fast," a man's voice said behind her.

She turned and met Bogart Mead's well-groomed countenance. He held up a container of double cream. "I hate that powdered stuff, and everybody else is into low-fat or nonfat. It's a crime to pour it into good coffee. So if I want cream, I have to buy it myself."

"That must cause a hardship," Ruby said.

He laughed amiably. "Would you prefer I sent my secretary out for it?"

"I really don't care what you do." She turned, but he stepped around in front of her, blocking her way toward the Porsche.

"Intriguing. You leave your sister's car innocently parked here at the grocery store and dash off in a car with a man."

Ruby glanced at Phyllis's car. "Then you noticed the car. Were you waiting for Phyllis?"

For an instant he looked caught out, then he grinned. "It's a distinctive car. I didn't think she'd let anyone else drive it, let alone take it out of her sight."

"I thought you had an important meeting," Ruby said.

"All finished. Really important business is completed a lot more quickly than minor business." He tossed the carton from hand to hand. "Would you like a cup of coffee? Mama Linda's is just up the street."

"No, thanks. I have to go home."

"Next time, then."

Once she was out of Albuquerque, Ruby rolled down the windows all the way and felt the rush of soft warm air. An elusive fragrance blew through the car, like blossoms on a hot, dry wind. No matter where she'd lived in her life, even though she enjoyed city life, in fact ached for its excitement when she was away too long, she never really felt herself untangle until she escaped its streets to the countryside.

She glanced over New Mexico's undulating hills, the gigantic sky, reminding herself this was only March, what Nick had called the best time of the year. If that was true, she couldn't imagine the parched glare of July. Maybe the air conditioner should rate right up there with the invention of the wheel and the zipper.

She entered the sloped and curving road that cut through the close hills about a mile from Phyllis's house, the Porsche effortlessly racing along, not another car in sight.

Suddenly, a hundred feet in front of her, a vehicle pulled straight out from the shoulder, blocking the entire width of the road. Ruby slammed both feet against the brake, gripping the steering wheel. The Porsche shimmied, brakes squealed and the car twisted sideways as it struggled to a stop. A surge of adrenaline lightened her head, making her see clearly a cairn of three rocks beside the road, stacked like a trail marker.

The car died facing into the hill on the left side of the road, the front wheels on the shoulder. She unbuckled her seat belt with shaking hands and flung open her door, half terrified, half enraged. She could have smashed into the idiot; they all might have been killed.

Ruby rounded the Porsche and stopped. The vehicle was still blocking the road and the driver climbed out. The blue pickup had a green hood and the driver was Leon Peppermill. His face was red, his short-sleeve shirt unbuttoned and untucked, flapping over a tank undershirt. His underarms were dark with sweat. He was alone.

Ruby remained where she was, leaning against the side of the Porsche, feeling the comfort of the warm metal. She forced herself to relax her shoulders, to cross her arms and take slow breaths, waiting for Leon Peppermill to come to her.

She didn't see any sign of a weapon on the advancing man. There was no telltale bulge in his pocket, his thick hands were empty, and she doubted he was the type to tuck a pistol into the back of his waistband. For one thing, it would be too difficult for a man of his bulk to reach behind himself.

A sound like ocean waves roared inside Ruby's head as she strained to hear approaching traffic. Anyone.

His foot slid on loose gravel thrown up by her desperate braking and he caught himself by flapping his arms as if he were struggling to take flight. Ruby wasn't reassured by the comic attitude; appearing silly would only enrage Leon more. She kept her face neutral, glancing up into the sky as if she hadn't seen him stumble. A hawk circled high overhead, spiraling lower until its golden beak was visible, then it flapped away, leaving her. She breathed, holding each breath before she exhaled.

"What are you doing here?" he asked when he was still twenty feet from her, his voice a harsh rasp, still walking, his arms and upper body swaying with each step. Just like at Cholla Engineering, he didn't wear sunglasses.

"I'm asking you the same thing," Ruby said. "You're blocking a public road."

"You're driving her car and you've got the same color hair," he continued, jabbing his thick index finger into his palm with each point. He stopped three feet from Ruby, standing with his legs splayed, his black-haired head thrust forward. "And you were at Cholla Engineering."

"Move your truck before I call the police," Ruby warned him, making a move toward the passenger door. She hadn't checked the Porsche's glove compartment; there *might* be a cellular phone there.

"And you're asking questions," Peppermill said, not to be deterred. "You people think you can hide your mistakes in the grave because people like me don't have the money to fight you. Grind up the little folks?" He leaned toward her, his weight shifting onto the balls of his feet, threatening. His breath would be hot, burning to blisters if it touched her skin.

Ruby knew she should remain calm, but a little

spark was being fanned and growing inflamed. "Back off," she ordered him. "Step back two paces, or not only will I call the police, I'll charge you with assault, and I'd make it worth the police's while. There'd be so much publicity it would ruin your chances for that big settlement you're hoping will make *you* one of the 'rich people.' "

"It's just money; it isn't my boy I'm going to get back."

Ruby almost softened at his words until she saw the coldness in his slitted eyes. Maybe the words had been said so many times they'd lost their impact; maybe his feelings for his son were as cold as Connie had claimed. Or maybe there was no room for grief in his eyes anymore; it had been replaced by rage at what he saw as an unjust world.

"I'm sorry about your son," she began, but he cut her off.

"Words aren't worth a damn, don't you understand that?" he demanded, taking a single pace back, then the second step.

"I'm beginning to. Why did you pull out in front of me?"

"I told you: to see who you were."

"Do you drive up and down these roads trying to get a peek at Phyllis? Are you the one who's been harassing her? The threatening phone calls and letters?" His eyes shifted, and she sensed him faltering and pressed her point. "You've already figured out where she lives and what cars she owns. What else do you know?"

He stared at her, then he pulled up the waistband of his pants. "I know she's still free."

"And she's going to stay that way." Ruby stood away from the car. "Now, please move your pickup so I can get through."

"Whoever you are, wherever you came from, if you value all that you have"—he spoke in a voice of thunder, as if he had the privilege to dispense and prophesize—"stay out of this. Go back where you came from, or you'll regret it."

And having delivered his message, he turned and stalked back to his truck, his heavy body perspiring in the heat, his untucked shirt billowing with each step.

Ruby stood beside the car and watched Leon Peppermill back up his blue truck and turn toward her. He passed her, gunning the engine and never once looking her way.

Chapter 16

"Car trouble?" a silver-haired woman asked, leaning out the window of her white BMW. Ruby stood beside the Porsche gazing down the road in the direction Leon Peppermill's truck had disappeared.

"Thanks," Ruby told her. "I'm fine. I nearly hit somebody and I'm letting myself cool off for a few minutes."

The woman nodded. She was overly thin and stylish, wearing chunky silver jewelry. "It's difficult to see on this stretch of road," she sympathized, motioning toward the slopes of sand to either side of them. "You take care." She smiled and waved and continued on her way.

The thought of Leon Peppermill patrolling Phyllis's road anytime day or night, recognizing her vehicles, learning her habits, caused a chill along Ruby's arms. If he was so familiar with the nuances of Phyllis's life, wouldn't he have recognized Phyllis's Jeep on the way to Bad Day? Is that why he'd driven so erratically? From shock at having been nearly caught?

A breeze ruffled her hair, stirring up loose sand on

the stony hill beside her. It was cooler than yesterday but not by much.

She got back into the Porsche and drove to Phyllis's, turning into the long, unmarked driveway, still thinking of Leon Peppermill.

When she reached the house, she saw Phyllis, Adam, Salina, and Jesse seated at the table in the courtyard, Salina and Jesse in shorts, Phyllis in jeans and a T-shirt. A blue and white umbrella shaded them. Ruby sat behind the wheel, taking in the tableau. They were playing cards, probably a simple game, and laughing. Jesse looked at Phyllis, and Phyllis touched her cheek. They could have been mother and daughter. Ruby suddenly felt the outsider, the fifth wheel arriving on the scene to disrupt the idyllic quartet with tales of murder, forgery, and harassment. She had the urge to take Jesse and flee back to Michigan, leaving Phyllis to sort out her own mess.

Watching Jesse in short sleeves, Ruby thought of snowy March in Michigan, of the mud and freezing temperatures, the dead earth. Time in Michigan was defined by the seasons, giving each day its stark shape. But Hank was there, too, and she missed his wry humor, his solidity.

She ran her hands around the inside of the steering wheel, touching them together at the bottom. "Why stay?" she asked herself aloud. She didn't have an answer, not now. She only knew she was reluctant to leave so soon.

All four card players looked up at Ruby as she entered the courtyard. They smiled at her as if she'd appeared in their refuge that instant, leaving behind a tumultuous and distant world that had nothing to do with any of them.

"We're playing Old Maid," Jesse told Ruby. She wore another new shorts outfit, this one green and white.

Phyllis held up her hand, palm toward Ruby. "Don't say it. I know, I should win hands down. How was your day?"

"Fine. Connie—"

"I don't want to hear about it right now," Phyllis said. "This is a very important game, the championship round."

Ruby sat in a wooden lawn chair and closed her eyes, listening to the chatter, wondering what mechanism Phyllis possessed that allowed her to flick her emotions on and off. But then, hadn't she always been that way? Keeping herself hidden away from scrutiny, exposing only the in-control, above-it-all facade.

"I'm the Old Maid," Jesse said. "Am I the winner or the loser?"

"Around here," Ruby heard Adam say, "I guess that makes you a winner."

"Hardee-har-har," Salina said like a vaudeville comedienne.

Ruby opened her eyes and sat up. "How was your walk this morning?" she asked Jesse.

"I saw eleven different kinds of cacti," Jesse told her. Then she turned to Phyllis. "Can we take Mom for a walk?"

"Sure," Phyllis said, already rising. "Better change your shoes, Ruby. If we still have the same size feet, I have a pair of sneakers that'll fit you."

"I think mine are dry," Ruby told her.

In her room the bedcovers Ruby had hastily pulled across the pillows had been remade to hotel perfection; the tissue she'd left on the bedside table had been thrown out.

She tucked her notebook into a bureau drawer and changed into shorts and the sneakers she'd worn at Bad Day. They were dry but stiff, slightly curled and dull. When she left the bedroom and entered the dining room, she glanced through the window and saw Salina and Adam walking toward Adam's pickup. They walked amiably together, their arms occasionally touching but not particularly romantic.

Suddenly they stopped and turned, both their faces expectant, and Ruby saw Phyllis catch up to them. They spoke a few moments and then Phyllis handed something to Adam that looked very much like green cash.

"That trail across the hill drops down into the arroyo," Phyllis told Ruby. "We can follow it and circle back to the road."

They descended into the arroyo, where there was no breeze and the sun burned hotter, trapped between the arroyo's walls. It wasn't an arroyo like Phyllis's project but a natural cut through the land made by flowing water, eroded through the hills over time. Its bottom was dotted by rocks and cacti, bone dry.

Jesse led the way, intent on examining every plant, meandering back and forth across the cut, picking up stones and putting them in a plastic bag Phyllis had given her.

The fine sand was loose, giving beneath their feet. "Does it remind you of walking on the dunes along Lake Michigan?" Phyllis asked.

"Without the view to compensate for it," Ruby said, glancing at the hill of sand beside her where prickly pear cacti grew like clumps of cartoon ears. Everything in this place was barbed, covered with spines and spears and needles, untouchable.

"I miss Lake Michigan," Phyllis said. "I've been to the ocean, but it smells wrong, do you know what I mean? Like dead things."

"You can always move back," Ruby said. She stooped and picked up a rose-colored stone, warm from the sun.

"Hah," Phyllis said. "So what did you think of my design notes?"

"I think it's possible they were altered," she said.

Phyllis stopped and frowned at her. " 'Think'?" she asked. " 'Possible'? Were they or weren't they?"

"I gave a written report to Connie saying the handwriting was inconsistent with yours."

"Is that the best you can do? Can't you say for sure?"

"That's not how document examiners operate," Ruby explained patiently. "We assess likelihood. It was a very small sample of handwriting: ten letters, ten numbers. Even though *I* believe there's been tampering, Connie says there's still a problem with my testifying."

"He told me," Phyllis said sullenly, kicking a stone.

"Because you're my sister and supposedly have an interest in my welfare."

"When did you talk to him?" Ruby asked.

"About an hour ago."

She stopped in the soft sand and rubbed her calves. "You talked to Connie? So you already knew what I reported to him?"

Phyllis nodded. "But I wanted to hear it straight from you."

"Did he call you to give you the report?" Ruby asked. She worked her jaws to unclench them, hating the way Phyllis held back information.

"I phoned him. I expected *you* to call me with the news as soon as you finished."

"Sorry," Ruby told her. "I didn't think of it."

"Why should you? I'm only a bit player in all of this. It's taken on a life of its own." She waved to Jesse, who'd paused a hundred feet ahead, looking back, her attention caught by their voices. "But that detective *did* call."

"Nick Powell? Looking for me?"

"No. To ask me about a truck you said nearly hit us on the way to Bad Day."

"Did you describe it to him?"

"I don't remember any truck." Phyllis picked up a stick of dried cholla that looked like silvery coral and broke it into pieces.

"Of course you do," Ruby protested. "The blue pickup with the green hood."

Phyllis shrugged. "I remember swerving when you grabbed the wheel, but I didn't notice what the other car looked like. What about it?"

"I saw the same truck today," Ruby told her. From a house tucked somewhere in the hills came the sounds of wind chimes.

"No kidding? Did you take down the license plate number?"

"I talked to the driver. It was Leon Peppermill."

Phyllis gasped. "So he was coming down from Bad Day? He killed Cesar?"

"He claims he wasn't on the mountain, that I'm mistaken."

"Could you be? I mean, I couldn't tell you whether it was a truck or car, but in a split second you caught oddities in the paint job?"

"A green hood on a blue pickup is noticeable."

"Mmm," Phyllis murmured. "What else did Leon say? I'm doomed? He's going to become a rich man and dance on his son's grave?"

"Something like that." Ruby mentally debated and then decided not to tell Phyllis about meeting Leon on her road. Phyllis was jumpy enough.

Jesse bent over a trail of tiny tracks that crossed the bottom of the arroyo. Phyllis knelt beside her. "Mouse tracks," she told Jesse.

Jesse followed the mouse's trail with Phyllis beside her, pointing out how the tracks of the mouse's front paws were smaller than those of its hind paws. She glanced up at Ruby. "See, I remember some of that stuff we used to know."

Phyllis stiffened and said to Jesse, "End of the trail, kiddo. Let's look for somebody else's tracks."

Ruby followed the mouse tracks and saw why Phyllis had redirected Jesse's attention: the trail abruptly ended, vanished, only a slight ruffling of the dirt to either side of the tracks, made, she knew, by an owl or hawk plucking the tiny mouse from the earth.

They rounded a bend in the arroyo and came upon a row of wire cages filled with large gray rocks. "What are those?" Ruby asked.

"Gabions. They hold back erosion when the water runs."

"Have you ever seen this arroyo run?"

Phyllis nodded, her eyes going dreamy. "Several times. It's always a shock when you're used to seeing a dry ditch like this. You want to pinch yourself."

Ruby couldn't imagine waves of water pouring down the arid, grassless channel. Somebody always dies, Phyllis had told her.

"He wants you to call him tonight," Phyllis said.

"Who does?"

"The detective. Dick Tracy or whatever his name is. After dinner, he said. Call him at home. I left the number on the dresser in your room, his *personal* number."

"After dinner rather than now?" Ruby asked.

"I'm only reporting what he said. I don't read minds."

The arroyo met the road, continuing beneath it through a six-foot culvert they could easily walk through. Jesse stood to the side of the pipe, ten feet back, staring, the vertical frown lines she'd developed after the accident deepening between her eyebrows, her body gone still, her hands at her sides.

"We don't have to go through that," Phyllis assured Jesse. "This is where we rejoin the world," and she led the way up a deeply grooved trail that climbed out of the arroyo to the gravel road.

Jesse relaxed, falling in line behind Phyllis. It was cooler on the road, the breezes ruffling their hair and dissipating the heat.

Other houses, even bigger and more expensive than Phyllis's, were tucked into the folds of the hills as tawny-colored as the sand under the day's shifting sunlight, each one politely invisible to the next.

"Are Adam and Salina gone for the evening?" Ruby asked.

"A night out. I gave them a little extra money to play. Why? You look like the disapproving aunt."

"I just thought Salina would be here to cook, that's all. Daniel said you'd invited him to have dinner with us. Are you cooking, then?"

"I don't cook," Phyllis said.

"But I remember you—" Ruby began, but Phyllis cut her off.

"I didn't say I *can't* cook, I said I *don't* cook. Daniel's bringing takeout." They passed a house where two women stood talking in the driveway. One of them waved and Phyllis waved back.

"Adam told me he works for you," Ruby said.

"When did he say that?" Phyllis asked casually, but Ruby sensed an attentive stillness about her.

"This morning. What does he do?"

After a moment's pause, Phyllis said, "Not to concern yourself, little sister. It doesn't have anything to do with Bad Day or Cesar's death."

"No?"

"No."

Two identical cars were parked in Phyllis's driveway, both of them new red Fords. Two men leaned against one of them, smoking and obviously waiting. Phyllis glanced at her watch. "Oh, damn. I forgot. I ordered a rental car delivered to the house for you."

"Why?" Ruby asked.

Phyllis shrugged. "Driving my Porsche around is probably like having a sign hung around your neck."

"Did Connie or the detective suggest it?" Ruby asked, for an instant absurdly wondering if Phyllis had given her the Porsche as a decoy: to draw off attention while she spent a relaxed day at home.

"No, I thought of it all by myself. Clever, aren't I?"

Before Daniel was due, Hank phoned Ruby from Michigan and she took the call in her bedroom, curling up on the bed and smiling at the sound of his voice.

"This is a cold and miserable place without you," he said.

"And if I was there, it wouldn't be?" Ruby asked.

"Well, it wouldn't be so noticeable."

"Why don't you come down here? The sun is shining; the temperature was seventy-three degrees today, and I've got a queen-size bed."

"So, I guess you're going to be there awhile, right?"

Ruby sighed. "Not long. I think I'll stay a few more days, though."

"I'll see if I can work something out." Ruby heard

the hesitation in his voice. "Don't go off on your own down there, Ruby," he finally said. "It isn't Sable."

"No lie."

Daniel brought takeout lasagna and a Styrofoam container of salad. "I even thought of beer and red wine," he said as he emptied a brown-handled bag onto Phyllis's kitchen counter. "And two different kinds of pop for Jesse."

"My sister brings my niece all the way from the frigid Midwest and we feed her *Italian* food?" Phyllis asked.

Daniel shrugged apologetically. "It seemed like a good idea at the time. I can go get something else."

"Don't be silly," Phyllis told him. "I was teasing."

"But I would," he insisted.

"I know you would."

He turned to Jesse. "Can I treat you to a Mexican meal at a restaurant called El Pinto while you're visiting?" he asked.

"Can Mom and Aunt Phyllis come, too?" the always literal Jesse asked.

"Definitely. We'll make a party out of it."

The conversation stayed light throughout dinner, eaten at Phyllis's more formal dining room table spread with a white tablecloth. They ate from paper plates, using plastic utensils, which Daniel had also pulled from his brown bag, brandishing them like a magician and announcing, "No muss, no fuss."

Daniel was in the process of xeriscaping the yard of his house in town and he discussed the merits of various cacti with Jesse. Phyllis rolled her eyes at Ruby. The lasagna was good, but Phyllis barely touched the food on her plate. She refilled her wineglass twice, and although Ruby didn't see Daniel do it, the bottle of wine ended up at his other side, out of Phyllis's reach.

At exactly eight o'clock Jesse asked, "May I sit outside and wait for the comet?"

"If you dress for Michigan," Phyllis answered for Ruby and then, seeing Jesse's puzzled expression, explained, "I mean, dress warm. It's chilly out there."

Daniel watched Jesse rise, push her chair in squarely, and leave the dining room. "She's a charmer," he said. "If you hadn't told me about her accident, I would have thought she was just an eccentric teenager."

"Maybe that's all it really is," Phyllis said with such earnestness that Ruby bit her lip to keep back the retort. How could they comprehend the long struggle, Jesse's battle to relearn life from the ground up, the subtle difference from the old Jesse, traits gone forever like tiny deaths?

"She's better all the time," Ruby said mildly.

"She should go to a better school," Phyllis said. "What is there in Sable but antiquated teaching methods? I found a school west of here that specializes in head injuries: small classes, lots of attention. We could—"

"She's responding well to her classes in Sable," Ruby said. "I'm satisfied."

"I'm . . . ," Phyllis began.

". . . not her mother," Ruby finished for her.

Daniel leaned across the table between them. "C'mon," he said in a teasing voice. "We have bigger fish to fry."

Phyllis turned her gaze from Ruby to Daniel and said abruptly, "Ruby said Leon Peppermill gave an interview outside the office today."

"That he did," Daniel said, sitting back, relieved, probably thinking he'd defused their exchange. "The press was eating it up, wringing out a few more tears." He glanced at his watch. "We missed the news. It's just as well; you don't need to hear his latest diatribe."

"If it's that good, they'll replay it at ten," Phyllis told him.

"Don't watch it, Phyllis," he said lightly. "Okay?"

"I probably won't," Phyllis said. She nodded toward Ruby. "My little sister here confronted the man himself."

Daniel turned to Ruby. "Leon, you mean? You should have gone out the back, as cowardly as the rest of us. Did he know who you were?"

Again Phyllis answered for Ruby. "Ruby says she saw Leon when we drove up to Bad Day, that he nearly ran into us tearing down the mountain."

"When you found Cesar?" Daniel asked.

Phyllis opened her mouth, but Ruby said, "I can talk for myself, Phyllis."

"Then what are you waiting for?"

"A chance."

Phyllis sniffed, and Daniel glanced out the door to the courtyard where Jesse sat watching the sky but not before Ruby caught the grin on his face.

"Yes," she told Daniel. "His pickup's blue with a

green hood; that's why I recognized it. He was driving like a bat down the mountain and nearly plowed into us."

Daniel frowned. "That's weird. Did you tell the police?"

Ruby nodded. "Yes, there's a sheriff's detective working on the case."

But Daniel's eyes were distant; his fingers tapped on the table beside his wineglass. "If Leon was at Bad Day . . . Could he have a reason to kill Cesar?"

"If Cesar was prepared to back up Phyllis's story . . . ," Ruby began.

Daniel shook his head. "You mean because he was afraid it would hurt his lawsuit? Do you really think he'd kill somebody for money after losing his son like he did?"

Phyllis leaned forward, pointing her fork at Daniel. "People do it all the time. Read the paper. Ask Ruby. If Leon had dreams of big bucks and Cesar was going to testify that my design had been tampered with, then Cesar was a hindrance. So Leon got rid of him. Case closed."

"But even if Cesar had testified," Daniel said, and Ruby could see he was musing, speaking before he thought, "that doesn't change the case. You're still . . ." He glanced at Phyllis, a pained expression on his face.

"Liable," Phyllis finished for him, speaking softly and dropping her fork on her plate. "I'd still be liable. Nobody's going to get me out of this one, you're saying, right?" And she stood and walked out of the room.

"Phyllis, wait," Daniel said, rising hastily from his chair, but the only sound was the slamming of Phyllis's bedroom door and the unmistakable clunk of the lock turning.

"Shit," Daniel said, and dropped back into his chair, rubbing his forehead. "Open mouth . . ."

"You were only stating what everybody's been saying and Phyllis can't accept," Ruby said.

"I didn't have to stab her through the heart to remind her." He leaned his head back, turning it as if he were alleviating kinks in his neck. "But Leon. I don't know the man, but I've seen his interviews on TV. An opportunist, a little greasy maybe, well, a lot greasy, but he doesn't strike me as a murderer. You sure it was him you saw?"

Ruby rubbed her hands together. "No. Actually I'm not. It was a blue truck with a green hood, traveling fast. I saw the driver's shadow—he looked big. That's all."

"Big?"

"That was my impression."

"Well, I hope your detective's hot on it." He leaned forward and rested his elbows on the table. "Phyllis is more relaxed now that you're here. Don't leave too soon."

Daniel left when it became apparent that Phyllis had disappeared into her room for the night. But before he did, he stood outside her bedroom door and spoke to her in a low, coaxing voice that brought no response. Ruby sat with Jesse for a while, watching the gauzy Hale-Bopp comet to the west, the waxing moon to the east.

"The paper said there's a lunar eclipse on Sunday," Jesse said. "Will we still be here?"

"I suspect we will be. Do you like it here?"

"Some of it. I don't like it when Aunt Phyllis thrums."

Thrums was the word Jesse sometimes used for herself when she realized she was growing overstimulated, before she reached the level of mechanical rocking. It was a warning and a plea that she was losing control.

"Your aunt Phyllis is under a lot of stress right now."

"She's in trouble, isn't she?"

"Yes, she is."

The phone rang, and Ruby slipped back through the door into the kitchen to answer it.

"Is dinner over yet?" a man asked, and Ruby recognized the voice of Detective Nick Powell.

"Sorry. We had company."

" 'S okay. I've only got a second here. I just wanted to tell you I talked to Leon Peppermill and he claims he was home watching TV with his wife when you thought you saw him up by Bad Day."

"And she confirms that?" Ruby asked.

"Right down the line. He even told me the questions on the game show they were watching. I checked with the station and he was right."

"Could she be lying for him?"

"Could be. Who knows? But it's an alibi. I'm meeting a guy in Santa Fe. I'll talk to you when I get back tomorrow." And he was gone before Ruby could tell him about Leon Peppermill's threat on the road to Phyllis's house.

Chapter 17

Phyllis stayed home the next day, too, not even calling the office, nor did anyone from the office call to ask whether she was coming in. She was overtaken by a curious languor, as if suddenly none of it mattered, not the lawsuit, nor her projects, not even the deaths. It was Jesse who occupied her attention. Phyllis's eyes followed her every movement. If Jesse spoke or appeared about to speak, Phyllis turned to her, patiently waiting while Jesse gathered her thoughts.

It's only temporary, Ruby told herself as Phyllis hovered over Jesse's breakfast, trying not to feel the old heat she'd felt when Phyllis had moved in on whatever possession of Ruby's that had appealed to her, usurping Ruby's boyfriends, whether younger than herself or not, or siding with their father over Ruby's belligerence. Phyllis had always taken what she wanted. But those days were in the past. Phyllis couldn't have children. "Something wrong with the plumbing," she'd said once years ago, her voice bright and careless.

"What are you planning to do today?" Phyllis asked Ruby.

"Poke around a little," Ruby began, but she saw the distant expression on Phyllis's face. She really wasn't interested. "Jesse can come with me."

"I was planning to take her to Zia Pueblo," Phyllis told her. "Play tourists."

"Alone?" Ruby asked.

Phyllis's eyes narrowed. "Salina's coming with us."

"Adam too?" Ruby asked.

"He has business in town," Phyllis told her. "Any other questions?"

"Is there an event at the pueblo? Sometimes too much activity—"

"Don't you think I know that? No 'event,' just a quiet day in New Mexico, all right?"

Jesse looked from Ruby to Phyllis, silently considering the two women. "Are you quarreling about me?" she finally asked.

"Yes," both Phyllis and Ruby answered at the same time. Phyllis laughed, and the situation was defused.

"We both want you to have a good time," Ruby told her.

"All right," Jesse said, "I will," totally accepting.

Just as Ruby had expected, the Peppermills' telephone number rang; no electronic voice told her the number had been changed or was no longer in service. Leon Peppermill courted publicity; why cut off the main access point?

"Hello?" a woman's voice answered, rough, as if she'd just woke up or hadn't had her first cigarette.

"Is Mr. Peppermill in?" Ruby asked, prepared to hang up if he was.

"No, but he'll be home in an hour. Can I take a message?"

"I'll call back later, then. Thank you," Ruby said, and replaced the black receiver in its silver cradle, turning and glancing through the Circle K's window at the teenager pumping gas into the tank of an aging convertible that barely cleared the ground.

She was a mile from the Desert View Mobile Home Park, the address listed in the phone book, in a small neighborhood of one-story tract homes and narrow streets, an early attempt at suburbs.

"Anything else?" the young Hispanic woman behind the counter asked Ruby when she placed a package of cashews on the counter.

"Can you tell me how to get to the Desert View Mobile Home Park?"

"Keep going up the street about six blocks, turn right on Del Oro, and follow it to the end," she said, turning her head briefly to the right, a recitation without inflection, and then asked, "Are you one of the reporters?"

"No. Have you been giving directions to a lot of reporters?"

"Not as many as at first."

Ruby judged the woman to be nineteen or twenty. "Did you know Eddy Peppermill?" she asked.

"When he was a kid. He was okay."

"What about when he was older?" Ruby asked.

She shrugged, and closed the cash register with a

thrust of her hip. "I didn't know him so well then. Here's your change."

Del Oro ended at the gates of Desert View Mobile Home Park: two square brick posts mounted with colonial-style lamps, one of the posts leaning precariously toward the road, its lamp broken.

A hand-printed sign, blue paint on a red background, read PEPPERMILLS: #17. Ruby wondered if Leon Peppermill had raised the sign himself or if residents of Desert View had, weary of directing reporters to the Peppermills' trailer.

The trailer park was small but with larger lots than more recent parks, the mobile homes mostly single-wides, a few silver Airstreams, nearly all with awnings and decks, some of those bigger than the trailers themselves.

Number 17 was a green-and-white single-wide, with a green-striped awning faded by the sun. A clay pot of surprisingly vigorous pansies and tulips sat beside the sidewalk, a chained refrigerator leaned against the trailer wall, and cheap plastic lawn chairs sat around a weathered wooden table. The driveway was empty.

Ruby parked in front and got out, locking the red rental car; at least it wasn't recognizable as one of Phyllis's vehicles. The morning was still too cool for air conditioners; windows were open throughout the park, spilling a mixture of talk shows, reruns, and the voices of small children. She imagined the whir and rumble of air conditioners and swamp coolers when the weather heated up, struggling mightily to cool the metal homes.

Back in an hour, Leon Peppermill's wife had said. Ruby glanced at her watch. She'd be out of here in forty-five minutes, sooner if possible.

No sound came from the Peppermills' trailer. Ruby knocked on the metal door, afraid that Grace Peppermill had left, too. Two gigantic plastic butterflies clung to the metal wall beside the door.

She raised her hand to knock a second time when she heard movement inside, footsteps coming slowly from the rear of the trailer. She took a step back and waited.

Grace Peppermill was short; even standing inside the trailer a step above Ruby, she still wasn't eye level. She was heavy, so heavy that her arms couldn't hang straight at her sides. Her purple sweatshirt was stretched taut across her bosom, skewing the image of two yellow kittens in a basket. Her body was distorted; her upper body was short and grossly overweight, while her legs, encased in black polyester pants, were long and comparatively thin, as if she'd been programmed to be a tall woman but only her legs grew while the rest of her body compacted.

"Mrs. Peppermill?" Ruby asked.

"Yes?" she inquired warily, glancing behind Ruby as if she expected cameras and a platoon of reporters. Her features had been altered by her weight to a smooth agelessness. Only her pale hair was sleek: thick and shiny.

"May I speak to you for a few minutes?" Ruby

asked. "I'm not a reporter. I'm doing some work for Conrad Tarcher, the attorney. My name's Ruby."

"My husband will be home in an hour," she said, raising her hand to the door as if she was about to close it. "You want to talk to him."

"It'll only take a few minutes," Ruby pressed, feeling a tinge of guilt, sensing here was a woman accustomed to being pressed, to giving in, who wasn't savvy enough to ask for identification or even Ruby's last name.

"Leon won't like it," she said doubtfully.

"I can come back later and talk to him, too," Ruby said, glancing at her watch. "But right now I'm in a hurry. I promise not to take more than thirty minutes of your time."

Grace Peppermill pressed her lips together, then stepped back from the door, and Ruby grabbed the door to keep it from closing. "Just a few minutes, then. My husband will be back soon and—"

"I understand," Ruby said, stepping into the shadowy trailer that smelled of cigarette smoke. It would have been the dining area, but there was no table, only a wide-screen television playing a children's show with the sound turned to a whisper. TV trays sat beside two oversize recliner chairs in the living room, a couch against one long wall. Plants stood on a small table beneath the window: gloxinia and ferns, a pot of white violets. No cactus here, only luxurious growth, and Ruby remembered her mother.

"Sit down," Grace said, motioning to the couch. "Would you like a glass of iced tea, or . . ." Her sentence trailed off, her voice disappearing.

"No, thank you," Ruby told her, and the small woman sat in one of the recliners, her bulk settling around her. She glanced to the left of Ruby, and Ruby followed her gaze to a table holding an array of photos depicting a boy's life, beginning in infancy, unmistakably a shrine to her son's memory. Around the mementos a row of sympathy cards stood open, arranged like Christmas cards.

"Is this Eddy?" Ruby asked.

Grace nodded, her eyes tearing up. The photos ended when Eddy Peppermill was about sixteen, shortly before his parents threw him out of the house, a photo of Eddy in front of the trailer, taken in profile as if he were turning away from the photographer.

"I'm sorry about his death," Ruby told her. Grace nodded again, and Ruby gently said, "I know you've heard that Cesar Peron died at Bad Day two days ago."

Grace jerked, her bulk quivering. "Leon was here," she said. "All day long." She motioned to the other recliner as if a trace of her husband still remained. "He isn't working right now because his back . . ." Her sentence trailed off. "We watch TV sometimes . . . all day. Does that sound awful to you? Just watching TV? I read too," she offered hopefully. "I have a weak . . ." She touched her chest with her thick hand.

"Tell me about Eddy," Ruby said, nodding toward the shrine.

Grace leaned back in her chair, relaxing a little. "He was the best baby. I'd given up on having children when he was born. He alway liked mechanical things; he used to take his toys apart . . ." Her eyes traveled over the array of photos, pausing at the sturdy little one-year-old challenging the camera, his eyes bright with curiosity.

"What went wrong?" Ruby asked quietly, guessing that something certainly had.

Grace shook her head. "He was a determined little boy, stubborn. Leon didn't like . . ." Again her words faded away.

"They didn't get along?" Ruby asked.

"No. It was like they say: bad chemistry." She glanced at Ruby, her eyes wide as if she'd suddenly realized what she was saying. "But he loved Eddy," she insisted. "Bad chemistry doesn't change that. He always wanted a son."

"Was it your lawyer's idea to sue Cholla Engineering?"

"Somebody called Leon to tell him there'd been a mistake and it was that woman's fault."

Ruby clenched her hands together, trying to keep her interest from showing. "Do you know who called?"

Grace Peppermill shook her head. "Leon didn't tell me."

"Was it a man or a woman?"

She shrugged. "I don't know, I really don't." She frowned at Ruby. "Don't you know all the details yourself?"

"Not this part. So then Leon found a lawyer?"

"We already had one, from when Eddy . . . Sometimes Eddy got in with a bad crowd." Grace wet her lips. "Leon said it was the right thing to do, so it would never happen to somebody else's boy."

"The lawsuit?" Ruby asked. The ultimate rationalization for a big-money lawsuit: so no one else will have to go through the pain I did.

"Yes," Grace said softly, looking down at her hands.

"I see. But on the day Cesar died, Leon was home all day?"

Grace nodded, and the recliner creaked. Ruby glanced around the trailer. No dirty dishes sat by the sink, and there wasn't a dishwasher. "Does Leon help you around the house?" she asked.

"Oh, yes. Always in the morning. He fixes breakfast and cleans up."

"That's nice. Then you can sleep in on the days you don't feel well."

"I've never been a morning person," she confided. "I'm more of a night owl. I could sleep all—"

"Did you sleep in the day Cesar Peron died?"

Grace's eyes shifted upward, her lips pursed. "I don't remember," she said.

"But you heard the television," Ruby said, "so you thought Leon was watching TV."

"He doesn't like to waste electricity," Grace said. "He always turns off the lights when he leaves a room; he wouldn't have left it on."

"But you didn't get up to see?" Ruby asked.

"Leon's a good man," she said. "He's . . . upset, but he'd never hurt anybody, I mean, not *kill* them."

Grace was excruciatingly uncomfortable. She shifted in her chair and worked her hands around one another, glancing toward the door as if hoping for intervention. Ruby remembered Leon's imminent return and checked her watch. She should leave within five minutes.

"He called here," Grace said, and from the tone of her voice and the expression on her face, Ruby knew Grace was divulging information she'd been warned to forget, hoping to deflect Ruby's questions about Leon. But the bait was too tantalizing not to take it.

"Who called?" she asked.

"The dead man."

"Cesar Peron?"

Grace nodded, and Ruby slid to the edge of the couch, as close to Grace as she could get. She tried to hold Grace's gaze.

"When?"

"The night before . . ." The words were being pulled from Grace, spoken with regret.

"Why?"

"I don't know. He left a message on our answering machine saying he wanted to talk to us and he'd call back."

"Did he?"

Grace shook her head. "Do you have to tell anybody that he called?"

"I don't know," Ruby told her. "Did Leon warn you not to mention it?"

"He said it would complicate the issue, especially since we didn't know why he was calling us."

Ruby wondered about that, too. Cesar must have called the Peppermills shortly after he returned to Albuquerque. Why? Had he already been to the death site at Bad Day?

"Can you remember anything else about Cesar's message? Anything at all? What time he called, any words or phrases that sounded out of the ordinary?"

"Our answering machine doesn't give the time, but, no, he didn't say anything else except he wanted to talk to us."

"Did he leave a phone number?"

"He said he'd call back."

Ruby had to get out of there. Leon Peppermill would be home any minute. She removed her notebook from her bag and tore out a page, quickly scribbled on it, and held it out to Grace. "This is the name and phone number of Nick Powell, the detective who's investigating Cesar's death. He also worked on Eddy's accident, so he knows what you've been through. If you think of anything else, call him."

Grace didn't reach out to take the slip of paper, and Ruby set it on the TV tray beside her chair, certain it would be out of sight before Leon returned, but Ruby hoped not into the trash.

"Don't get up," Ruby told the woman. "I'll let myself out. And thank you very much."

Ruby drove out of the trailer park through the brick gate confident Grace wouldn't tell Leon she'd visited her, asking questions. She wouldn't want her husband to guess how much she'd spilled.

Chapter 18

From the same Circle K Ruby used the pay phone to call Phyllis's cellular phone number.

"We're about to turn in to the pueblo," Phyllis told her. The connection was filled with static, hollow-sounding.

"Is Jesse okay?"

"Of course she's okay. If you're so worried, you should have come with us."

Ruby refrained from reminding Phyllis exactly *why* she'd come to New Mexico, why she wasn't playing tourist with Phyllis and Jesse. "What reason would Cesar have to call the Peppermills?" Ruby asked her.

"Just a second. Let me pull over." Ruby heard the faint sounds of the engine ceasing and then Phyllis say to Jesse, "I have to talk business with your mother for a second, and then we'll be on our way." To Ruby she said, "He did? When?"

"The night before he died." Ruby related her conversation with Grace Peppermill, pausing while Phyllis asked, "You *actually* went to see her chin-to-chin? Gutsy."

"Thank you," Ruby said, "I think."

"Probably not very smart, though. I can't think of a single reason Cesar would call them." She paused. "But he was a direct person, the type who believed in right and wrong and that a man does the right thing, no matter what the rules and conventions are."

"So if he knew your design had been tampered with, would he have called to tell them so?"

"It's possible," Phyllis said. "I wish he'd called me first. Maybe . . ." She sighed. "What else did she say?"

"That her husband would never kill anybody. They were watching TV when Cesar was murdered."

"How sweet," Phyllis said. She was silent for a moment, then cleared her throat and asked in a softer voice, "How's she doing?"

Ruby pictured Grace Peppermill's shrine, wondering what to say, when Phyllis said brusquely, "Never mind, that was a stupid question. Oh, Daniel called me from downtown. He said if I heard from you to let you know he'll be late. He's stuck at city hall with a cranky design reviewer. Do you want his number or should I call him back for you?"

"Could you?" Ruby asked. "I'm out of quarters. Tell him I'll wait for him."

"All right. I'll see you tonight."

Daniel arrived at the deli looking harried, a sheaf of papers in his hand. He waved to Ruby, made a quick order at the counter, and joined her where she sat beneath a window overlooking the outside dining area. She'd already eaten half her Reuben sandwich.

"Sorry," he said. "There's a new design reviewer who's a stickler. Hold on a second while I put these in order. I still have to go back after lunch and pick up the blueprints."

Ruby sipped at a glass of iced tea and watched him sort through the printed pages filled with lines of numbers and descriptions, catching glimpses of red ink. He zeroed in on his task to the exclusion of every noise and movement in the deli.

Finally he sat back, squared the pages, and smiled. "It's the paperwork that kills us, isn't it?" he asked.

"Actually paperwork is my livelihood," Ruby said.

"In a way I guess it's mine, too. So that's what you wanted to hear about today?"

Ruby nodded. "Specifically, work orders. Phyllis explained the process to me, but I'd like to hear about it from somebody else, too."

"Okay. They're done different ways, depending on the company. A change order modifies a contract. We're talking time and money. If there's a fifteen-percent change in original estimates, we do a change order. A work order is an adjustment in the field and isn't such a big deal."

"Which would Phyllis have done if she caught the aluminum/steel error in her design, a change order or a work order?"

Daniel frowned. "To change aluminum back to steel? A work order. The contractor's bid was based on steel. Aluminum's more expensive but the only aluminum was in the cantilevered section of the walkway so the price change was minimal. She might have planned to follow up with a change order, but it wouldn't be necessary."

"Who gets copies?" Ruby asked.

"The work order itself is in triplicate, one for the engineer, one for the contractor or project manager or CAD person or whoever's directly impacted, and one for the office's project files."

"Are there a lot of work orders on a job?"

"Can be." The waiter brought him iced tea and a sandwich brimming with sprouts and lettuce.

"So it's easy for a work order to get lost?"

Daniel realigned his papers and set them aside. "No, that rarely happens. There are procedures, too many copies. One copy might get lost but not all of them."

"So then Phyllis should have had a copy of the work order herself?"

He nodded. "If she'd followed standard practice."

Ruby ate her last potato chip and asked, "You don't believe she ever wrote a work order, do you?"

He scraped half the sprouts off his sandwich before he answered. "I want to. But there oughta be a copy somewhere, a note, some kind of record." He lifted his hands and dropped them. "But there's nothing."

"And she claims she never mentioned the work order to anyone," Ruby said. "She can't remember giving it to anyone, only that she wrote one up."

"Your sister's a good engineer," Daniel said.

"That's what everybody keeps telling me. Until this past year, that is. What happened?"

He shrugged. "The problem wasn't in the office, as far as I know. Business has been good."

"What about in her personal life?"

He looked steadily at Ruby. "She'll have to tell you anything private; it's none of my business."

"But you probably know."

"I won't gossip about her. We've been friends a long time."

"Anything more than friends?" Ruby asked.

He smiled, and Ruby thought she caught a hint of regret. "A couple of dates when I first started at Cholla, but we make better friends."

Exactly what Phyllis had told Ruby. Daniel finished the first half of his sandwich and asked, "Did the police discover if that was Leon Peppermill you saw on the mountain?"

"His wife told them he was home watching TV all day, but she also said she slept late every morning and she *heard* the TV."

"But she can't swear he was in the room watching it, am I right?"

"You are."

"So he could have slipped off and killed Cesar without the missus realizing he was gone." He turned his glass. "But how would Leon have known Cesar was at Bad Day?"

"Leon might have called Cesar and asked him to meet him at Bad Day," Ruby offered. "Leon probably learned from his lawyer that Cesar was involved in the design." She decided not to mention Grace's statement that Cesar had called and left a message on their answering machine. Grace had given her that information too reluctantly, and she had yet to share it with the detective.

"I guess, but it's hard to believe a man who's playing the press and lawyers and hoping to make a financial killing—sorry—would risk it all for a clandestine meeting with a man destined to testify *for* Phyllis."

"Unless Leon's plan was to stop Cesar from testifying," Ruby said. "Tell me about the CAD person you said Phyllis fired."

"Allen? He was a smart-ass kid from the East Coast. One of those take-charge-and-the-process-be-damned types. He got everybody riled, but for some reason Phyllis liked him. Finally he screwed up one of Peter Stern's designs big-time and Phyllis was forced to fire him. But then she got him a job with one of the contractors on Bad Day as a laborer. That didn't last long. I heard they had a run-in and he headed south to become a cowboy or gunslinger or something."

"Cowboy?" Ruby asked, pausing as she brushed her crumbs off the table. "He was from the East Coast?"

"Yeah, pretty funny, huh? Fulfilling his boyhood fantasies, I guess."

"Did he have an accent?"

Daniel laughed. "As if he stepped out of a mob movie."

Ruby sat back, stunned. Around them the tables were emptying out. A busboy filled a gray plastic tub, the dishes clattering together dangerously. She tried to absorb what Daniel was telling her. "And his name was Allen?"

"Right. His last name was Kentzner, I think, or Kaiser. They can tell you at the office."

"Did he hold a grudge against Phyllis for firing him?" Ruby pressed.

Daniel shrugged. "He made some noise."

"Do you know which contractor he worked for? Can I talk to him?"

"Sure. Steve Fox. He's working on a development east of town. I can take you out there if you want. It's about fifteen minutes from here."

Ruby stood. "Let's go. Oh . . . what about your blueprints at city hall? Don't you have to pick them up?"

He rolled his eyes. "Hopefully the human-contact portion is finished. I can pick them up when we get back, if you don't mind leaving your car here. It would be easier than trying to follow me through traffic."

Fifteen minutes later they pulled into a nascent development, a subdivision that followed the curve of the land overlooking Albuquerque in the distance. They entered between pillars, the bare bones of a future gate to be built of slabstone like Anasazi ruins. Every necessary amenity was rendered harmonious: curbs the same color as the sand; no utilities in sight. Even in the midst of gigantic yellow machinery and the confusion of construction, an aura of money and dearly purchased serenity hovered over the area. There weren't any houses built yet, but Ruby imagined them appearing like the houses where Phyllis lived: low to the ground, exclusive and unobtrusive.

Daniel pointed out bridges and subtle arroyos, invisible riprap, large lots with exposures facing away from one another. "For a project like this," Daniel told her, "the developer gives us the basic plans and we design the infrastructure: streets, water systems, parks, all the underpinnings."

"No expense spared," Ruby commented.

"You got it."

A backhoe dug a trench along a new street, and beyond it a grader smoothed dirt. A tank truck sprayed water in front of the grader.

"We have to keep the dust down," Daniel told her, nodding to the tank truck. "Rules is rules. The city'd love to fine us for threatening the air quality."

He drove past a row of pickups and cars to a construction trailer. "There's Steve," he said, braking beside a young man in a blue hard hat. He was baby-faced, smaller than either of the two men walking past him, thirty years old, if that. He glanced into the Jimmy, eyes narrowing, then acknowledged Daniel with a brief wave and nod.

Daniel left the motor running and opened his door, stepping to the ground. "How's it going?" he asked the young man.

"Better, now that the storm sewer pipe's arrived. We'll play catch-up, but we'll make it by next Wednesday."

"I believe you," Daniel said.

So did Ruby. She got out of the Jimmy and came around the front to the two men. Steve Fox was one of those rare beings who got a handle on life at a very young age. A child, she'd wager, who at age six didn't giggle into video cameras and spoke in complete intelligible sentences when surprised by the principal during a prank.

"This is Ruby," Daniel said, nodding to Ruby, who was grateful he'd left off her last name. "She's asking a few questions about the Bad Day incident." So now it was an "incident."

Steve Fox removed his sunglasses while he shook Ruby's hand, his hazel eyes gazing steadily into hers, taking her measure. "How can I help you?" he asked.

"Do you remember one of your employees who originally worked as an AutoCAD technician in Cholla Engineering's office and then for you at Bad Day? You let him go. His first name was Allen."

"Allen Kentzner?" he asked. "The kid Phyllis fired?"

"That's the one," Daniel said.

"I remember him." Steve Fox shook his head. "You couldn't trust him to follow directions. He always had big ideas to improve a situation. Fine in some businesses, but not this one. I finally told him to be innovative on his own time, not mine."

"What was he doing at Bad Day?" Ruby asked.

"General laborer. We started him on foundations, then framework, and finally out the door."

"Did he work on the walkway that collapsed?"

Fox looked at Ruby without surprise, as if he'd been expecting this question all along. "Some. Everybody on the crew did, depending on the stage of construction.

"We build according to blueprints," he said without apology or regret, putting on his sunglasses again. "I learned years ago that was my job: follow the plans to the letter. And that's what I do." He made a move to be on his way. "This wasn't Kansas City." Again the evocation of the collapsed overhead walkways. It was a bogeyman in the back of engineers' minds, the worst in engineering disasters.

"You didn't think that using aluminum in the walkway landing instead of steel was unusual?" Ruby asked.

"It isn't common around here, but it's not unheard of, especially near water."

"Then you haven't worked with aluminum very often?"

"Maybe three or four times."

"Thanks," Ruby told him. "Have you seen Allen Kentzner since he was fired?"

Fox nodded. "Once. In a roadside bar down south about a month ago. He'd gone the cowboy route. Didn't talk to him, though."

Ruby caught the hesitancy in his voice. "Was he with a woman?" she asked.

"He was," Steve Fox said, his eyes behind his sunglasses smoothly shifting away from Ruby's.

As they drove back toward downtown, Daniel asked Ruby, "Why'd you ask if Kentzner was with a woman?"

"It was just a guess. I was curious that the two men didn't speak to each other."

"Might be bad blood between them."

"Maybe, but sometimes a woman's presence keeps bad blood from erupting," Ruby said, wondering if the woman Steve Fox had seen with Kentzner had been her sister, Phyllis.

* * *

"You're not driving one of Phyllis's cars," Daniel said when he dropped her off beside her rental.

"Phyllis thought it made me too conspicuous," Ruby told him.

"Good for her. Do you want to come with me to city hall? See how the Design Review Committee works?"

Ruby hesitated. "Bad Day didn't go through the review process with the city, did it?"

"No. It wasn't in their jurisdiction."

"Thanks, but I'll pass."

"Okay. Tell Phyllis to call me."

"I will."

Ruby drove through town, heading in the general direction of Phyllis's house but avoiding faster-moving traffic on the main road. She slowed at a school crossing and watched a line of elementary school students, each holding on to a white rope that was held by their young teacher, trailing after her like ducklings. She remembered Jesse at that age when the future held only possibility, unlimited possibility.

A few blocks farther she parked at the curb beside a park that was no larger than a city lot. A politically incorrect park, with brilliant green grass, a towering cottonwood tree, and a small grove of struggling maple trees. Tulips and pansies bloomed in raised beds.

Ruby climbed out of the Ford and followed a gravel path to the trees. STAY OFF THE GRASS, a sign warned. Precious commodity. She breathed deeply the familiar odor of green growing things. She chose a concrete bench and stretched out her legs, closing her eyes and picturing Blue Lake back in Michigan, mushily frozen, spring still a fantasy.

Phyllis might be having an affair with a man she'd fired and who may have had the opportunity to sabotage the plans for Bad Day while he worked in Phyllis's office. What was Salina's role in all this? A front?

And Leon Peppermill, who obviously kept his wife Grace on a tight rein. Ruby didn't doubt that the little fat woman did her husband's bidding. What did he do in return? Abuse her? Or fix her breakfast while she slept in? Do the dishes?

The Peppermills had every right to sue. If it had been Jesse instead of Eddy Peppermill, Ruby doubted she'd have felt any emotion beyond grief *except* revenge.

In a court of law what chance did a sister's assertion have that ten letters and ten numbers in an entire binder of design notes had been tampered with? Or that Phyllis swore she'd put in a work order that mysteriously disappeared? Ruby rubbed her hands together, feeling a surge of panicked frustration over her inability to get a handle on it all, realizing she had little affect on events as they careened toward an inevitable outcome: the ruin of Phyllis's career and probably her life. Hidden away somewhere was the key that would bring everything into focus, if only she could find it.

Her bag containing all her notes sat on the bench beside her. She opened it and pulled out the roster of engineers at Cholla that Phyllis had given her. Each entry included a home address and telephone number. Peter Stern's name was one below Phyllis's, and Ruby checked his home address against her street map of Albuquerque. His house was a little over a mile away.

Peter Stern lived in an older subdivision of comfortable homes, three to a cul-de-sac, each cul-de-sac branching off a single main street that meandered a ridge taking advantage of the view. The front wall of his house was decorated by a larger-than-life depiction of the flute player, the Kokopelli, in relief. Xeriscaping ruled. Cacti and buffalo grass, chamisa and yucca, all native plants. She parked in the wide driveway next to the white Volvo she'd seen at Cholla Engineering the first day. Red cinder crunched beneath her tires.

The yap of a small dog sounded from behind a courtyard wall, the constant single-noted irritation of a bored animal.

Before Ruby could set foot on the sidewalk, the front door opened and a perfectly groomed woman emerged, carrying a purse over her shoulder and dressed in a creamy linen suit. Ruby recognized Charlotte Stern and stopped.

The woman started at the sight of Ruby, flashed a cool smile, and asked, "May I help—?" before she stopped and said coldly, "Why are you here?"

"Mrs. Stern, I'm Ruby—"

"I know who you are. Did she send you here to intercede on her behalf?"

"Would it do any good?" Ruby asked, uncertain what Charlotte Stern was talking about.

"Definitely not. Their minds are made up. Your sister's no longer an asset to the firm. She can return to Wisconsin with you."

"Michigan," Ruby corrected. "And it's my understanding that Phyllis is a founder of the firm."

"She's a partner," Charlotte said. "Only one of the partners."

"Without as much influence as the spouses of the partners, apparently," Ruby said.

Charlotte's face reddened. "Your sister used her position as a . . . dating service."

"Is that more of an issue than the death at Bad Day?" Ruby asked.

"Deaths," Charlotte spat out. "There were *two* deaths at Bad Day."

"But Phyllis's culpability is being questioned in only one of them," Ruby reminded her. "It's impossible for her to be involved in the other."

"I heard that, because she was supposedly with you. How convenient. And I suppose there isn't a soul on earth who can verify that, is there? And isn't it interesting that the two sisters found the body?"

That anyone could have conceived of Charlotte's scenario hadn't occurred to Ruby before that moment. She caught the glint of triumph in Charlotte's eyes and asked, "I understand you were an engineering student at one time, that your husband was your instructor?"

"That's right," she said, raising her chin.

"Between your education and your interest in your husband's position, you probably have a clear understanding of engineering practices."

"And if I do?"

"You also clearly have access to the offices at Cholla Engineering."

"What are you implying?" Charlotte asked.

"You would know that substituting undersized aluminum for steel in a cantilevered walkway would pose a disaster."

"How dare you?" Charlotte Stern demanded. "I wouldn't stoop to tampering with her designs. That she would even think so shows how low she's fallen, how self-deluded she is. She's forgetting that my husband *didn't* leave me for her, that he chose *me*. I won. She lost and she'll just keep on losing until she has nothing left. When she loses everything she has, maybe she'll understand what a cheap failure she really is."

Ruby felt sick to her stomach. The air crackled with rage. The lovely woman's face was distorted by hatred. Ruby turned and walked back to her car, leaving Charlotte raging on as if she couldn't stop herself. "And you're welcome to repeat every word I've said to her," Ruby heard Charlotte say as she opened her car door. "In fact please do."

A mile from the turnoff to Phyllis's, Ruby passed the remains of an automobile accident: pieces of orange and red taillight glass on the shoulder, a long black swerve of tire marks. She saw three police cars parked beside the arroyo a hundred yards off the road and two policemen looking into the arroyo before she resolutely turned her head away, not caring to view the details of another tragedy. Her fears were ungrounded, she was sure, but she couldn't dismiss them until she reached Phyllis's house and saw her sister's vehicles safely parked inside the garage, the doors still raised.

Adam's truck was gone, and Phyllis sat alone in her courtyard, staring at her hands folded on the table in front of her. She didn't look up as Ruby closed the door of her car and entered the courtyard.

"Where's Jesse?" Ruby asked.

Phyllis raised her head and looked at Ruby from a far distance, her face curiously slack. Ruby smelled alcohol, but there was no bottle visible, not even a glass. "She's taking a nap." The words weren't slurred, only flat, detached. "The pueblo tired her out."

"Are you okay?" Ruby asked.

"Connie called."

"Does he want me to call him back?"

"I don't know. Maybe. He wanted me to be among the first to hear the news."

"What news?"

"Leon Peppermill's dead."

Ruby dropped into the chair opposite Phyllis, saying the first thoughtless words of shock that most people uttered, "Are you sure?"

"Well, *I'm* not, but I guess Connie and the police are."

"What happened?" Ruby asked, wondering if Grace Peppermill knew yet.

"A one-car wreck, sometime today."

Ruby sat up. "Where was the accident?" she asked, She bit her lip, trying to recall the accident scene she'd just passed. She hadn't seen the vehicle, only the police.

Phyllis shrugged. "I don't know. He rolled his pickup." She made a tumbling motion with her hands. "The plot thickens, as they say."

"I'll call Connie," Ruby told her, rising from her chair.

"Wait a minute," Phyllis said, nodding toward the road.

A familiar dark car slowed and turned into Phyllis's driveway. At the wheel, Ruby made out the long face of Detective Nick Powell.

Chapter 19

Phyllis rose from her chair before Detective Powell's car came to a complete stop. She didn't falter, didn't sway, despite Ruby's suspicion she'd been drinking heavily. "Siesta time," she said. "You talk to him. If you need me, knock three times on something or other."

"Phyllis . . . ," Ruby began.

"He's all yours," Phyllis snapped, and disappeared into the house.

Nick Powell's face was grim. He didn't waste any words on cordial finesse but opened the gate and entered the courtyard, seating himself in Phyllis's chair. "Why'd your sister run inside?" he asked.

"She didn't run; she walked," Ruby corrected. "She's tired and she's upset about Leon Peppermill's death."

"Who told her?"

"Connie Tarcher, her lawyer."

Using both hands, the detective lifted his left leg beneath the knee and rested his foot on the chair across from him, wincing as if it caused him pain. "Were you with her today?"

"No. We split up this morning. She and Salina took my daughter to Zia Pueblo, and I drove to town. I came back a few minutes ago."

"I saw you."

"The accident down the road?" Ruby asked. "Is that where Leon died?" knowing before he nodded that she was right, that Leon Peppermill had died so close to Phyllis's house. Had he been on his way to confront Ruby or Phyllis? She pressed her hand to her heart. Or had he been hoping to intercept Phyllis while Jesse was in the car?

"What happened?" she asked.

"It looks like he was forced off the road. No seat belt, either."

"Then it happened this afternoon?"

"I'd say earlier. A kid shooting rabbits saw the truck in the arroyo, belly-up."

"And no witnesses?" Ruby asked.

"None so far."

Salina stepped through the kitchen door. "I'm making more iced tea," she said. "Would you like a glass?"

Both Ruby and the detective agreed and Salina turned around, but Nick stopped her. "What time did you get home today?" he asked.

She blinked, looking confused. "From where?"

"From the pueblo," Ruby reminded her, "with Phyllis and Jesse."

"They . . . I . . . ," Salina began, fidgeting with one of the hoops in her right ear.

"You didn't go with them," Nick finished for her.

Salina shook her head, looking miserable. "No," she said. Phyllis had lied to Ruby again.

"Have you been here all day?" Nick asked.

Salina nodded. "I did the laundry and cleaned the house."

Nick turned to Ruby. "I'd like to talk to your sister."

"My daughter was with her," Ruby said. "She wouldn't have forced Leon Peppermill off the road."

"I'd like to talk to your daughter, too."

"No," Ruby told him emphatically.

"I'll be gentle," he assured her. "I'm good with kids."

"That's not the point. Jesse was severely injured in an automobile accident eighteen months ago. She suffered a head injury and her memory isn't dependable."

"Maybe if your sister can help me out, I won't need to talk to Jesse," he said.

Ruby stood and went inside the house through the kitchen, passing Salina, who leaned against the counter, her arms crossed as if she were cold. "Did I get Phyllis into trouble?" she asked Ruby. Her dark eyes were wide with worry.

"No, definitely not," Ruby told her. "But why didn't you go with them to the pueblo?"

"Phyllis didn't ask me."

"Did Allen leave?" Ruby asked.

Salina glanced through the glass doors at Nick Powell. "Just for the day," she answered, not even catching that Ruby had asked for Allen, not Adam. "He'll be back tonight."

Ruby nodded—one more lie confirmed—and continued to Phyllis's room. She knocked sharply on the wooden door three times.

"What?" Phyllis asked.

"Let me in," Ruby told her.

"Turn the knob; that's how it's usually done."

Ruby opened the door and entered the tumble of Phyllis's sanctuary, letting her eyes adjust to the comparatively shaded room. Phyllis wasn't lying on her bed but sitting in the wooden rocking chair that had once sat in their living room in Sable. Simple construction, its arms worn bare of varnish, one rung clumsily repaired. Ruby smelled alcohol again, the smoky odor of whiskey, but still there was no bottle or glass in sight.

"Jesse liked the pueblo," Phyllis said. "She told me it was a safe place. She's too young to be looking for safe places."

"It's not that," Ruby told her, sitting on the edge of Phyllis's bed. "Since the accident she feels more comfortable in worlds with boundaries. They're less confusing to her."

"But still she got tired so fast."

"Anything new exhausts her. Why did you lie about Salina going with you to the pueblo?"

Phyllis shrugged. "Pure selfishness. I wanted Jesse all to myself." She rocked, a staccato back-and-forth put into motion by her foot. "This was Gram's chair."

"I know."

"You got her quilts. You got the cabin on Blue Lake, but I got the rocking chair. Lucky me."

"Gram gave it to Mom when you were born. You should have it."

"Big of you."

"The detective wants to talk to you," Ruby told her.

"Why?"

"About Leon Peppermill's death."

"No, thanks, I don't know anything about it."

"He died a couple of miles from here."

Phyllis continued to shake her head. "It's none of my business. The less I know the better."

"Did you see the police cars along the road?"

"No."

"Please, Phyllis. Will you talk to him?"

"Why in hell should I?" she asked, stopping the chair's motion.

"Because if you don't, he intends to ask Jesse questions."

Phyllis raised her hand to her mouth, her thumbnail going between her teeth, then jerked it out. Ruby waited, glancing around the room, noticing a small picture of their mother sitting in the deep windowsill, taken when she was young, before her marriage had driven her inside herself.

"I stole that from Dad's bedroom a couple of years ago," Phyllis said, nodding toward the picture.

"Does he know?" Ruby asked.

"I took every picture of her I could find," Phyllis said. "He didn't deserve to be left a single one."

Ruby said nothing, and Phyllis set the chair to rocking again. "If I talk to him, will he leave Jesse alone?"

"I don't know. I hope so."

"All right, then. Let me brush my teeth first, or gargle with Listerine or something."

"You can't hide it that easily, Phyllis," Ruby told her.

"No, I guess not. What the hell." And she rose, leaving the rocker swaying behind her.

Nick Powell hauled his leg off the chair and stood when Ruby and Phyllis returned to the courtyard. "Do you want your lawyer here?" he asked Phyllis.

Phyllis paused, her eyes rapidly blinking. "My lawyer? In case I incriminate myself, you mean? Not yet. Where did Leon Peppermill die?"

"About two miles south of here. His truck went off the road and turned over in an arroyo. What time did you and Jesse return from the pueblo?"

"Early this afternoon. One-thirty maybe. She was worn out."

"Did you see the accident site?"

"Not a thing. When was he found?"

"About two-thirty."

"I have no knowledge of it," Phyllis said as solemnly as if she were under oath.

"Is there any reason he might have been on his way to visit you?"

"None. Nada. I don't think he knows . . . knew, I mean, where I lived."

"I saw him out here yesterday," Ruby told the detective.

Phyllis gasped. "When? Why didn't you tell me? Is he the one who—?" She stopped.

"Who what?" the detective asked, giving Ruby a stern look, as if she'd withheld information, which Ruby supposed she had.

"I get phone calls sometimes," Phyllis told him.

"Ruby said she told you about those, the tape she gave you, remember? Things disappear from outside the house now and then, trash thrown into my yard, the usual petty forms of harassment."

"How long has this been happening?"

"Mostly since Eddy was killed at Bad Day, but off and on the past several months. All of it little stuff."

"Have you reported it to the police?"

Phyllis rubbed her arms. "No, I thought it was someone I knew."

"Who?"

"I don't want to say. It's another issue completely."

"Somebody's wife?" he asked, lowering his voice to a confidential level meant to be reassuring: you can trust me.

Phyllis glanced at him sharply, then seeing that he already knew about her affair with Peter Stern, she nodded.

Nick turned his attention to Ruby. "So tell me about seeing Leon yesterday. Why didn't you tell me last night?"

"You didn't give me a chance." She explained how Leon Peppermill had blocked the road, threatening her and demanding to know why she was in New Mexico. "I had the impression he was very familiar with the territory out here."

"And the next day he ends up dead in that very same territory. Where were *you* all day?"

"In town. I talked to Daniel MacSimon and Steve Fox, and"—Ruby took a deep breath—"this morning I stopped by Desert View Mobile Home Park and spoke to Grace Peppermill."

The detective leaned forward in his chair and stabbed his index finger onto the table. "Grace Peppermill? Jesus H. What did you do that for?"

"I was curious. I thought she might tell me more than she told you."

"Why should she?" Nick asked. "You're Phyllis's sister, the defendant in their lawsuit. She must have had a screaming meemie when you told her who you were."

"I didn't tell her," Ruby admitted.

"How much worse can this get?" he asked, shaking his head. "So what did she tell you?"

"That she slept in on the morning Cesar died. I gather she's a night owl, in bed until noon. Leon often fixed her breakfast. She heard the TV, but . . ."

"She didn't see Leon," Nick finished. He narrowed his eyes. "What else did she say?"

"Cesar Peron left a message on their answering machine the evening before he died."

"Saying what?" The detective's voice was rising, his words brisk. He was still bent toward Ruby, his jaw tight, in full interrogation mode.

"Only that he'd call back, but the next day he was dead."

He leaned back in his chair, letting out his breath in a whoosh. "Busy girl," he commented. "Getting in over your head, aren't you?"

"I don't believe so. Have you talked to Grace since Leon died?"

"Haven't had time to do more than come up here," he said tersely. "She's been told of her husband's death, though."

They were silent, each of them thinking of Grace Peppermill. Between the distant houses sunlight flashed on the windows of a passing car. Finally Nick said to Ruby, "I'd still like to talk to your daughter, to ask her if she saw the truck in the arroyo on her way home."

"It'll have to be another time," Ruby said firmly. "Right now it's more important that she sleep. But I'll ask her when she wakes up and let you know."

"Fair enough," he said, rising from his chair. "I'll be expecting you to call."

"I'll walk you to your car," Ruby told him.

"One other thing, ma'am," he said to Phyllis as if he'd just thought of it. "Which vehicle were you driving today?"

"The Jeep," Phyllis told him. "Why?"

"Mind if I take a look at it?"

Phyllis stared at him. "Are you looking for damage? Maybe a suspicious dent or two with vestiges of blue paint?"

"Let's just say I'm officially eliminating you from the equation," he told her mildly.

"Help yourself. Take Ruby with you as your witness." Phyllis pulled her legs onto her chair and stared pensively across the hills.

Detective Powell walked around each vehicle in the three-car garage, with Ruby close behind him.

"What type of damage are you looking for?" Ruby asked.

"Definitely a damaged front fender area, possibly a broken turn signal and headlight." He circled the Jeep last, which, except for the long scratches Ruby had noticed the first time she rode in Phyllis's Jeep, was clean. "So that's that," he said, dusting off his hands.

As they left the garage and stepped into the bright sunshine, Nick lowered his sunglasses and said, "I should tell you I called your sheriff back in Michigan."

"Carly Joyce? Why?"

"Just to find out what I could expect from you. He warned me you have a bad habit of going off on your own."

"That was thoughtful of him. Did he also tell you I was good at what I do?"

The detective laughed. "He did." Then he grew more serious. "But don't be a loose cannon, Ruby," he said, sounding like Carly. "Keep me posted." He walked once around her red Ford, saying, "Just being thorough," before he went to his own car.

"Also, be prepared," he said as he reached for the door handle. "There's going to be some bad press about the way this looks."

"Because the man threatening to ruin my sister's life was found dead near her house?" Ruby asked.

"On top of Cesar's death, yes. Plus, you, her sister, were threatened twenty-four hours ago by the deceased. *That* we'll try to keep under wraps, but you know how word gets out."

"What about the men Cesar fired?" Ruby asked as he slid behind the steering wheel. "Did you find them?"

"One's dead of an overdose; poetic justice, eh? One's in jail in Texas, and the other one's still eluding our best efforts."

"And the tape from Phyllis's answering machine?" Ruby asked.

"I sent it to the big boys for analysis. Of course if it turns out to be Leon's voice, it'll be moot. He harassed Phyllis, maybe killed Cesar."

"But who killed Leon?" Ruby asked.

"Now that's the big question, isn't it?"

When Ruby reentered the courtyard, Phyllis asked, "I know this is tacky when the body's not even cold, but what do you think will happen to the lawsuit now that Leon Peppermill's dead?"

"What did Connie say?"

"He didn't. It was too soon when he called. He'd just heard the news."

"Lawyers rarely wait until the body's cold to sort out the legal ramifications. I'll call him if you want me to."

"Would you? I can't think right now." Phyllis was drooping. Whatever artificial means had kept her going was now wearing off. She punched a number on her cordless phone and handed it to Ruby.

Connie came on the line in seconds. "Hello, Ruby," he said. "Where are you?"

"With Phyllis. Detective Powell just left."

"Then you know the details."

"What he'd tell us: that Leon Peppermill died in a rollover one-car accident. No seat belt. There's evidence he was forced off the road and it all happened within two miles of Phyllis's house."

"That's more than enough. What can I do for you?"

"What's the effect of Leon's death on the suit?" she asked, watching a hawk soar above them, its wings still, like a paper airplane.

"It looks like none. I already talked to Jake Webber, the Peppermills' lawyer. He's intending to carry on."

He paused and Ruby jumped on it. "But what?" she asked.

"He didn't actually say it, but I had the impression Mrs. Peppermill was never too keen on the lawsuit in the first place. He'll have to convince her to go it alone."

"Hasn't the suit already developed a life of its own, with all the publicity?"

"That, too. Is Phyllis sober?"

Ruby glanced over at Phyllis, who was slumped in her chair, toying with the cuffs covering her wrists. "Not exactly."

"Well, keep her under wraps if you can. The press will be in your backyard any minute, and a camera shot on the six-o'clock news of Phyllis stumbling through the cactus won't help her any."

"I'll try."

"Later," he said, and the phone went dead.

"From the dire expression on your face—not very attractive by the way," Phyllis said, "the suit goes on."

"So far. *Did* you see a truck in the ditch on your way home?"

"Arroyo, not "ditch." Ditch is Michigan. Arroyo is New Mexico. Local idioms for the moving of excess water. In Idaho they sometimes say 'barrow pit,' did you know that?"

"No. Did you see Leon Peppermill's pickup?"

Phyllis shook her head. "Not on the road and not in the arroyo. I have *never* seen his truck."

"Were you drinking?"

Phyllis rose from her chair and leaned across the table toward Ruby, supporting herself with both hands flat on the tabletop. "You ass. I wouldn't touch a drop when Jesse's with me."

"You've obviously touched more than a drop," Ruby pointed out.

"Only after we came home, only after Jesse fell asleep, only with Salina here. And, I might add, only after Connie called me with the latest twist in the case from hell. And I am not"—she jabbed her finger at Ruby—"even now, impaired."

"Then what are you?"

Phyllis sat down again, tipping back her head against her chair. "I am tired, wearied to death, bored with being under siege." She swayed her head back and forth. "And get this, little sister, I'm scared."

The air was soft. Somewhere behind the house a bird chirped in a long, breathless volley, as if it were holding a conversation.

"Tell me about Peter Stern," Ruby said.

"Oh, God, *that*." Phyllis rubbed her temples. "We had an affair. Hearts and bells. You know how you read all those Dear Abby letters about the husband who assures his mistress he's going to ask his wife for a divorce but never does?"

"Peter promised you that?" Ruby asked.

"No," Phyllis told her. "He *did* it. Everything hit the fan. I mean everything. When we firmed up the partnership, we neglected to add a clause that protected us from avenging ex-spouses. Her lawyer worked out a formula that would have sunk the ship, not that she cared, as long as she got her portion—and her vengeance."

"So Peter recanted?"

"Yeah. It got messier and messier until the flames were doused."

"Were they?" Ruby asked.

Phyllis rubbed her arms. "They have to be. Charlotte emerged victorious, queen of the dung heap. Peter in chains and me out in the cold."

"But still present," Ruby pointed out. "You spend every day with her husband. It must drive her crazy."

"What is this? You sympathize with her? She'd rather chew the man to pieces with her own teeth than see him get away."

"Sympathy didn't cross my mind. I was thinking about your harassing calls and letters."

Phyllis leaned forward. "You're doubting Queen Charlotte dirtied her hands with threatening notes and calls?"

"No. It wouldn't be unusual. Remember the notes you told me about when I first arrived? Are you sure you didn't save any?"

Phyllis frowned. "If I did, it was by accident. They'd probably be in one of the drawers by the telephone. Or else with the mail that gets stacked up."

"Can I look?"

"Be my guest. Any other questions now that I'm in a cooperative mood?"

"Yes. About Adam."

Phyllis stood. "Not now. I don't want to discuss him."

Ruby stood, too. "But Phyllis," she said. "I know who he is."

"Well, good for you, but I still don't want to discuss him."

Ruby's attention was caught by a white van slowly passing on the road. It stopped at the end of Phyllis's driveway, and Ruby recognized the same TV news logo she'd seen on the van when Leon Peppermill was being interviewed at Cholla Engineering.

"You have company and they have cameras," she told Phyllis. "Let's go inside."

"Shit," Phyllis said. "Talk about harassment."

As they walked to the house, Ruby stayed beside Phyllis, blocking the cameras' view of her sister.

Chapter 20

Although nothing was said in front of Jesse, she reflected the moody tension between Phyllis and Ruby, silently eating her dinner, jumping when a white plastic bag blown from somewhere else slapped against the kitchen window, fluttered there a few moments and then blew away, tumbling across the open land.

"I hate it when the wind blows," Phyllis said, rising from the table and moving to the window to watch the plastic bag disappear. "It's relentless."

The winds had begun an hour earlier. Long, sweeping blasts that whistled and thumped and pressed against everything in their path, leaning the landscape. "Relentless" was an apt description, as if a window somewhere had opened and the pent-up winds were escaping in a continuous fury.

"Why is the air gold?" Jesse asked.

At first Ruby thought it was the hazy light of early evening, but now she realized there *was* something in the air, riding the winds like golden clouds.

"Is it sand?" she asked Phyllis.

"Pollen from the juniper trees," Phyllis told her.

"In the spring it covers the trees until the winds shake it loose. Pure torture if you have allergies."

The TV news van had driven past the house twice and once turned into the driveway until Salina had walked out and asked the crew to leave. Now Salina sat at the table with them, quieter than usual, concentrating on her dinner, and, Ruby was certain, avoiding her eyes. Adam still hadn't returned.

The wind blew into the night and Phyllis turned up her stereo to block out its moans and cries. CDs, not the radio. The television remained dark, the telephone switched off. They sat by lampglow, each of them reading, reluctant to talk during the continuous blow. We are under siege, Ruby thought. Next we'll be turning off the electricity and sitting in the dark, waiting for the wind to breach our walls. Better the wind than reporters.

While she helped Jesse prepare for bed, Ruby casually asked her, "Do you remember when you were in your Aunt Phyllis's car today, coming home from the pueblo?"

Always it was necessary to make a question as complete as possible in order to keep Jesse focused. Her memory was uncertain, sometimes prodigious, often simply erased.

"Yes," Jesse said gravely.

"When you were almost home, did you see a truck off the road, lying on its top?"

Jesse thought, the frown lines appearing. "No," she finally said. "I didn't see a truck."

"A blue pickup truck?"

"No."

"Did you see anything unusual? Anything that surprised you?"

Again the frown. "I saw a red-tailed hawk try to catch a rabbit, but it got away."

Ruby kissed Jesse's forehead. "Lucky bunny," she said.

Phyllis was cold sober. She sat alone in the living room, a book in her lap with pages she didn't turn, her head tipped as if she were listening for voices in the wind. Salina had gone to her room.

"Why did Allen change his name to Adam?" Ruby asked, sitting across from her.

Phyllis closed her book. "You don't let up, do you?"

"No. Was it your idea after you fired him?"

"I thought you said Jesse was the one who had to discover the logic behind anything that mystified her," Phyllis said.

"If he changed his name and you slipped up and mentioned it, nobody would realize who you were talking about, right?"

Phyllis shook her head. She looked out the window at the moonlit night, tipping her head when a metallic bong sounded, like a distant bell set to ringing by the wind. "Little pig, little pig," she murmured. Finally she answered, resignation in her voice. "It just made sense. There was so much speculation and enough complication in my life."

"When did you begin having an affair with him?" Ruby asked, and Phyllis sank deeper into her chair.

"I was a wreck after Peter. It wasn't just a casual

affair, like I told you. It's corny, but I thought the pain of it was truly going to knock me dead." She took a deep breath, replenishing herself.

"Is that when you called me last summer?" Ruby asked.

Phyllis nodded. "I was, to put it mildly, in very bad shape. Adam was sweet, a take-charge kind of person, exactly what I needed at the time. I didn't expect it to go any farther, but . . ."

"Here you are, hiding him in your house."

"He's not hiding."

"He disappears whenever you have company."

"Only when Daniel came, I mean purposely. Daniel would recognize him immediately. I'm not being secretive, Ruby, really. Every damn thing I do has been under scrutiny and I'm just not up to explaining this aspect of my life. I'd like to keep this to myself as long as possible."

"He worked in your office and at Bad Day, fired from both jobs."

Phyllis smiled slightly. "He's far happier being the cowboy from New Jersey. Better suited, too."

"And Salina's a party to all this?"

"She's his sister."

"Sister?" Ruby sat back in disgust. "Come on, Phyllis. She's Hispanic."

"Shows how much you know. Salina's Puerto Rican. Their mother's dead and neither father is in the picture. They've stuck together for years. They came out here together; everybody here is from somewhere else."

"The story you told me was that she was an illegal alien from Mexico."

"I lied."

"No joke." For a few moments Ruby didn't trust herself to speak. "What other lies have you told me?"

"None that matter. The facts are the same: Eddy Peppermill died because my design was tampered with; the work order disappeared."

"And Cesar and Leon Peppermill were both killed, don't forget."

"Doesn't that reinforce my story? Why would Cesar be dead unless someone knew he could have backed me up?"

"But why kill Leon Peppermill?" Ruby asked. "That's almost as if somebody did it *for* you."

"*That* should certainly narrow the suspect list, shouldn't it? Let's see: who loves Phyllis?" She made a fist and raised a finger with each name. "Adam, Jesse. You realize I'll have to add friends in order to create a pool. Daniel, Monica. Maybe even you, sneaking back from town to run Leon off the road, thinking in your small-town way that if he was dead, you could steal Jesse from me and go home to the tin woodsman."

Only one sentence roused Ruby. "I wouldn't be *stealing* Jesse, Phyllis. She's my daughter."

"Don't rub it in, okay?"

"What about adding Peter Stern to your list?" Ruby asked.

Phyllis's face softened for a moment. "He's happily reunited with his wife, have you forgotten?"

"But it's obvious he still—"

"Don't say it, please," Phyllis begged, childishly squeezing her eyes closed.

"All right," Ruby conceded. "Maybe there are two criminals at work: one who killed Cesar and one who killed Leon."

"Maybe Leon wasn't murdered," Phyllis said. "It could have been an accident: hit and run."

Ruby doubted it. "It may have been," she said anyway.

The wind didn't let up and Ruby couldn't sleep. She found herself waiting for the intensity to drop, for the continuous rush to blow itself out. But it persisted until it seemed to stir the air inside the house, agitating the molecules to sullen rebellion. The night felt as disturbed inside as it sounded outside. Currents whistled and howled across the hills and around the house, maybe moving the barren landscape under cover of darkness, like the winds of the Sahara.

When the digital clock beside her bed read 1:48, she gave up and turned on the bedside lamp; she was wasting time lying there. No sounds but the wind disturbed the house, and Ruby followed the dimly lit hall to the kitchen, intending to find something to eat, opening cupboards until she discovered crackers, then peanut butter. The path of the nearly full moon shone in the window and lay across the floor, nearly bright enough to show colors outside, if there *were* colors in this land.

She opened the wrong drawer looking for the silverware and instead discovered a junk drawer filled to brimming with loose bits of notepaper, pencils, old notes from friends, string, tape, and a flashlight.

Phyllis had invited her to search her house for any threatening notes she might have accidentally kept. Ruby struggled with the drawer, pulling it off its tracks with a jerk that almost tipped the contents to the floor. Her crackers and peanut butter forgotten, she carried the drawer to the table and turned on the overhead light.

Grocery receipts filled one corner, reminding Ruby of the way their mother had saved receipts, a certain percentage of the proceeds going to one vague charity or another. She looked at each one, front and back, smoothing them flat. Phyllis ate a lot of yogurt.

There was a birthday card from Monica, a letter from their father that Ruby didn't read, last year's calendar, and a list of native plants written in Phyllis's hand.

Something touched her shoulder and Ruby gasped, dropping a note that read *P. called,* and spinning around to see Jesse's pale face. She was barefoot, wearing a terrycloth robe over her pajamas, another gift from Phyllis.

"I didn't hear you, with the wind," Ruby said. "Did it wake you up?" Jesse rarely woke up once she fell asleep, usually a deep drop into unconsciousness.

"I think so," Jesse told her. "What are you looking for?"

"Just a note your aunt Phyllis might have received."

Jesse studied the piles of paper to either side of Ruby, then the drawer. "It's like the refrigerator drawer at home on Blue Lake," she said.

"That's exactly right," Ruby told her. The top drawer next to their refrigerator held a hopeless tangle of detritus from their everyday life. "Would you like a glass of milk?" Ruby asked Jesse. "You can sit here with me for a while if you want."

Jesse shook her head. "I only wanted to see what you were doing. Who wrote the note you're looking for?"

"I don't know," Ruby told her.

"What does it say?"

"I don't know that, either." Ruby laughed. "It sounds like an impossible task, doesn't it?"

"Is this what you call 'I'll know it when I see it'?" Jesse asked.

"Yes, I believe it is."

Jesse was more talkative than usual, under the influence of night and wind and moon. She leaned against Ruby, and Ruby went still, reluctant even to breathe, as if a rare bird had alighted on her finger. Since the accident Jesse hadn't spontaneously offered affection; it wasn't that she repulsed it or avoided it when it was offered but as if its concept simply was no longer a part of her personality. For eighteen months Ruby had been longing for this moment: a simple sign that Jesse might someday regain her impulsive affectionate side. Jesse's body was warm against her arm and Ruby felt a thickening in her throat. She warned herself not to put as much stock in the simple gesture as she longed to. One minuscule step at a time. It was a hard lesson to learn for a woman with as little patience as she had.

"Aunt Phyllis tries not to show how sad she is. You're that way sometimes, too."

"I know. Are you?"

Jesse stepped away and Ruby longed to pull her back, missing her touch so much that her skin ached. "No," Jesse said solemnly. "When I'm sad, I can't think of any other way to be."

"Then you're being honest," Ruby told her.

"Did I used to be dishonest?" Jesse asked. She knew she was different now than before the accident, but the why and the how puzzled her. It had only been in the past month or two that she'd begun to ask about the "old Jesse," as if she were some other girl who'd left home.

"No, my dear," Ruby assured her. "You've always been as honest as the day is long, as right as rain, true blue, and cute as a button."

"That's silly," Jesse said, when her usual response would be to decipher each simile, trying to find its literal meaning.

"It's easy to be silly in the middle of the night," Ruby told her.

Jesse yawned. "I'll go back to bed now. Are you looking for a note with somebody else's handwriting on it?"

"Yes, but I don't know whose."

"If I find one, I'll give it to you."

"Thank you, sweetie. Sleep tight."

She watched Jesse leave the dining room, her bare feet soundless on the cool tiles, and went back to sorting through the drawer's contents.

The wind persisted, and she found nothing more

incriminating in Phyllis's junk drawer than a postcard from her dentist telling her she'd missed an appointment and to please reschedule. There were other drawers, a huge wooden bowl of papers and old mail on top of the refrigerator, a rolltop desk against the dining room wall.

But sleep was finally nudging its way into her consciousness. She slid the drawer back onto its guides, turned off the lights, and returned to bed, falling asleep immediately.

Ruby opened her eyes, thinking Jesse was in her room. It was still dark; a faint glow came from the hallway through her open bedroom door. The moon hung above the horizon, shining into the room.

"It's me," a voice whispered, and Ruby recognized Phyllis, ghostly in a white T-shirt. She sat on the end of Ruby's bed and pulled up her legs. "I know why Leon Peppermill was killed."

Ruby rolled over and sat up, bracing the pillow behind her back. It was just four o'clock. "Why?" she asked. Emerging wide awake from sleep had never been a problem for her.

"Let's pretend you really *did* see Leon coming down the road from Bad Day," Phyllis said. "You said he was driving like a bat, right?"

"Erratic, fast."

"Okay. Again, what if it *was* Leon and he was hightailing it down the mountain, not because he was trying to escape the scene where he'd committed a murder but because he'd *seen* something up there: the murderer, the body, maybe the act itself."

Ruby hugged herself, thinking. "And Cesar's murderer killed Leon so he wouldn't tell anybody what he'd seen," she finished. "It makes sense. But why wait until two days after Cesar's death to kill Leon? And how did the murderer know Leon had seen him?"

"Maybe the murderer didn't have a clue there was anyone else up there until you started mouthing it around that you'd seen Leon coming down from Bad Day, and then he pieced it together."

Ruby felt a chill. *Could* that be? She herself might be responsible for Leon's death, even indirectly?

"Who did you tell?" Phyllis asked.

"The police, the lawyers, casual friends. Anybody could have heard it. But why was he killed practically in your backyard?"

"A sense of irony?" Phyllis suggested.

"Maybe whoever killed Leon was watching him," Ruby said. "Leon made one of his little forays up here to throw garbage on your yard or just to see what you were up to, and he was followed."

"And maybe for fun," Phyllis said slowly, "Leon's killer decided to throw suspicion on me, to thicken the stew. Maybe the police won't be able to prove what kind of car forced him off the road."

"No witnesses, no alibis," Ruby said.

"Jesse was with me. I have an alibi," Phyllis said.

"Jesse would be easy to discount. Besides, I'd never allow her to testify; it would be too stressful for her."

Gray dawn was approaching and Ruby suddenly realized the night was silent. "The winds have stopped," she said, looking out the window at the glow from the setting moon.

"That's what woke me up," Phyllis said. "And I started thinking. Do you feel like a cup of coffee?"

"No, thanks," Ruby told her. "Maybe I'll sleep another hour or two."

Phyllis hesitated, then rose from the bed, and Ruby realized a moment had been lost. "That was good thinking, Phyl," she said.

"It's just an idea. Use it if you can," she said, and left the room.

Chapter 21

After breakfast on Saturday morning Ruby called the three automobile yards on the north end of Albuquerque. "I'm with Chimera Insurance," she said. "Was Leon Peppermill's pickup truck brought to your yard yesterday?"

"We've got it," the man who answered at the second yard, Auto Body Experience, said.

"Thanks," Ruby told him, jotting down the address on a piece of notepaper.

Jesse, Salina, and Phyllis sat outside in the courtyard, all three wearing sunglasses, deep in conversation Ruby couldn't hear. She folded the piece of paper, stuck it in her pocket, and reached for her cup of coffee.

"Morning," Adam said, entering the kitchen, heading for the coffeepot.

"Hello," Ruby said, picking up her cup and turning to leave the room, in no mood to sort out Phyllis's private life.

"Chimera Insurance?" he asked, stopping her in her tracks. "That's pretty good. What is it, some kind of rationalization that you're not really lying?"

She turned and faced him. His hair was freshly combed and shiny wet; he smelled of the shower. He wore narrow-leg jeans and a blue shirt with pearly buttons. "*You* talk to me about lying?" Ruby asked him. "Phyllis told me your story, Adam or Allen or whatever your name is."

"You can call me Adam," he said lazily, pouring coffee into a black mug.

"Where were you yesterday?"

"Running errands. Where were you?"

"The same."

"So neither one of us has an alibi," he said, toasting her with his cup of coffee.

"Are you looking for one?" Ruby asked. He was maddeningly calm, unperturbed by her questions. Maybe even amused.

"Don't need one." He sat down at the small table in the kitchen and reached for a piece of cold toast. "I bet you hang tough when the world goes to hell, just like Phyllis."

"She hasn't been so tough on this one, has she?" Ruby asked, surprised at the sense of betrayal she felt as soon as the words were out of her mouth.

"Do you mean the drinking? There are worse habits. She'll be okay, whether you come through for her or not."

"Will you still be here?" Ruby asked.

"I don't try to predict the future. Never have."

Ruby pulled off the road at the scene where Leon Peppermill died, parking behind the set of skid marks that blackened the pavement and led off down an embankment where they became unreadable gouges in the arroyo's bottom sand.

Ruby got out of her Ford and walked down to the arroyo, feeling the sun's heat on top of her head. She carried lip balm in her pocket now and she moistened her lips with it as she walked. A roadrunner zipped from behind a woody shrub and raced to another one farther away, its black-crested head stretched out in front of it.

If Leon had been thrown from the truck, other items would have fallen from the cab as well. She found a pack of Camels still holding two cigarettes and a baseball cap that advertised beer, caught on the spines of a cholla. Any paper would have been scattered miles away by last night's wind. She hoped the police had picked up everything else.

She turned in a circle, avoiding a tuft of green on the rocky ground, and examined the site: tire tracks where the police cars and probably the ambulance had driven down to the arroyo, bits of broken glass, swerving black marks on the road. That was all.

Despite its name, Auto Body Experience was a standard junkyard covering several acres and surrounded by a solid wooden fence reinforced by chain link. It was located in a barren industrial area near the freeway. A sign warned that the premises was patrolled by guard dogs. Ruby spotted two doghouses as she drove through the open gate but no dogs. Car parts lined the walls of the single-story office, inside and out. A wooden cutout of a giant saguaro cactus stood beside the front door. Nothing green grew here.

A bald man in his late fifties stood in front of a computer behind a high counter. Thick black sideburns rose from his lower jaw and ended abruptly at the tops of his ears as if they'd been razored straight off.

"The Peppermill truck? Yeah, it's out back. Came in yesterday." He punched plastic-covered computer keys, using two fingers. "It's in Row thirty-three, Spot seven. That's just behind the office." He pointed to the left with his chin. "If you don't mind waiting until Jack gets back, he can show you."

"I think I can find it," Ruby said.

"You can't touch anything," he said doubtfully. "There are laws."

She patted her purse where Jesse's instant camera rested. "I'll only need to take a couple of photos." She paused at the door. "The sign says there are guard dogs?"

"Yeah, Sadie and Radar, but they're trained to attack when the gates are locked up. A couple of pussycats during the day."

"Thanks," Ruby told him, and left the office, walking in the hot sun in the direction he'd indicated. Like grocery aisles, each row of automobiles was marked. At the back of the lot Ruby spotted vehicles pancaked five and six bodies high, their tops mashed to seat height, but closer to the office the newly acquired were tightly positioned in double rows one-high.

At Row 33 she counted back seven vehicles and there sat Leon Peppermill's blue Chevy pickup, crumpled, its windows broken out, the cab roof crushed nearly to the steering wheel, the green hood hanging by one latch. The driver's door was detached and lying in the battered truck bed.

She winced, imagining the large and unbuckled Leon Peppermill in the out-of-control pickup.

A variety of possessions were strewn throughout the cab, the items that had been thrown onto the ground, and, Ruby suspected, tossed back inside by the police: pop cans, oily rags, pencils, a tire iron, a sports magazine, and a rat's nest of rope. There was no blood.

Ruby carried a penlight with her and she shone it beneath the driver's seat, pulling out a stiff leather glove and two Snickers bar wrappers and an old-fashioned beer can opener. She wasn't sure what she was looking for, some indication of where Leon had been going, whether he'd had an appointment with his killer.

She glanced around the lot and, not seeing anybody, pulled herself into the cab, hunching over beneath the collapsed roof. The pickup rested at an angle, sloping toward the passenger door; it smelled of oil and gas. The glove compartment was stuck and Ruby pried it open with the can opener. A profusion of papers fell out: maintenance records, credit card receipts, lottery tickets, and proof of Leon's legitimate insurance: State Farm. Ruby quickly sorted through the papers, pulling out two with telephone numbers scribbled hastily in pencil, and slipped them into her pocket. A tire gauge, toothpicks, a melted Nestlé's

Crunch, and two condoms sealed in their wrappers. Now *that* was curious.

But nothing else that Ruby could see was related to Phyllis or Cesar Peron. Only more junk beneath the passenger seat, a thick foam pad was wedged between the seat and passenger door, too tightly for Ruby to pull out.

A soft growl behind her made her freeze. She turned to see a bullheaded rottweiler studying her from the driver's side, its big front paws up on the seat. Was this Sadie or Radar? The dog bared its bone-white teeth, its upper lip quivering. What had the man in the office called his dogs? Pussycats?

"Hey, dog," she said in a low and what she hoped was a friendly voice.

Growls continued to rumble in the rottweiler's throat. It didn't take its eyes off Ruby, immune to sweet talk.

"Sadie," she said firmly. The dog didn't blink, and Ruby hoped she hadn't accidentally called for canine reinforcements. She thought of gentle Spot at home and how ferocious she could appear to strangers. She imagined a fierce-appearing but sweet-tempered Spot in front of her, a "pussycat."

"Radar," she ordered from her crouched position in the crushed truck cab. "Get down. Sit, Radar."

The dog looked at her uncertainly and Ruby repeated the command with more self-confidence, and then again, until Radar backed up and reluctantly sat on its haunches on the beaten earth, its eyes still on Ruby but showing tongue instead of teeth.

"Good dog, Radar," Ruby said as she climbed out

of the pickup cab. "Good dog." She slowly backed away from the truck and walked backward to the office, all the time talking in a low voice. The rottweiler rose and followed her on stiff legs. Its coat was glossy black in the sunshine; the muscles behind its front legs and over its haunches rippled.

Ruby walked in through the open office door, and the dog bounded in after her, its cropped tail wagging as it bumped its head against the man at the counter.

"Get what you needed?" he asked.

"I hope so," Ruby told him.

"Well, you know where the truck is if you need any more pictures. Get down, Sadie," he told the exuberant rottweiler.

"I thought that was Radar," Ruby said.

"No, Radar's a boxer—German shepherd mix."

"Thanks," Ruby told him.

"Anytime."

Phyllis sat at the dining room table in shorts and a sleeveless shirt, her wrists covered by blue cuffs, surrounded by paper. Adam and Salina were outside with Jesse.

"Daniel brought me some work I need to finish for the arroyo project," she told Ruby, and glanced through the door at Adam. She pulled back her short hair with both hands. "He didn't tell me he was coming."

"Was Adam here?" Ruby asked, dropping into the chair opposite her.

"In the flesh." Phyllis looked grim. She palmed her

mechanical pencil and clicked it until the lead was two inches long and then gently pushed it back in again. "Daniel was surprised to see Adam, to say the least."

"And did *that* surprise you?" Ruby asked.

"Frankly, yes. Why should he care whether Adam's here or not?"

"He probably doesn't," Ruby told her, "but you fired Adam, remember? He disappeared and now suddenly Daniel discovers him camped in your house. *I'd* expect him to be surprised, maybe even feel tricked. I did, when you finally admitted you were having an affair with Adam."

"You felt tricked?" Phyllis asked.

"Yes, I did."

"Oversensitive," Phyllis commented, bending over her papers.

"I found two notes for you," Jesse said proudly. "Do you want them?"

Ruby was in her bedroom sitting on her bed. She'd just dialed one of the numbers she'd found in Leon Peppermill's glove compartment and it had been answered by a Pep Boys Auto Parts Store employee.

"I do, very much," Ruby told her. Jesse was wearing another new outfit: a lime-green one-piece romper.

Jesse climbed on the bed, a piece of paper in each hand.

"Where did you find them?" Ruby asked her.

"This one"—she raised her left hand—"I found in the basket where Aunt Phyllis keeps her magazines, and this one I found in *The Wind in the Willows*." It was one of Jesse's favorite books, read over and over, before and after her accident. Ruby had read it aloud a chapter a day in the first bleak days of Jesse's recovery, keeping it up whether her daughter responded or not. Jesse had been thrilled to find it among the books Phyllis had placed in her room.

The first was a note Phyllis might have scrawled herself. *Monica's birthday,* it read. *May 23.* The other was a florist's card, the kind that came attached to a bouquet.

The loose, looping handwriting, in ballpoint pen, read, *Thanks for a perfect evening,* and it was signed, *Daniel.*

Daniel? Ruby stared at the card and its graceful penmanship.

"Are these what you were looking for?" Jesse asked.

"Hmm?" Ruby asked, turning over the card and lightly running her finger over the back. No impressions had come through. The author had been relaxed, not pressing hard as he wrote, word endings casually feathered. She remembered the crabbed and schoolboyish penmanship Daniel had showed her in his office. She looked up at Jesse waiting expectantly and said, "You did a very good job, Jesse. Thank you."

"You're welcome," Jesse replied, smiling.

As soon as Jesse left the room, Ruby found a plastic bag in her equipment and slipped the florist's card inside, sealing the bag closed. It was probably pointless after all the hands it had been through, but it was a habit that was too ingrained to deny.

She stood, and the other slip of paper from Leon

Peppermill's glove compartment fluttered to the floor. She picked it up and dialed the number written there.

"You have reached Cholla Engineering," a mechanical voice said. "Our office hours are . . ." Ruby hung up, and with the plastic bag containing the card in her hand, she went in search of Phyllis.

"She and Adam are in back of the house," Salina told her. "My bedroom window's stuck."

"Tell me," Ruby asked, "when you and your brother are alone, what do you call him, Adam or Allen?"

"Now I call him Adam."

When Ruby rounded the corner of the house, she came upon Phyllis and Adam embracing, Adam bending protectively over Phyllis. Phyllis's back was to Ruby, but Adam raised his head, gazing at Ruby with an unreadable expression. He wore his beige cowboy hat tipped back so far it touched the back of his neck.

"Excuse me," Ruby said.

Phyllis turned in Adam's arms. "Ruby," she said. Her face was flushed.

"I'd like to ask you something."

"Sure. Go ahead," she said, still in Adam's embrace.

"Alone."

"Top secret," Adam commented. "I'll go back inside. Call me when the cloak-and-dagger's finished."

Ruby handed the plastic-encased florist's card to Phyllis. "Who's this from?"

"Isn't it obvious? Daniel."

"Daniel MacSimon?"

"The very one. Why is this card in a plastic bag?"

"Habit. What was the 'perfect evening'?" Ruby asked, nodding toward the card.

"That was ages ago, not long after we hired him. We'd gone out and had a nice time. I don't remember the details now. Sweet, though, wasn't it?"

"Did you drink?"

"Maybe. I do sometimes when I go out."

"I have to leave for about an hour. Will you stay here while I'm gone?"

"I wasn't planning to go anywhere. What's up?"

"I don't know. I'm trying to figure it out. Keep an eye on Jesse."

"You don't need to worry about Jesse when she's with me," Phyllis said. She paused. "You believe *that,* don't you?"

"Yes, I do," Ruby told her. "Completely."

Chapter 22

Ruby drove fast. She'd taken her rental car, but on her way out of the house she'd stopped beside Phyllis's unlocked Jeep and grabbed the cellular phone from the glove compartment. The florist's card with Daniel's note to Phyllis sat on the passenger seat; she didn't intend to let it out of her sight. It lay there, the sun glistening off the protective plastic, a catalyst to thinking.

The handwriting Ruby had seen in the Cholla office, when Daniel had asked her to analyze his personality, had been cramped, childish, totally different from the writing on this card. Which was the real specimen? And why would he disguise either one of them?

She tapped the brakes behind a slow-moving sedan, then gunned the engine, passing the car so quickly, she had no impression of its driver or passengers.

She was too prone to operate on her own; hadn't she been told that often enough? Disregarding protocol and safety. Not this time.

Phyllis had said Daniel had moved to Albuquerque

from California. Now, from memory, she tapped out Ron Kilgore's Palo Alto phone number.

Ron had given Ruby her start, back when she'd still been a high school dropout. She'd been the receptionist, his secretary, the organizer when he'd opened his detective agency following his third failed attempt at the California bar exam. He'd recognized something in her and steered her into forgery detection, changing her life.

Ron himself answered. Ruby glanced at the clock. It was nine o'clock in California.

"Where's DeEtta?" Ruby asked.

"Late. You calling from a car?"

"I am. Can you run a quick check on a Daniel MacSimon for me? He's from the Bay Area, or at least lived there four years ago. He lives in Albuquerque now."

"Sure. What's happening? Are you in Albuquerque? Where's the report on the Fosey-Henderson job?"

Ron only operated on one speed: rapid-fire.

"I'm in Albuquerque," she affirmed. "I'll get the Fosey-Henderson back to you next week. Can you call me right back on Daniel MacSimon? I'll tell you the details later."

"Can do. How's Jesse?"

"She's fallen in love with cacti."

"Good practice for the world. What's your number?"

Ruby gave him the number and then hung up, feeling as she always did after she talked to Ron: that

Gordian knots were simple slipknots: Tug the proper end and it all unraveled.

With one hand Ruby flipped her wallet open until she found Detective Nick Powell's card and phone number. Let him shoot down her growing theory. At least this time no one could accuse her of being too independent.

She'd tapped out five digits of the detective's number when suddenly it hit her.

"Oh, shit," she said aloud, dropping the phone on the seat and taking her foot off the gas. "How could I be so damn thick?" She steered to the side of the road and pulled onto the shoulder, grateful she hadn't shared her theory with the detective. This was one reason she preferred to work alone; it was bad enough to see your own stupidities; why inflict them on the world?

The sedan she'd overtaken earlier now passed her, slowing down. Inquiring faces peered out the windows and Ruby waved them on.

Of course the handwriting on the florist's card was different from the penmanship she'd seen on Daniel's pad of paper. He'd called the florist's shop and dictated the message over the phone. She'd asked Phyllis if the card was from Daniel, not if he'd *written* it. In Sable it was more common to drop by Evelyn's Flowers, write the greeting, and seal the card in an envelope yourself, just so Evelyn wouldn't share it with her coffee klatch the next morning.

"This here's the real world, honey," she told herself, and leaned back, wondering what to do now, return to Phyllis's?

Instead she guided the car back onto the road, driving more sedately, and let her mind play with the facts, allowing it to "unfocus," the same way she first looked at a questioned handwriting specimen: instead of studying individual letters, viewing it as a whole, searching for patterns and anomalies.

A billboard advertised the gondola ride to Sandia Crest, and Ruby thought of Bad Day, the way it had looked on the day Cesar died.

It was a long drive, but she retraced the route she'd taken with Phyllis and drove up the road that rose into the mountains through national-forest land. Signs warned of the new three-dollar parking fee at the picnic grounds, and since it was Saturday, the roads were busier than the last time she'd been here.

The chain-link gates had been removed from the entrances to the picnic areas; voices filtered into the car as she passed. Again Ruby gratefully breathed in the pine fragrance, welcoming the comparative lushness after the parched dryness of the lower elevations.

No vehicles were parked at Bad Day. The gate had been reinforced with a second fence, and Ruby had to walk fifty feet farther into the trees before she found a gap she could squeeze through. She carried the cellular phone in her pocket in case Ron called.

Snow remained only in the deepest shade: tattered little patches gone crystalline like piles of dirty salt.

The silent park felt broody, even in the sunshine, tainted by death and an aura of abandonment. Ruby followed the concrete path toward the walkway and the stream, wondering briefly if the park would ever be completed. A chickadee accompanied her, chirping from the tree branches.

This time Ruby hiked closer to Eddy's death site, stepping gingerly off the path, consciously avoiding new growth. Above her the walkway hung suspended against the cliff, but Ruby's attention was focused on the ground beneath it. The spillway hissed and splashed. She walked through the broken beer bottles, stepping across an intact brown bottle, its cap still on and the label faded to white by sunlight.

She gently pushed aside the branches of low bushes with her hands, bending and peering beneath them, eyeing stones and winter-broke limbs.

Finally she found what she was looking for, what she doubted even existed. She crouched beside a small bundle of stems lying on the ground amid the beer bottles. At the end of each stem was the remains of a flower, gone brown and decayed. Ruby didn't touch the dead bouquet, only studied it. Then she moved back toward the path, trying to approximate the spot where she'd stood with Phyllis looking at the collapsed walkway and thinking she'd seen a clump of spring flowers.

The cellular phone rang and Ruby jumped, raising her hand to her heart before she reached for the phone in her pocket, almost turning it off instead of answering it in a place like this. She turned her back to the broken walkway. The chickadee went silent.

It was Ron Kilgore. "Got your information," he said. "Daniel Martin MacSimon, thirty-nine, engineer, Cal Tech, class of '81, married and divorced."

"Any record?" she asked. Her voice sounded overloud to herself, an assault on the surroundings.

"Not really."

"What does 'not really' mean?"

"One speeding ticket six years ago—"

"That's not a record."

"Let me finish. About the same time as his speeding ticket he got divorced." Ruby heard the shuffle of papers. "From Pamela Maureen Pace. It seems Pamela sought a restraining order against your Daniel, claiming he was stalking her. So who is this guy? Is he making a move on you?"

"A friend of my sister's. Did Pamela get the restraining order?"

"She didn't follow through. He left town not long after, anyway, and now she calls him 'sweet.' "

"You talked to her?"

"I like to be thorough. Said I was doing a security-clearance check. Pamela left him, I gathered."

"Why?"

"I'm not *that* thorough. She gave me some chick talk about feeling smothered, that he took the divorce hard, they haven't spoken in years, she hopes he's happy yadda-yadda."

"Thanks, really. I appreciate it."

"Is your sister in trouble?"

"Yes."

"Watch yourself," and as if he thought she hadn't heard him, he repeated it, adding, "I mean it. Don't forget, your job's here whenever you want to give up Hickamerica."

"I'll remember that. Thanks again."

Ruby returned the phone to her pocket and turned back to face the collapsed walkway, fixing the position of the bouquet in her memory.

The chickadee didn't return and all Ruby could hear was the water from the spillway. No wind, no birds; everything else was still.

And suddenly she wanted away from this sad place where lives had ended. She hurried back to the path and through the fence to her car, twice glancing behind her.

There were no vehicles parked in front of Space 17 in the Desert View Mobile Home Park, and Ruby hoped Grace Peppermill was home—and alone.

Television voices in theatrically earnest conversation sounded from the Peppermill trailer and the same voices came from the trailer next to it so that as Ruby waited for Grace to answer the door, she stood in stereophonic sound. A curtain moved on the window beside the door, and Ruby rapped on the metal door again, harder this time.

The door cracked open a few inches, exposing the left half of Grace's face above pale yellow. Her hair was tangled. "What do you want?" she asked.

"Just to ask a couple of questions," Ruby said. "I'm sorry about your husband."

"I don't want to answer any questions," she said, not firmly but like a sulky child being told it has no choice.

"Only two questions," Ruby said. "That's all."

"What are they?"

"Do you want me to ask them out here, where someone might hear?"

Grace looked behind Ruby, then the door opened all the way. Ruby marveled that she was being allowed inside again. Grace didn't even know Ruby's name. Ruby felt unexpected tenderness toward the too-trusting little woman.

Through the open bedroom door Ruby spotted a suitcase standing open on the disheveled bed, folded clothes piled around it. Dirty dishes sat in the sink. Eddy's shrine was partially dismantled, a cardboard box on the floor beside it held half the photos and memorabilia from Eddy's short life.

"Are you leaving?" Ruby asked her.

"Is that one of your two questions?" Grace returned, surprising Ruby.

"No."

"I'm going to my sister's in Gallup for a while," Grace said. She pulled at the hem of her yellow sweatshirt, which was stretched as if this were a chronic habit.

"Have you seen the spot at Bad Day where the accident happened?" Ruby asked.

Grace shook her head. "I don't have a car."

"On the day Cesar Peron died . . . ," Ruby began, stopping when Grace put her chubby little hands over her ears and closed her eyes. She waited until the woman removed them and looked at Ruby, her eyes still tight as if she were peeking, pulling again at the hem of her sweatshirt.

"That wasn't Leon we met coming down from the mountain, was it? It was you."

Grace shook her head and looked down at her hands.

"I thought it was Leon because I could see his body. You're so short, it didn't occur to me that it might be you. But when I went through Leon's pickup at the junkyard this morning, I saw the cushion you sat on. It would have raised you up to almost his height."

Ruby gave Grace a few moments to respond, but she didn't. Her breathing was harsh, fast as if she couldn't catch it. Her bosom heaved, and Ruby lightly touched her shoulder. "Let's sit down," she said.

Grace obediently followed her to her chair and dropped into it. Ruby found two glasses in the cupboard and filled them with water from the kitchen faucet.

"You'd been visiting Eddy's death scene," she went on, giving one of the glasses to Grace. She nodded toward the photos. "Like a memorial. I saw the flowers you left at the bottom of the cliff."

Grace raised her head and glanced over at the potted plant sitting on top of the television. A stalk of large white violets was just opening.

Go for broke, Ruby thought. "Did you kill Cesar because you were afraid he was going to testify on Phyllis's behalf?"

Grace's eyes widened. She gasped. "Oh, no! Not me."

"Then you saw who killed him."

Grace bit her lip, shaking her head with little conviction.

"You were afraid," Ruby said, keeping her voice calm and soft. "That's why you were driving so erratically down the mountain, afraid that the killer had seen you and would be after you next, isn't that right?"

Slowly, just perceptibly, Grace Peppermill nodded.

"Please, Grace," Ruby pleaded. "Tell me what you saw at Bad Day."

Grace heaved a sigh and eased back into her recliner, folding her hands tightly together over her abdomen. Ruby set her own glass on the TV tray near her and leaned toward Grace.

"I'd gone up there alone once before," she said hesitantly, gulping air between sentences. "I knew how to get in. I didn't park by the gate because I was afraid if somebody saw the truck, they'd come looking for me and throw me out. So I parked farther up the road, behind some trees. You couldn't see the truck from the gate."

"And then you walked back down the road and went through the gate?"

"No, through the trees."

Ruby pictured the fat little woman on her lonely trek through the woods to visit the spot where her son had died, avoiding the patches of snow and mud, carrying a few flowers to leave where her son's body had fallen. She swallowed and waited for Grace to continue.

"Eddy was a good boy," Grace said, her voice catching. "But something happened when he got older. He changed, there was all that trouble. He shouldn't have been at Bad Day. It wasn't open. I saw the No Trespassing signs. But Leon said it was the engineer's fault, that she had to pay for killing Eddy and in a way we'd be paid back for the heartache Eddy had caused us."

"Who did you see at Bad Day?" Ruby asked gently.

"I left the flowers and started back to the truck," Grace went on, gazing toward Eddy's photos. "There was still dirty snow in the shade. Then I heard voices, so I stopped behind a tree. I was wearing green," she added.

"Men's voices?"

Grace nodded.

"Were they loud? Quarreling?"

"No. Just talking. Friendly like. I thought they were together."

"Then what happened?"

"I didn't move and they came closer to me. I was standing above them, and the bushes were in the way, so I couldn't see everything." She paused again, and Ruby squeezed her fingernails into her palms to keep from telling the woman to just blurt it out.

"Were they facing you or were you looking at their backs?" Ruby asked.

"Their backs. Kind of their sides, too, but mostly their backs. They came to the stream; it was spread out from all the snow melt that was coming out of the mountains, and the Mexican man stepped in front of the other man. The other man had been carrying a rock, not a really big rock, more like he was interested in it, like he might take it home. Then he just lifted it up and hit the Mexican on the head. Right here." Grace touched the side of her head, her eyes distant in memory.

"I couldn't believe it was real. It wasn't like on TV."

She shivered. "He didn't make a sound. He fell into the water and the other man bent over him. I was so scared . . . I didn't look anymore." She gazed down at her hands, working her pudgy fingers around and around.

"Then what did you do?"

Tears spilled from Grace's eyes and she began to rock her body back and forth. "I didn't . . ." She hiccupped. "I didn't go down to the stream to help him. I didn't even go down to see if he was dead or alive. The other man was gone; I heard him running through the trees, but I was afraid he'd come back, so I waited a while longer. The man in the water didn't get up so . . . I left."

"And that's why, when we saw you, you were driving wildly down the road? You were in a panic?"

Grace nodded. "Did he die because I didn't help him?" she asked, her voice broken.

"No, Grace," Ruby assured her. What was the point of saying anything else? "The man you saw murdered Cesar Peron. He stabbed Cesar after he fell in the water. You couldn't have saved him. Can you describe the other man?"

"Not really. Just a man. Medium. I couldn't see his face very well. He wore a cowboy hat."

"What color?" Ruby asked.

"Black."

Adam's hat was fawn-colored, but that didn't mean he didn't own other hats.

"Have you seen the man who killed Cesar since that day?"

"No. But Leon knew who he was."

"He did? How?"

"I told him what I'd seen. He said he was going to flush him out. He went on TV and talked to the reporters. He said things so the killer would know Leon meant him, like talking about a black hat and Eddy's death made him feel like he'd been hit in the head with a rock."

"Why?" Ruby asked. "Why not tell the police?"

Grace flushed. "Leon had a plan. He was going to blackmail the killer."

"In case he lost the lawsuit?" Ruby asked. "For insurance?" Outside, an ice-cream truck drove through the park, playing "Pop Goes the Weasel," followed by the voices of children.

"I didn't like it," Grace said.

"But Leon was obviously successful in flushing the killer out. Did he contact Leon?"

Grace took a drink of water and nodded. "Leon told him how much money he wanted and the killer agreed. He arranged with Leon where they could meet."

"And that was yesterday while I was here; that's when Leon was killed. Did Leon tell you who it was or where he was going?"

"He said it was better if I was ignorant." She shifted in her chair. "Sometimes when I get rattled, I say things before I think."

Which Ruby was very grateful for. She rose from the couch and touched Grace's shoulder. "Thank you, Grace. You know you'll have to tell of this to the police?"

She nodded, working her hands again. "I knew I'd have to someday."

Ruby had her hand on the door handle when she thought of something else. "Remember when you told me that Cesar had called you: Now that he and Leon are both dead, can you remember what he said on your answering machine?"

Grace flushed again. "He said he had proof there'd been tampering."

"Proof?" Ruby asked. "Are you sure he used the word *proof*?"

Grace nodded.

Ruby pulled into a mall parking lot and dialed Detective Powell's number. When she told him what Grace had said, he whistled.

"So we have a very busy mystery killer. I'll go talk to Grace and get her statement."

"You'd better hurry," Ruby warned him. "She's on her way to her sister's in Gallup."

"Will do. You should have called me before you dropped in on her."

"I didn't know I'd hit gold," Ruby said.

"Didn't you?"

"Any word on the answering-machine tape you sent to the state lab?"

"Yeah, but there's a screwup. They're closed on weekends, so I'll call Monday morning to straighten it out."

"What was the screwup?"

"The message I got—over the phone, not written—

I don't know why those guys couldn't send a fax, through two secretaries, is that they're both the same, whatever that means." Ruby heard him whistle two notes through his teeth. "Listen, Ruby. Promise you'll call me if you have any other brilliant deductions or if any murderers walk up to you and confess their sins, okay?"

"I'll do my best."

He groaned. "Better yet. Forget it all and have a nice weekend. Watch the eclipse tomorrow night. Relax."

"Gotcha," Ruby said, and switched off.

She backed out of her parking space and drove to a snack shop at the edge of the mall parking lot, thinking of the garbled message Nick had received from the lab. "They're both the same." Both what? Had they confused two different pieces of evidence? Two different tapes? But then why would they both be the same?

She ran into the snack shop and paid too much for a six-pack of diet pop. She'd never drank so much and peed so little. She opened a can and nearly drained it before she started her car.

She was the second car in line waiting to turn in to the street when she remembered there were two different messages on the machine: the threatening voice and one other . . . from Daniel MacSimon.

Is that what the lab had meant? Both *messages* were the same? They'd both been spoken by the same person? Daniel?

The florist's card still sat on the passenger seat. Ruby looked at it, frowning, until she was aware of a car horn honking more and more insistently behind her. She pulled onto the street, heading back toward town, toward Cholla Engineering.

It was Saturday and the office was closed, but from what Ruby had seen of the pressure the staff worked under, someone was bound to be there.

Three vehicles were parked outside the building, two of them four-wheel drives. A newspaper and a Taco Bell wrapper were wound in the shrubbery out front, left over from the night's wind.

Ruby was surprised to find the front door unlocked and she entered the silent and empty reception area, her footfalls sounding harsh and out of place, like unexpected movement in the forest.

She heard the distinctive sound of a photocopier and followed it to a small room holding two photocopiers and a blueprint machine. Standing at one of the copiers, wearing jeans and a purple T-shirt, was Monica, Phyllis's CAD designer.

She glanced up at Ruby, the perplexed smile on her face clearing as she recognized Ruby, not Phyllis. "Hi," she said. "I'm here for a couple of hours, trying to catch up."

"Hi," Ruby told her. "Has Daniel been here?"

"I haven't seen him."

"Damn," Ruby said. "I must have missed him. He was going to give me a book explaining cantilevered walkways."

Monica gave Ruby a sympathetic glance as she flipped one page off the copier's glass and another one on. "Maybe he left it on the bench outside his office. Want me to look for you?"

"I know where it is. I'll check. Thanks."

Ruby passed an office where a man was bent over a tilted drafting table, one hand to his forehead. Nearby she heard the soft *click-click* of computer keys.

When she reached Daniel's windowless office, she quietly tried the doorknob, but the door was locked. She tried twice more, then returned to the copy room. Monica was gone, so she found her way to the CAD room, where Monica was just sitting down in front of her screen, the cursor blinking over a line of numbers.

"No luck?" Monica asked.

Ruby shook her head. "Maybe he left it on his desk. I don't suppose you have a key?"

"I don't, but I can tell him tonight," Monica offered.

"Tonight?"

Monica blushed. "Employees are definitely *not* encouraged to date each other around here, but . . ."

"How long have you and Daniel been dating?" Ruby asked.

"Almost a year." She smiled. "We keep it outside the office."

"Must be tough. When you both have to work late, do you sneak in a few minutes after everybody's gone?"

Monica rolled her eyes. "This time of year we're so busy, we're lucky to get that much time."

"Well, this room is at least"—she glanced around at the other three silent computers—"private." The binders of design notes stood on the shelf to the left of

Monica's computer. "Lots of projects," she commented. "Does Daniel put together his designs the same way Phyllis does?"

Monica leaned toward the shelf next to the second computer and ran her finger along the spines of the three-ring binders. "I don't do Daniel's designs anymore, Jim does. Phyllis's are generally clearer."

"You mean better penmanship?"

"No, just her specifications." Monica chose one of the binders and handed it to Ruby. "Take a look."

Ruby tried not to show her eagerness as she took the binder. The page she randomly opened to was carefully written in precise draftsman's print: block letters and numbers. She flipped back a few pages, then to the front, where a description of the project was written in longhand.

And there it was: the same fluid handwriting as on the florist's card: lightly pressed with consistent and smooth connections, proportioned letters. Why had he offered her a sample of his handwriting that was crabbed and childish? There was only one reason: to throw her off track. To remove himself from Ruby's subconscious if she came across any of his handwriting at Phyllis's. Why? Had he expected Phyllis to save every threatening note she'd received and he was worried he'd slipped up somehow, falling back into the style of his own penmanship, and that Ruby would spot it?

It wouldn't have mattered. Given the two handwritings side by side, with careful study, Ruby would have found him out.

"See what I mean?" Monica asked.

Ruby cleared her throat. "If I knew more about engineering, I probably would. Phyllis said you're one of the best. Has Daniel ever helped you out when you've had to stay late?"

"Now and then. He's so sweet." She put her finger to her lips. "Don't tell."

"I'd better get home. It was good to talk to you again, Monica."

"Sure. Anytime. Tell Phyllis hi."

Back in her car Ruby removed the phone from the glove compartment and called Phyllis. She picked it up on the second ring.

"We were just about to leave," Phyllis said. "Should we wait for you?"

"Where are you going?"

"Daniel's taking us on a picnic. Does that sound hometowny Michigan or what?"

"Daniel? Where is he, Phyllis?"

"Outside talking to Adam. I'll get him for you. He's just outside the window." Ruby heard the muffling of the mouthpiece and Phyllis call out, "Daniel, Ruby's on the phone."

"Wait, Phyllis," Ruby shouted into the tiny phone.

But it wasn't Phyllis who answered her; it was Daniel. "How are you, Ruby?" he asked.

Ruby took a steadying breath and answered as calmly as she could, "Hi, Daniel, Phyllis said you're taking everyone on a picnic. Sounds like fun."

"Come on back and join us," Daniel invited.

He sounded cheerful, ebullient, as if she'd caught him in the middle of a lighthearted conversation. She could hear Phyllis's voice behind him in the same room, saying something about ice for the cooler.

"Thanks, I'd love to," Ruby told him. "I can be there in twenty minutes."

He chuckled as if she'd said something humorous. "We can wait for you," he said, his voice warm and friendly, yet sounding regretful.

"Great. Can you put Phyllis back on the line?"

"I don't think so."

"I beg your pardon?"

"All right, then," he said warmly. "But we'll miss you. Jesse made the lemonade."

"Please," she couldn't help begging. "Don't."

"Bye now," he said, and the phone went dead.

"Damn," she whispered, and ran back to the car, scraping her hand on the keys as she yanked them from the steering column.

She frantically fumbled with the keys, unlocking first the lock in the doorknob. The door swung open; the deadbolt hadn't been locked, only the door handle, which would have locked automatically when the door was closed.

Ruby swallowed and used one hand to push the door open the rest of the way without stepping inside, casting her eyes across the foyer into the living room and kitchen. No one was there. The sun shone on the kitchen counters through the skylight. She heard a rhythmic buzz and at first she thought it was in her head, but she traced it to the telephone on the kitchen counter where the receiver lay beside the phone. She replaced it and checked the counter, the refrigerator door, the table, vainly looking for a note from Phyllis.

One slow step after another, Ruby walked through the house, taking a breath before she entered each room, her relief mixed with dread as she discovered each one empty. She had no idea where they'd gone. None. This wasn't her country; she couldn't even guess.

Jesse's room was perfectly tidy, Ruby's untouched, Phyllis's such a disorderly cave that Ruby couldn't detect whether anything had been disturbed or not.

At the end of the hall Ruby turned the knob of the wooden door that led to Salina's room. She hadn't set foot in here before and found herself in a young woman's domain, a rock poster tacked to the wall over a tiny dinette set, colorful prints of horses and flowers, a bright patterned blanket on the bed. A cot was set up on the opposite side of the room, a green sleeping bag spread across it.

The house was empty. Ruby banged her fist against the wall, at a loss. She barely knew her way to and from Albuquerque; how could she possibly find her sister and daughter? She glanced at her watch; they had at least a fifteen-minute start. Fifteen minutes: fifteen miles if Daniel took the freeway, maybe even farther. All she could do was wait for Nick Powell and hope he had an idea where to look next.

She was leaving Salina's bedroom for the living room when her attention was caught by the dark silhouette of a large bird circling the house, no higher than thirty feet in the air, its wings outstretched. She stopped and gazed through the window.

There in the rear courtyard lay Adam, facedown, a streak of red through his blond hair.

"Oh, no," Ruby said aloud. She unlatched the glass door and in a moment was beside the prone figure, feeling his neck for a pulse.

"I'm alive," he gasped, turning onto his side, his eyes unfocused, panting. "Where's Phyllis?"

"Gone. Do you know where?" She removed a tissue from her pocket and wiped at the dazed man's head. Blood seeped from a wound above his ear. The flesh was swollen, discolored.

"Can't think right now," he said. He reached to touch his cut and she pushed his hand away.

"Is Jesse all right?"

"Last I knew. My hat." He limply waved his hand toward the edge of the courtyard.

His tan cowboy hat had rolled against the stucco wall. Ruby retrieved it and left it on the ground beside him while she went inside for a glass of water and a towel.

When she returned, he was sitting up, dabbing at the cut with the blood-saturated tissue. "Here," Ruby said, holding the towel to his head. "Bleed into this while I find Phyllis's first-aid supplies."

"It's white," he said, trying to shrug off the towel.

"It's the first one I found," she said, pushing the towel against his wound. "We'll buy Phyllis a new one. Do you know if she has a first-aid kit?"

"In her bathroom," he said. "Under the sink."

Ruby returned to the house and the bathroom off Phyllis's bedroom. A plastic first-aid kit sat beneath the sink next to a fire extinguisher. Ruby leaned down and grabbed the kit and as she raised up, through the mirror's reflection of her frantic face she caught sight of printing on the mirror's surface, not written in lipstick but probably with a spit-wettened finger. It was barely visible. Holding the first-aid kit close to her chest, Ruby leaned forward, then back, so she had an oblique view of the mirror and the faint letters became readable.

Petro, it read. Petro? There was a mark after the *o* as if Phyllis had been interrupted before she could finish the word. For she was sure that was who had written it. The *P* was formed in one stroke, exactly the same as Phyllis formed the *P* in her name.

Ruby left the bathroom and hurried back to the courtyard. Adam had poured water from the glass onto the towel and wiped away most of the blood from around the wound.

"You might need a couple of stitches," Ruby told him as she knelt beside him and finished the job, dropping the towel on the ground. It lay there, a flag of red and white.

"Later. We have to find Phyllis."

"And Jesse. Where's Salina?"

"She went to town. A haircut. Phyllis let her take the Porsche."

He winced as Ruby poured Betadyne on a gauze pad and covered his torn and swollen skin. "Does the word *Petro* mean anything to you?"

"Petrol?" he asked. "Like gas?"

"I don't know. The letters *P-e-t-r-o* are scrawled on Phyllis's bathroom mirror. It could be half of a word."

Adam thought, taking deep breaths. Ruby could see the struggle to concentrate. He was woozy, disoriented, and in pain.

"Petro," he murmured. "Petro. Retroactive."

"Petro," Ruby repeated. *P-E-T-R-O.*" She taped the gauze bandage, trying to fasten it to the flesh beneath his hair. It was a sloppy job. "You might have to hold that," she told Adam.

"Petro," he said, not hearing her. "She might have meant petroglyphs."

"Are there petroglyphs near here?" Ruby asked.

"On the ridge behind us, about six, eight miles. The Desert Fox Petroglyphs."

"Is it a tourist attraction?" Daniel wouldn't take Phyllis to a public place. Ruby didn't know what Daniel was planning, but she did know Phyllis, and in a public setting her sister was sure to create a scene.

"Not these. I've been there with Phyllis. The locals keep quiet about them so they'll stay intact."

"Tell me how to get there," Ruby said, repacking the kit and latching it closed.

"I'll come with you," he said, trying to rise to his feet. He would have fallen if Ruby hadn't caught him, stumbling herself under his weight.

"Wait here. I called the detective. He'll be on his way."

"I'm coming, or I won't tell you how to get there."

"I'm not playing games." She stepped away from him and he remained upright, straightening his shoulders.

"It'll save time," he said. "Let's go."

"I'm not patching you up if you come apart," Ruby warned him, "or waiting for you if you can't keep up with me."

"Fair enough," he agreed, and she thrust the first-aid kit into his arms. "You carry this," she told him.

"Will we need it?" he asked stupidly, and Ruby didn't answer.

Before they left the house, Ruby wrote *Desert Fox Petroglyphs, seven miles west* in large letters on a piece of paper and left it on the counter. She turned the inside door knob, leaving the door unlocked for the detective.

Adam headed for his pickup, and Ruby said, "I'm driving and we're taking Phyllis's Jeep."

"I have to get something first," he told her, opening

the unlocked passenger door and reaching under the seat. He pulled out a tooled leather belt and holster with a long barreled revolver strapped into it.

"Is that real?" Ruby asked. It looked like a prop from a Western movie.

"Definitely," he told her, a touch of bravado in his wounded state. "I bought it from an old cowboy in Las Cruces."

Ruby backed the Jeep out of the driveway and spun around, throwing up gravel. "Go right," Adam told her.

"What happened?" Ruby asked once they were on the road.

"After you called, Daniel got nervous," Adam said, leaning back his head and gingerly touching the bandage. "He started yammering that we had to leave right away, but Phyllis wasn't ready and she got pissed at him for prodding her. He sniped back at her and I called him on it and the next thing you know we decided to discuss it outside so Jesse wouldn't hear."

"And when you got outside, he hit you on the head. With what? A rock?"

He touched the bandage again. "It felt like a cannonball."

"But why did he take Jesse and Phyllis?"

Adam shook his head, then winced. "But he was definitely surprised when he found me at Phyllis's this morning."

"Surprised in what way?" Ruby pulled a tissue from the box on the console and handed it to him. "You're bleeding."

"Like I was on his territory," he said, wiping at the blood trickling toward his ear.

"You're saying he was jealous?"

"Yeah, that's exactly what I'm saying. He fussed around, first like an old hen, then he started pawing the earth like a bull."

"But Jesse?" Ruby asked. "Why did he take Jesse?"

Adam raised his head from the headrest and looked at Ruby as if she were hopelessly slow. "Because he knows Phyllis will do anything he wants in order to keep Jesse safe. Jesse's his insurance."

"He's crazy."

"I could have said that a year ago. Turn left by that For Sale sign."

"Then why didn't you?" Ruby asked.

"Who would have listened? He was an engineer; I was an insubordinate draftsman."

"What did he do that was so crazy?" Ruby asked. She turned left, feeling soft earth slew beneath the tires.

"Nothing, really. It's his eyes." Adam looked behind them, then scanned the empty land. "I had a mutt with eyes like that: rolling over on his back all the time, trying to lick your face, begging you to love him, but if you didn't do it *right*, he'd go for your throat."

"Daniel looked at Phyllis that way?"

"He was always doing things for her." Adam shrugged. "Phyllis liked him. I didn't think—"

"We never do," Ruby snapped. She took her eyes from the road, searching for a glimpse of Daniel's Jimmy, hoping that what Adam had said was true:

Phyllis would do anything to keep Jesse safe, and admitting to herself that yes, she *did* believe Phyllis cared more about Jesse than anyone else in her life. The knot of jealousy had unraveled; at this moment she *wanted* Jesse to love Phyllis with all her heart and to do whatever Phyllis told her.

"What are you looking for?" Adam asked.

"Daniel's Jimmy, the police, some sign."

He opened the glove compartment, put his hand inside, and then pulled it out, empty. "Damn. I thought the cellular was here. We could have called your cop again."

Ruby hit the steering wheel with her fist. "I took it to town with me," she told him in despair. "It's still in my car."

He closed the glove compartment. "But you already called them once, right? They're on their way."

"On their way to Phyllis's house, where I left a note on the counter." In her panic over Jesse's disappearance she'd forgotten the cellular, had slipped into a low-tech mentality, her communication reverting to pencil and paper.

"Careful," Adam warned. "This road isn't good enough for how fast you're driving."

"I can't go fast *enough,* damn you," Ruby said. Tears of fear and frustration spilled down her cheeks. The terrain rose toward a long, narrow mesa that was still a mile or more away. If that's where Daniel had taken Phyllis and Jesse, he already knew they were following him. Their dust alone was visible for miles. The road was little more than a depression through the soft sand and rock, meandering around juniper and hollows in the terrain. She held the wheel with both hands, fighting the pull of the tires. The engine groaned, but she didn't let up.

"Veer to the left at the Y. It'll take you right up onto the mesa."

The closer they got to the mesa, the fainter the road grew. As soon as she took the left fork, she spotted a flash of light on the mesa.

"There they are," Adam said at the same time. He leaned forward, pointing out the windshield.

"Do you see anybody?" Ruby asked.

"No."

"He *wants* me to come up here," Ruby said. "He thinks I'm the only one who knows the whole story."

"What is the whole story?" Adam asked.

"Later. He's using Jesse and Phyllis to lure me."

"How do you figure that? *I* didn't even know where he was taking them."

"He knew that somehow Phyllis would leave me a message. Maybe he wrote the message on the mirror himself. He likes to play with handwriting, I suspect."

They ended their ascent and drove onto the mesa. Golden boulders and pillars of rock rose to their left, all of them rounded and worn as if they'd been sanded by time. Daniel's car was fifty yards in front of them, temporarily out of sight.

"Slow down here and I'll jump out," Adam told her.

"What?"

He grabbed his tooled leather gun belt. "He

doesn't know I'm with you. He probably thinks I'm dead. I'll come up from behind. But give me a little time to get there."

"I'm not planning to stall around when Jesse's life is in danger."

"Just don't do anything radical until I get there, that's all I'm asking."

Ruby slowed the Jeep and Adam rolled out, letting the door swing closed.

She glanced in the rearview mirror and saw Adam dust himself off and run, half crouching, toward the rock-strewn hill. The mirror might as well have been a tiny TV screen. The feel of the tableau, all of it, was otherworldly, impossible: the bright mesa and big sky, a bleeding cowboy with a six-shooter fading into the rocks.

To her left the ridge rose fifteen feet high, and she drove alongside it, following it farther onto the mesa, dropping her speed to fifteen miles per hour, watching to either side for signs of Jesse or Phyllis. But there was nothing, only the desolate mesa, void of vegetation except for a few branched plants struggling in the thin dirt of the shadier spots, no humans in sight.

Daniel's beige Jimmy loomed in front of her and she slammed on the brakes. The windows were tinted and in the sunlight she couldn't see whether anyone was inside. When the driver's door didn't open, she turned off her engine and cautiously climbed out into the silence, standing in the protection of her open door for a few moments before she took two cautious steps into the open, away from the Jeep toward Daniel's vehicle.

But there was only silence. The wind blew a shiny square of paper across the track, fluttering it against a rock, and Ruby recognized the orange of a Reese's Peanut Butter Cup wrapper. There'd been several left in the bowl on Phyllis's counter.

Every door of the Jimmy was locked, and she cupped her hands around her eyes, peering in through the windows, feeling her heart pounding in her chest, her ears whooshing like breaths.

No one was in the car, not lying on the seat nor huddled on the floor. The fact that the right front side of Daniel's Jimmy was damaged, the turn signal light broken, barely registered.

Ruby turned away from the Jimmy and shouted, "Jesse? Phyllis?" toward the ridge above her, hearing the whisper of an echo and vainly listening for an answering call. A trio of birds rose up from behind a rock and flapped away.

"Jesse! Answer me," she demanded, turning in a lonely circle. Beneath the mesa the vista was empty, without a sign of Detective Nick Powell's sedan or a posse of rescuers. Had he found her note and understood where she meant?

Ruby returned to the Jeep and blasted the horn. What had Hank once told her; if she was ever lost in the woods, three of anything signaled an emergency: three whistles, three shouts, three gunshots. Three times she leaned on the horn, holding it while she counted to three, waiting between each honk while she counted to three again. Then she paused, reciting the alphabet before she did it all over again. And again.

"I hear you."

Ruby whirled around. Daniel stood twenty feet behind her, on an outcropping of rocks. Relaxed, casual, a slight smile on his face.

Chapter 24

Daniel gazed down at Ruby from the rocks, his hands hanging at his sides, empty. She didn't see signs of a weapon anywhere on his body. He wore a polo shirt, and unless he'd hidden it behind him in his waistband, he was unarmed.

"Where's Jesse?" Ruby asked him. Her own hands were in fists so tight they corded her arms. "If you've hurt her, I'll—"

"Not so fast. I don't hurt little girls. She's fine."

Ruby stepped to the side, out of the line of the sun. "I want to see her."

"You will. Later."

"Now. Where are they?"

"Ruby, this is all a misunderstanding." He spoke reasonably, confidently, squatting down and smiling at her, looking as if he might pluck a blade of grass and chew its end, if only there'd been any. "You must have realized how much I care for Phyllis."

"So much that you'd kill for her?" Ruby asked.

A truly pained expression crossed his face. He rose and took a step toward her and she took a step back. "I never meant for anyone to die." He raised his hands, holding them out, empty, as if pleading. "I'm not a killer."

"Yes, you are," Ruby told him. She kept her voice even, matching his. "Let's get Jesse and Phyllis and go to the police. Don't add kidnapping to the list."

"Give me some time to talk to Phyllis, to make her realize I was trying to help her. When she understands that, everything will be fine. You and Jesse can go home to your cabin on the lake."

"How do you justify ruining Phyllis's career as acting in her best interests?" Ruby asked him. They'd each taken a few wary steps closer to each other; Ruby was tensed, keeping her eyes on Daniel, ready to spring out of the way if he made a threatening move. He stood above her with every advantage.

"She was so alone," Daniel told her, "too proud to let anyone help her."

"Is that how Pamela was?" Ruby asked. "Did you make yourself so helpful, so protective that she felt smothered and then frightened, finally forced to seek a restraining order against you?"

Daniel tipped his head and considered Ruby, his eyes widening in surprise and an expression that was almost proud, as if he was pleased by how clever she was. "Now, I wonder how you discovered Pamela?" he asked. "Did you learn little tricks like that in forgery school?"

He drew the words in the air as he spoke them: "Snooping One-oh-one," and even in air-writing, Ruby saw the rounded strokes of his writing, not the tight penmanship he'd shown her in his office.

She'd led him onto dangerous ground, away from

Phyllis and Jesse to a past that still caused him rage, threatening to take over the conversation. She didn't care about his history or his ex-wife and she tried to bring him back to the present. "Did you encourage Phyllis to drink?" she asked, her voice loud, insistent.

Daniel jerked his head and blinked. "Phyllis's drinking was a cry that she needed someone to stand by her, a man she could depend on."

Ruby remembered the florist's card. "What was the 'perfect evening' you thanked her for when you sent the flowers? She couldn't remember."

Daniel's mouth contorted; he wet his lips, then wiped the back of his hand across his mouth. "I know she couldn't. She forgot completely."

Ruby was beginning to understand. She leaned forward and said in a lower voice, "You took her out, you drank, you professed your love and fell into bed. Great meaningful sex, you thought. But Phyllis has blackouts and as far as she was concerned, the perfect evening never happened, right? To her it was just an evening out with good old Daniel."

Daniel looked away, into the impossible distances beyond the mesa.

"So you decided to alter her design notes for Bad Day. Dating Monica gave you easy access to the CAD room. Did you actually believe that killing some stupid kid would make her turn to you during troubled times? Solid Daniel, always there when you need him? Is that your idea of the foundation for true romance?"

"I thought the weakness would be discovered by an inspector. I didn't expect the job to lag over the winter. I never intended for anyone to die."

"You keep saying that," Ruby said. "But both Cesar and Leon are dead."

"I don't know anything about their deaths," Daniel said with complete confidence, gazing directly into Ruby's eyes.

Ruby briefly debated how much to say, afraid further accusations would set him off and put Jesse and Phyllis in greater danger. She looked away from him, searching for some sign of her daughter or sister. A breeze ruffled her hair, too weak to affect the cacti or sand on the mesa.

"At first," Ruby began quietly, "I thought Leon had killed Cesar because I saw his pickup coming down from Bad Day the day we found Cesar's body. I told you that the night you brought lasagna to Phyllis's for dinner. And the next day Leon was dead."

"So?"

"So you of course *knew* Leon didn't kill Cesar, but now you feared he'd witnessed *you* knocking Cesar in the head with the rock and then stabbing him in the neck. You called Leon—exactly what he'd been waiting for—and he demanded money to keep quiet. You arranged a meeting—while you told me you were hung up at city hall with the Design Review Committee. You met him near Phyllis's house and ran him off the road and then you met me for lunch, hardly even late. Efficient."

"That's crazy."

"Maybe the police should examine the dent in your Jimmy and the broken turn signal," Ruby suggested.

"I hit a coyote."

"You were right on one account," Ruby went on.

"There *was* a witness, only it wasn't Leon. Leon didn't drive up to Bad Day; it was Grace Peppermill, gone to leave flowers at the site of Eddy's death." Ruby paused. "She saw everything."

Daniel froze. Ruby could see his mind furiously working, unable to accept that he might have failed, wondering if Ruby was bluffing.

"Where are Jesse and Phyllis?" Ruby asked.

"If you leave, I'll release them."

"On what conditions?"

"That you don't call the police until after you see them."

"I don't believe you."

"You don't have any choice," Daniel told her, confidence returning. "Do you think you can find them up here?"

Ruby bit her lip, sickened by a wave of hopelessness. She couldn't leave the mesa just on Daniel's word, not knowing Jesse was nearby.

A speck of blue moved in the pale rocks above Daniel. It was Adam's blue shirt.

"It won't work," Daniel said, shaking his head at her, "pretending you see someone behind me so I'll turn around, and what could you do, butt me with that hard head of yours? Throw stones? I only want to talk to Phyllis, that's all. If you leave right now; I'll release your daughter in a few hours. You'll see her safe and sound."

"What about Phyllis?"

"When she understands what I've done for her, when she truly understands how much I care about her, she won't want to join you; she'll come with me."

Soundlessly Adam rose, his revolver aimed at Daniel's back, his eyes narrowed, cold and purposeful, every inch the dangerous man of the West.

"Don't do it," Ruby warned him as he closed one eye and steadied the gun.

The safety clicked and Daniel's eyes widened. He spun around, reaching behind him, and as he turned, Ruby saw the gun in his waistband and threw herself at him, knocking him to the ground as Adam's gun went off, the shot too close.

Daniel collapsed, falling on top of Ruby, pushing her face-first into the dirt, for a second unable to breathe. His body was inert, heavy, and she struggled beneath its weight, feeling sticky liquid dripping onto her neck.

Then Adam was there, pulling Daniel off her. "Are you okay?" he asked.

"What in hell did you do that for?" Ruby demanded, rolling over and frantically turning Daniel, feeling for a pulse.

Adam shrugged, reholstering his gun. "I was listening to him," he said, "hearing how he'd killed those people 'for' Phyllis—and I just got so damn mad."

A pulse beat wildly in Daniel's neck. Blood spread from his upper right chest. "Well, you'd better hope he doesn't die, because not only is he the key to this mess but he's the only one who knows where Jesse and Phyllis are."

"I was aiming for his leg," Adam said. "If you hadn't knocked him down, that's what I would have hit. His leg. I'm a good shot."

Daniel moaned as Ruby straightened out his limbs.

The pistol was on the dirt beside him, and Ruby picked it up and tossed it with all her might into the rocks. "Where are Jesse and Ruby?" she shouted into his face.

His eyelids fluttered, but it was obvious he was in no shape to answer. She turned to Adam. "Check Phyllis's car for a blanket. If you don't find one, smash the windows of Daniel's Jimmy and look there."

"He doesn't deserve—"

"Adam!"

"Okay, okay."

Ruby watched him bypass Phyllis's Jeep, pull his revolver from the holster, and shoot out all the windows of Daniel's vehicle. The shots reverberated. Glass collapsed into the Jimmy and to the ground around the vehicle in a million tiny chunks.

He returned with a red-checked tablecloth. "This is all I could find," he said.

Ruby tucked the tablecloth around Daniel's neck, covering him to his knees. She stood, gazing first at the rolling land beneath them, then at the rock faces around them. "We have to find Jesse and Phyllis," she said.

"I know where they are," Adam told her. "Or probably are."

Ruby turned on him. "Where?"

"There's a cave a little way from here. Phyllis showed me. She probably showed Daniel, too. I'll go check it."

"Tell me where it is and *I* will," Ruby told him. "You stay here with him."

"You'll never find it."

"I will if you give me decent directions." She nodded to Daniel, who moaned again, turning his head back and forth. "This is your doing."

"He might not be alive when you come back," Adam said sullenly.

"He'd better be. Give me your gun."

"No. Go find Daniel's that you threw away."

"I don't have time," Ruby told him. "Give me yours. If I run into trouble, I'll fire three shots."

He resignedly pulled his revolver from the holster and checked the chamber before handing it to Ruby. "It shoots a little high," he said. "It's a Hartford. Try not to bang it up."

Ruby followed Adam's directions along the mesa top, at first easily able to see Daniel's tracks, losing them when the ground turned rockier. She stopped every few yards and called, "Jesse? Phyllis?"

Past the rock shaped like a chair, Adam had said, and between two nearly identical facing slabs. She slipped once, falling to one knee and scraping her palm, but managing to keep Adam's revolver from getting "banged up."

On the other side of the facing slabs, Ruby ran headlong into a wall of petroglyphs. They eerily glowed along the wall under an overhang, shoulder-high: long rows of dark minimal shapes carved into the rock—humans and animals, geometric and circular designs, all of them protected from weather, to preserve the lost symbols for eternity. Even in her haste she stopped and gazed at the ancient pictures, holding her hands to her sides so she wouldn't touch them as she longed to do.

She rounded the next large rock and realized she'd lost her way. "Keep to the left," he'd said. "It'll be right in front of you."

Well, she had and it wasn't. Ruby retraced her steps past the petroglyphs and tried again. Still no sign of a cave. On a hunch she retraced her path yet again and this time turned to the right instead of the left, working her way along the wall. A small dark object wedged between two rocks caught her eye and she reached down to pick up a wadded piece of fluted paper. She remembered the Reese's wrapper. This was the paper cup the candy was formed in.

But again she reached a blank wall with no sign of a cave. "Jesse? Phyllis?" she called, then standing perfectly still, holding her breath and listening. She moved a few feet farther and repeated the calls, then twice more, each time listening so hard she could hear her heart beat.

Finally there came the slightest sound, like a cat's mewing. It came from beside her.

She saw it: rocks piled against the wall to the height of her thigh. If she'd been more familiar with the terrain, less panicked, she would have spotted its dissimilar arrangement immediately.

Ruby dropped the gun and began clawing away the rocks, tossing them behind her. They hadn't been stacked very securely and they tumbled around her, exposing the cave's entrance.

She knelt and looked inside. Not five feet from the entrance sat Phyllis and Jesse, their hands and legs bound, silver tape across Phyllis's mouth, another piece hanging from Jesse's cheek. Blood ringed Phyllis's legs and wrists, and Ruby could see the long scrape marks where Phyllis had crossed the floor of the cave to Jesse.

Jesse was in Phyllis's arms, rocking the way she did when her senses had been overloaded, when she could no longer deal with the world. Her eyes were blank, as if she'd gone into her own cave and left her body behind. Phyllis had somehow reached her bound wrists over Jesse and she rocked with her, holding her while tears streamed down her dirty cheeks.

Ruby scrambled inside and pulled the tape from Phyllis's mouth. "What have I done to Jesse?" Phyllis cried out as Jesse rhythmically continued to rock, not even seeing Ruby.

"Shhh, shhh," Ruby crooned. "It'll be all right," and she wrapped her arms around Phyllis and Jesse, holding them both close until help arrived.

Chapter 25

Hank Holliday sat across from Ruby in Phyllis's courtyard, with Jesse lying on a lounge chair between them, a light blanket across her legs, even though it was in the low seventies. Jesse drifted in and out of a doze; the effects of her episode the day before had worn off, but she remained dreamy and listless, as she often did after a traumatic experience. Ruby knew this fugue state was temporary, that by tomorrow Jesse would return to normal, but she noted her daughter's every move and glance, judging Jesse's progress, her mother's heart never completely at ease.

Phyllis sat beside Ruby, the rope burns on her wrists and ankles bandaged, the skin around her mouth blotched red from the strip of tape Ruby had ripped from her mouth. "Think of all the money I saved," Phyllis said in a bright voice that strained to be humorous, raising her wrists. "I was ready to pay a fortune to have these tattoos removed and all I needed were a few serious rope burns."

"Sorry I missed all the excitement," Hank said. He'd flown in that morning and had driven a rental car to Phyllis's from the airport. He and Phyllis had taken to each other at once when she'd looked up as he followed Ruby in the door and declared, "You're better looking than I expected," and he'd grinned and responded, "You're not exactly my idea of an engineer."

"That excitement I hope never to see again," Phyllis told him, leaning back in her chair and raising her eyes from her damaged wrists.

Inside, the phone rang again, and nobody moved, letting the answering machine pick it up. Adam had parked his pickup across the end of the driveway, barricading the entrance after a reporter had driven up to the house, a photographer in the passenger seat.

"There's still a long way to go before it's over," Ruby reminded Phyllis.

"I know." She sighed. "No matter what happens, Eddy's death is ultimately my fault; I'm trying to accept that. I could still lose everything, including my engineering license. If it happens, I hope I'll be ready for it. But I trusted Daniel. . . ."

"Maybe it'll go easier now that Daniel's confessed his involvement," Hank said.

"And Cesar's wife has the drawings the two of you made in the bar," Ruby reminded her. "Connie said they show you were planning to use A36 steel for the cantilevered landing. Each piece of evidence contributes to the case. Elements of what he called 'extenuating circumstances.' "

"Maybe," Phyllis said somberly, "but three people are dead."

Neither Ruby nor Hank said anything. Phyllis was

right. Dealing with her culpability in the deaths would last her lifetime.

"Did you call the Center?" Ruby asked gently.

"I did. They're shoehorning me in next week. Notoriety has its advantages. I don't know if I really need it now. This has scared me out of ever wanting to drink again." She held up her hand before Ruby could respond. "But I'm going through the entire program, I swear it. By the trial I'll be deep into official sobriety."

Adam emerged from the kitchen carrying a sweaty brown bottle of beer. His head was shaved around the wound above his ear and black stitches pulled at his skin. He pulled a chair closer to Phyllis's chair and sat down.

"Big lunar eclipse tonight," Hank said, looking up at the clear sky. "It was cloudy when I flew out of Michigan. Nothing in the way of seeing it here. The Hale-Bopp comet and an eclipse of the full moon at the same time: celestial ecstasy."

"Can I watch it?" Jesse asked, stirring on the chaise longue.

"You get the front-row seat," Ruby assured her, and Jesse smiled, closing her eyes again.

"Then will you go home?" Phyllis asked.

Hank looked at Ruby, and she told him, "As long as you're here, we should look around this part of the country, see what attracts so many people."

"Not many trees," he commented.

"We can find trees," Phyllis offered. She gazed at Jesse, then Ruby, her face still. "But you'll still go back to Michigan, won't you?"

"It suits me better," Ruby told her.

Phyllis nodded, looking down, and Ruby leaned over and touched her bandaged wrist. "It's not so far away," she said.